KINGDOM OF FIRE AND ASH

LILIANA HART

Also by Liliana Hart

Whiskey and Gunpowder

Whiskey Lullaby

The Scarlet Chronicles

Bouncing Betty

Hand Grenade Helen

Front Line Francis

The Harley and Davidson Mystery Series

The Farmer's Slaughter

A Tisket a Casket

I Saw Mommy Killing Santa Claus

Get Your Murder Running

Deceased and Desist

Malice in Wonderland

Tequila Mockingbird

Gone With the Sin

Grime and Punishment

Blazing Rattles

A Salt and Battery

Curl Up and Dye

First Comes Death Then Comes Marriage

Box Set 1

Box Set 2

Box Set 3

The Gravediggers

The Darkest Corner

Gone to Dust

Say No More

CHAPTER
ONE

Winter was a cruel and spiteful woman, scraping her icy fingernails over New England. She pummeled, battered, and decimated—plants and creatures alike—happily destroying those who wouldn't bend to her will.

Despite the chilled temperature of my room, my body was slicked with sweat, and the last dregs of a nightmare filled my belly with a heat so intense I curled up in a ball on my damp mattress to protect myself against the pain. The stench of smoke and burning flesh was trapped in the back of my throat, and every breath was a struggle.

I was used to death. Between my family and my job, I came in contact with it much too often—often enough where the sight of wasted life didn't bother me as much as it used to. As much as it should have.

Icy rain pelted against my windows and the wind howled into the straining glass. I looked at the glowing red numbers of the clock on my bedside table and saw it was just after midnight. I'd barely had more than an hour of sleep. It was all I was likely to get for the foreseeable future.

I was too late to save her—the woman from my dream. By the time the visions came, I was always too late. But I got out of bed anyway and headed into the bathroom. I splashed cold water on my face and dried off quickly without looking at myself in the mirror. I was afraid to face the terror I was sure would be looking back at me.

I grabbed a pair of worn jeans and a black sweatshirt from my closet and slipped them on before using the house intercom to wake my assistant.

"Rise and shine, Cal," I said. "We've got a body. Meet me at the car in five, and don't forget my bag."

Cal mumbled something unintelligible, and I clicked off. I pulled on thick socks and my old black boots. The ground was muddy where we were going. I brushed my long black hair into loose knot at the base of my neck. I didn't bother with a coat. The nightmare I'd just witnessed was enough to keep me warm for a while.

They'd killed close this time. Practically in my own backyard. But I couldn't think about that now—about what it meant for me.

My name is Rena Drake, and I'm the closest thing to a cop the Drakán has. They call me an Enforcer. I keep law and order, and right the wrongs of any crimes my people commit—meaning I bury the bodies and erase the evidence. I'll occasionally accept a job from a human just to keep things interesting. But humans are easy.

For the past two months I've been hunting one of my

own. The problem is, dragons are really good at not being found. And they're even better at killing. In all honesty, it isn't the killing that bothers me so much. Killing is in our nature, and it certainly doesn't violate any of our laws.

The hardest part of my job is being the one responsible for keeping our people a secret, making sure we blend in with the human world. But this rogue group was making it very, very difficult to fulfill my duties.

They'd become unnecessarily violent, and the feedings were happening more frequently. Feeding wasn't even the right word. We were all meat eaters, and some of our kind preferred only human flesh. But this group of Drakán wasn't eating for survival. They were simply out to destroy. And now here they were, less than a twenty-minute drive from my house. They were running out of chances. I was going to have to draw up a contract to execute if they didn't lie low for a while. They were putting our entire race in danger.

Cal was already seated in the passenger seat of my dark green Land Rover by the time I made it to the garage. The heat was on full blast and the windows were fogged over with the humidity. I shot out of the garage, barely clearing the still-opening garage door, Muse blaring from the speakers.

The icy rain turned into sluggish drops, then nothing at all, so I flicked the windshield wipers off. I drove fast, and I didn't take it personally when Cal cringed in the corner of the passenger seat as I hit a patch of ice and slid close to the ditch.

"Maybe you should slow down a little," Cal said, eyes still closed.

"Relax, Cal. A car crash won't kill you."

"That doesn't mean it won't hurt."

"You should have a little faith. I'm an excellent driver."

"You've wrecked three cars in the two months I've been working for you. That doesn't qualify you as an excellent driver."

"The last one doesn't count. I was in Mexico. Everybody drives like they're insane in Mexico. And I had the right-of-way."

Calvin Rutledge was a distant cousin of some sort on my father's side. I liked Cal. He was young—still less than a century old—but he had a sharp mind and knew how to follow orders, which was more than I could say for my last assistant, whose ashes resided on the fireplace mantel in my formal dining room.

The threat of more rain concealed the moon, and the night was completely black except for the beams of my headlights against the asphalt. But my vision was perfect. I watched a wolf chase a small rabbit through the adjacent forest, and it made my pulse jump in anticipation and my mouth water with need. There was nothing like the hunt, but I reeled myself back in. Now wasn't the time.

I pressed the pedal to the floor and sped along the winding road. A thick copse of trees stripped of all its leaves hunched over the road like bony arms, and the weight of ice on the breaking limbs echoed like gunshots.

I heard the crime scene before I saw it—the slurp of boots as they sucked against the mud, the murmur of voices, coffee being poured into Styrofoam cups. My senses were primed as I stopped the car at the edge of the road and turned off the ignition.

"There are more than a dozen cops," I told Cal. "You take half."

"But what if I don't get them all?" He chewed on his bottom lip nervously. "I don't want it to be like the last time."

There was a small part of me that felt somewhat maternal toward Cal. Maybe it was the smattering of freckles across the bridge of his nose, or the mop of curly white hair. His eyes were guileless and pure onyx—so dark his diamond-shaped pupils were barely visible. He was naïve despite his age, and he lacked the instinct that was needed for this line of work. In all actuality, I was scared to death I was going to get him killed.

I put the sympathy away and answered him like I would have anyone in my employ. "Speak with confidence. Don't break eye contact. Don't second-guess yourself. And don't screw up." I gave him a hard smile and got out of the car. He followed behind me, lugging my equipment, and I relaxed a little. He wouldn't screw up this time.

Wet leaves squished beneath my feet as I made my way down a steep incline thick with trees and fallen branches. I wasn't visible yet, the trees still hiding us from view. When I stepped into the clearing, no one even gave me a second glance.

The problem was we were exactly on the border between Canada and Maine, and there was a jurisdiction argument going on between the Maine State Police and the

Canadian Border Patrol. The air was filled with the scent of burnt meat and blood. It was a nasty scene, and the cops had at least taken the time to cordon off the area with yellow crime scene tape before arguing. What was left of the body was being ignored.

I was almost on top of the crowd before two cops noticed me and veered away from the excitement to cut me off. The one on my left opened his mouth to speak, but I didn't let him get any words out. A cold numbness grew inside me as I easily breached the walls of his mind, and I watched in satisfaction as he grabbed his throat and his eyes widened with fear. His partner reached for his weapon, but he wasn't able to get it from his holster in time.

"Follow me," I said to them. And they did. Powerless as marionettes on a string. I turned to Cal. "Go herd the stragglers and wipe their memories. I'll take care of the big boys."

The big boys were currently acting like children. A circle of cops had gathered around the two men who headed each unit, and the argument over jurisdiction quickly escalated with raised voices. I understood the need to fight for territory. It was a natural instinct for any creature. But enough was enough.

"Stop," I breathed out softly, the single word floating across the air like mist. The circle of men froze in place, but the two in the center of the ring were stronger—truly alpha—and tried to fight my orders. "Look at me," I commanded. They had no choice but to obey.

"You are finished here," I told them. "There is no body. No crime scene. All paperwork on this incident will be destroyed. You were never here. I was never here. Go home."

The men turned and started back up the hill, disappearing one by one into the trees. All except one—one of the alphas. He was tall and muscled. Anger vibrated off his body in waves. The hair at his temples was matted and his street clothes were damp with perspiration. He was strong, much stronger than any of the others, and he probably had the blood of a Drakán somewhere in his family tree.

"What are you doing to me?" he asked, his jaw clenched with pain.

He wasn't aware of his power or he wouldn't have asked. I decided to look a little deeper and find something that would send him on his way without a fight. I focused on the pulse pounding in the side of his neck and felt the rush of liquid just under the surface, masked by the sickly smell of fear. And I saw.

"Go home, Lieutenant," I said softly. "Take something for your headache. Make love to your wife. If you stay here you'll be hurt. Don't try to fight me. Be afraid of me. And when you wake up in the morning you'll barely recall the nightmare. Be afraid. Run."

I picked him up by the front of his shirt and threw him in the direction the others had gone. He hit the ground hard and stumbled to his knees. Even from that distance I could hear his whimpers. He looked back at me once, got to his feet and ran. Smart man.

I heard Cal approaching and gave him my attention, the lieutenant already forgotten. "Any problems?" I asked.

"No," Cal said, unable to keep the grin from his face. "They didn't have any will at all."

"Well our victim sure as hell didn't," I said, turning to the remains on the ground behind the yellow police tape. "Let's take a look."

I sucked air in through my mouth and held it—tasting the particles of death and rolling them across my tongue as if they were a fine wine before squatting next to the body. I knew from my vision the kill was recent, but the taste of death lingered and I was able to narrow the time down to the minute.

Don't let your guard down, I whispered in Cal's mind. *They could be close. Watching.*

He paled visibly, but nodded his head.

Dragons don't have fingerprints, so I didn't bother to put on gloves before touching her. We're also a very clean race, which is what made this particular case so difficult. There were no pieces of skin to gather and analyze. No hangnails, no strands of hair. And no visible footprints. There had been no clues at any of the scenes. I had nothing, and it was beyond frustrating.

I was an expert tracker, my senses keen, and my mental capabilities greater than almost all others of my kind. The job of Enforcer was a hereditary trait passed only through those of my grandfather's blood. A dragon's mental powers were strong. We could all read minds with ease, except those of the most ancient Drakán. But an Enforcer was the only one gifted with the ability to control minds. With the centuries of human blood diluting our race, I was the only one who'd gained the power in several thousand years. Someday Cal would get there, but not yet.

Whoever I was hunting knew me, knew my abilities, so each kill was always made by someone different—someone whose scent I wasn't already looking for. This was a sport to them—an initiation of some kind. My fists clenched against my thighs, and the bite of my nails against skin brought my rage under control. They were playing with me, but they'd made a mistake this time.

Someone had torched the body after killing her. Despite the fairy tales, not all dragons could breathe fire, so my list of suspects decreased from a few thousand to less than a few hundred. I was among the many who'd never been blessed with the skill. Human blood diluted our Drakán powers, and many of us were missing the genes to carry on the magics of our ancestors to the next generation.

"None of the other victims were burned like this," Cal said. He held a handkerchief over his nose and mouth, and he was ghostly white under his freckles.

"No," I agreed. "And it was stupid of them to start now. There has to be a reason they torched this one. At least it'll make them easier to find."

"How do you know they didn't just douse her in gasoline and light a match?"

"The smell, first of all. Torch fuel makes my throat raw. Besides, look at her body closely. She's still burning." The embers of the inside of her body glowed red as she burned from the inside out. "If we had shown up two hours from now there would be nothing left of her. Only dragon fire

9

can burn that hot. Once the fire starts it can't be extinguished."

"What do we do?" Cal whispered.

"I can slow the deterioration enough so we can get her home to Erik. He'll want to take a look at her." I dug through the black bag at my side until I came up with a can of cooling spray—a special formula my brother had come up with. But despite Erik's best efforts, he'd never been able to invent anything that could stop dragon fire completely.

"Why do you say 'she'? Cal asked.

"Really, Cal? I'd figured you'd be able to tell the difference between a man and a woman at this point in your life."

Cal flushed red, and I took pity on him. Surely I hadn't managed to hire the only hundred-year-old virgin in our society. And maybe the charred meat in front of us did look rather androgynous.

"Look at the shape of the pelvis," I told him, blanking my mind as I pointed to the charred areas that identified her as woman. "Definitely female. And the size of her in general is consistent with that of a female."

"Right," Cal muttered. "I knew that."

I opened her thighs and the burnt skin crackled. There were several tears in the flesh. Made from teeth sharp enough to leave nothing but ragged pieces behind. They hadn't killed her for food, but for fun. There was too much meat left on the lower half of her body, and dragons never wasted a meal. If they'd meant to use her for food they would have taken the body back to their lair with them.

"They always travel in a pack," Cal said. "But I don't

understand why they tried to cover their tracks with this one. They didn't burn the others."

"Maybe there wasn't a member of the pack who could breathe fire before. Maybe they're traveling with someone new." I moved to the head and picked up the skull gently, just in case there was anything I missed. Her hair had been dark and probably long, but it was now melted against the bone like plastic. Where a nose had once been was now an empty cavity and the mouth was drawn and open in the parody of a scream.

"Let's get her bagged and back home so we can dispose of her properly," I said. "I've found all traces of the different scents of her killers I'm going to find. None of them are familiar to me. I'll start hunting as soon as we get back. We'll have to dig up all the ground underneath her and bring it with us. You know the drill. I don't want any sign that she was ever here."

"You got it," Cal said. He'd already taken a shovel out of the bag.

I laid the skull back down and moved to stand up, but as I did her eyelids crackled open and immediately sloughed away like dust, leaving her eyes big and round in their sockets.

"Kill me," she wheezed.

Cal dropped the shovel and jumped straight up into the tree above us—more than fifty feet.

"Oh, gods," I said. It was the only thing I could think of as I stared into a pair of pale yellow eyes with pupils in the shape of diamonds.

She was Drakán—one of us. And it was now glaringly

11

obvious why they'd chosen to burn this woman. There was no other way to get rid of the body. All of their other kills had been human, so the last thing I'd expected to find was that the victim was one of us.

I moved down to her calves where the fire hadn't spread yet and inhaled deeply. Her scent was faint, but it was there. And it wasn't the scent of my clan. What I had to figure out was what she was doing in our territory. I opened my mind and let my power flow, trying to read the last images she'd seen, but she was already too far gone, and I saw nothing but the blackness of impending death.

"Kill me," she said again.

"Who did this to you?" I asked. I knew I didn't have a lot of time to question her. She had no chance for survival, and I winced at the pain she must be suffering. I couldn't even fathom the torture of burning to death slowly.

Cal jumped back down, and took the recorder from the bag to start documenting.

The woman tried to answer, but she was turning to ash in front of my eyes, little bits of her blowing into the wind with every small movement she made.

"What's your name? What clan are you?"

"Jillian." Her voice was no more than a whisper.

I wasn't going to get anything helpful out of her, and I couldn't stand to see her suffering any longer. "Be at peace, sister." I took her head in my hands and twisted hard and fast so the break was clean. I held the skull between my hands and crushed it so the only thing left was a fine bone dust that fell in gray flecks to the frozen ground. She wasn't in pain any longer. "Let's get her home to my brother," I said when it was done. "Maybe he'll be able to tell us something that will help us catch them."

Dragons were hard to kill. The head could be separated from the body to slow us down, but the skin would reknit itself if the two pieces were brought back together. The heart could be taken and crushed, rendering us unconscious for a day or two, but eventually the organ would regenerate itself. Ashes to ashes was the only way to truly kill a dragon, but killing one of our own was an automatic death sentence by the High Council.

The tortures that Jillian had just experienced were nothing compared to what would happen to her killers.

I just had to find them first.

CHAPTER

TWO

I t was almost dawn by the time we made it back to our lair. The sky was a solid wall of gray, heavy with rolling storm clouds and almost bursting with the promise of rain. I made the sharp turn into our drive at high speed, kicking up wet leaves and mud.

The big house I'd called home for the last hundred and fifty years came into view—an intimidating fortress built of dark stone, standing three stories high and barely visible amid the towering forest of trees. Stone arches and a covered courtyard surrounded the entire outer bailey, and massive gardens of evergreen shrubs sat in neat rows between the drive and the house.

We'd lived in this house longer than any of our other lairs. With the growth of the human population, all Drakán have had to move their lairs more frequently or make major adjustments to their lifestyles. Our clan members lived in either a remote location, where people were scarce and animal hunting was convenient, or they lived in a major city where the overwhelming population wouldn't notice if humans went missing every once in a while. They had jobs, found mates, and lived among the humans, guarding the secret of their blood fiercely. The diamond pupils could be covered with contacts and their violent natures toned down with small doses of animal tranquilizers taken like vitamins. We were experts at blending.

Our home was the main lair for our clan. It's where we had our yearly gatherings and where our people would come if there was danger. The hunting was plentiful, though not so much for my father. He was an Ancient, and all Ancients I'd ever met only ate human meat, so he had to fly to more populated areas for good hunting. I'd never been able to hunt humans the way the Ancients did. There were a lot of things I couldn't stomach that the Ancients did. Ancients were more dragon than human—animals without a conscience trapped in a human body, tyrannical in their need for power and possessions.

The cobbled driveway crunched beneath my tires as I followed the serpentine curves around to Cal's side of the house. Everyone in residence had their own entrance that led to their own specific wing. We didn't spend a lot of quality time together in my family, so separate quarters were a necessity.

"I'll get the body to Erik," I told Cal. "Get some sleep."

"I want to go hunting with you."

"Not this time, Cal. They're too close. And it's too dangerous." I stopped the car at the door to Cal's private entrance on the west side of the house.

He shoved the car door open with enough force that I was surprised it wasn't ripped from the hinges. "Stop treating me like a newling," he said, the calm of his voice ruined by the clenched fists held at his sides.

I wasn't in the mood to deal with a temper tantrum. I didn't like working with anyone on my best days. Seeing this side of Cal made me question my sanity at agreeing to mentor him in the first place.

"You are a newling. You barely have a grasp on your powers of persuasion against humans. What makes you think you'll be able to do anything but be an easy kill for an Ancient?" Drakán didn't hit puberty till they were almost fifty years old, so even though he was a hundred in human years, he was still a very young dragon.

"I'll never learn if you don't give me a chance." He was close to pouting, and I wouldn't have been surprised in the least had he stamped his foot in protest.

I threw open my own door, not bothering to wince as it flew far into the wooded area surrounding the house. I jumped across the hood of the car from a standing position and had Cal's face pressed against the cold stone of the drive before he knew what, or who, was happening to him. I squeezed my hand around the back of his neck and yanked his arm a little harder than necessary behind his back. I heard the pop of cartilage as his shoulder slid out of joint.

"I'm not going to kill you," I whispered in his ear, "but I can make you wish you were dead. Continue your training. And only when I feel you're ready will I let someone besides me try to tear the limbs from your body. Understood?"

He whimpered in agreement and I let him go, throwing

myself back behind the wheel of the Land Rover and squealing around to the front of the house before Cal had the chance to get up. I was shaking with anger. The instinct to kill was close to the surface, and if I'd lost control for even a second I could have hurt Cal badly. Sometimes I hated our power, even though I knew I'd die before I ever gave it up.

I stopped the car in front of the garage and got out, taking a moment to stare at the gaping hole I'd created where the door should have been. I kicked at the front tire and couldn't control the growl that spewed from my throat as the tire exploded in a *whooft* of hot air. The skies opened just as I grabbed the black bag that contained the remains of Jillian from the back of my Land Rover.

"Figures." I closed my eyes and controlled my breathing before I did something I'd regret.

I ran to the front of the house in a blur of speed, and my brother, Erik, opened the door for me before I could turn the handle. I'd called him as we left the crime scene to let him know what had happened.

"Is there anything left of her?" he asked.

"Not much. She's turning to ash as we speak. Just do your best. I only need a miracle." I followed him down the curved stone stairs that led to his lab. There were no lights —the space so dark a human wouldn't be able to see a hand in front of their face—but we had our dragon-sight to find the way.

Erik's body blocked most of my view. He was a large man—strongly built—broad through the chest and slim through the hips. It was the body of a warrior, and in his

17

time that's exactly what he'd been. He skimmed just under six feet and carried himself like a general. His black hair was cut close to the scalp and his goatee was neat and trimmed. His eyes were a pale green, and despite the relaxed jeans and T-shirt he wore, he never looked comfortable in modern clothing. Erik's mother, Claudia, had been the first wife of Augustus Caesar. When my father seduced her and left her pregnant with a half-Drakán child, Claudia was exiled from Rome for her adulterous treachery.

Erik hadn't been blessed with any powers at all, other than Drakán longevity. This wasn't unusual because of the human blood that tainted us, but it was extremely rare for someone like Erik since he was the grandson of a pure blood. His attempts to develop his powers had been fruitless over the years. Dragons could sense the strength of others around them, and Erik was no more powerful than a stronger than average human.

But Erik hadn't let his deficiencies harden him over the years. He'd spent the early part of his life training the Roman armies and leading them to victory (I always assumed he spent so much time with humans so he felt like he had a purpose). When he'd gotten tired of a soldier's life, he'd turned his interests to medicine and research. He was now known as a doctor of our clan. His lack of powers made him somewhat of an outcast, which worked out well because my ability to control minds made me one as well. We spent a lot of time together, and we were as close as anyone of our race could be.

Erik took the black bag from my arms and laid it on a metal sterile table. Some of the most advanced computers in the world lined one wall, and weapons and medicines he'd invented lined another. It was a state-of-the-art lab that any scientist would dream of.

"Are you going to tell Alasdair?" he asked.

Alasdair was our father, though we never called him so to his face. He was also the Archos—leader—for our clan. And I used the term leader loosely. He was a bastard by any definition. There weren't many Ancients in our clan, but I'd known a few over the last five centuries. Their dragon natures always overpowered the minute amount of human blood that flowed through their veins. I'd read many times that the only difference between humans and animals was that humans had the ability to feel. They had a soul. But I could say with certainty that Alasdair had never had a soul, and the longer he was confined to the Earth Realm, forced to spend more time in his human body than dragon form, the more cruel and depraved he became. I tried to keep my distance.

"Eventually," I said.

The human killings I'd been tracking over the last two months wouldn't have drawn Alasdair's notice. Humans were like cattle to him—nothing more than a source for food. But he would hear about Jillian's death. And soon. Finding an enemy clan member's body in our territory could cause Alasdair problems from the other Council members if we didn't act swiftly—the Council consisted of the Archos of each of the five Drakán clans.

The Drakán were banished to Earth after the Atlanteans destroyed our Realm eleven thousand years ago. There'd only been five Drakán survivors after the attack—the strongest warriors our people had ever known—and the gods had given them the chance to rebuild our world and reclaim the once-awesome powers the Drakán had been feared for. All the warriors had to do was pick a king among them—someone to lead our people back to greatness. But the warriors fought bitterly—because it's dragon nature to be selfish. The warriors were equals in strength, so the king couldn't be chosen by a duel. It made the gods angry that the warriors couldn't decide on a king, so they banished them to the Earth Realm—where our powers have steadily been diluted with every human mating.

After the Banishment, the warriors continued to feud, and that's when the five clans were created. And why my job as Enforcer isn't what it once was. Enforcers of old were meant to serve the royal family and make sure Drakán were loyal and obeyed the law. The Earth had been no more than a fertile hunting ground where we came for food, and the Enforcers traveled with the hunting parties to control the human minds so we remained invisible. My job now is much the same, but it's hard to be an Enforcer when you're not allowed to go into enemy territory. I had my hands full just looking out for my own clan.

But with the death of an enemy Drakán in our own backyard, this was a problem that was now out of my hands. As much as I hated being in Alasdair's presence, I was going to have to seek him out and let him know what had been happening. I had no other choice, though the scars on my back burned with remembrance at the thought of facing him.

Alasdair loathed what the Drakán had become. With

every generation born we were less and less of what we'd once been—more human than dragon—more prey than predator. And Alasdair hated that he was forced to rule over what he considered to be no more than food. My clan was terrified of him, but they had no choice but to bow to his wishes or face death. He kept us all under his watch, taking what he wanted and hoarding it away. And deserters were not dealt with quickly. They were tortured, eventually begging for death. They got it if they were lucky. It was a way of life my clan had learned to tolerate because they had no other choice. It wouldn't change until someone could challenge Alasdair for Archos and win.

I turned to leave Erik and head to my rooms, but a strange scent wafted across my path and caused me to stop. It was the scent of pain and torment, and the human in me shuddered in misery. Alasdair had taken captives since I'd been gone.

"Don't do it, Rena," Erik said, grabbing my arm from behind. "Alasdair is out hunting, but he'll punish us both if they're gone when he returns. He wants to try and breed with the female. She's the last woman in our clan to have a successful Drakán birth, and Alasdair said her scent is that of one who is fertile."

"I'm not going to just sit by and let the innocent suffer. I can't believe you can."

His gaze shuddered, and I saw guilt in his eyes. "Think before you act, Rena. This could be a breakthrough for our people."

"You want me to keep them prisoner so you can play scientist and gather information after Alasdair rapes her?

What is wrong with you? There are children in there," I hissed between my teeth.

"They're children in body only, not in mind. There because their father challenged Alasdair for his position as Archos. It was a fight to the death, and Alasdair only collected the man's wife and children to make sure they understood where their loyalty should lie. I'm not saying it's right, but we don't have any choice in the matter."

"Like hell I don't," I said and jerked out of his grasp. I ran for the door under the stairs, not bothering to flip on lights as I went. I had to set them free before Alasdair came back.

The hall to the dungeon area was dank and musty. The stone walls covered with moss and cold to the touch. My dragon speed swirled dust through the air as I followed the U-shape curve of the hallway. There was only one way into the dungeon and one way out. And gods help us all if Alasdair came back before we'd left.

My feet skidded to a stop, and I came face-to-face with a woman behind thick iron bars. Hatred blazed in her eyes as she stood in front of her children, shielding them with her body. Her face was a wreck, one eye completely swollen shut and her nose broken and bleeding. Bruises marked her skin in shades of black and purple. Her clothes were torn, and I wondered if Alasdair had already raped her to begin the breeding process. I took in another deep breath, but didn't catch the distinct smell of semen. I only smelled blood, fear, and hatred.

"I'm not here to hurt you," I said, taking another step toward the steel cage. My mouth curled in a smile at the snarl that came from her lips and the way she pushed her children farther behind her. She'd been a worthy Drakán mate.

"Get away from us," she spat. "I won't let you have my children. Even if they are Drakán."

I took the keys from the wall and made slow movements so she wouldn't do anything rash. I rifled through her mind until I found her name. She'd been the wife of Marcos, one of the strongest Drakán in our clan, and I cursed Alasdair for taking the life of someone we could use in battle if our existence ever came to that.

"Be at peace, Sarah," I whispered. "I won't hurt you or your children." The cool breeze of power rushed over my skin as I took momentary control of her mind. Just long enough to calm her heart and ease her fears. I needed her cooperation if she was going to escape.

The tension in her shoulders went slack as my orders relaxed her body. Slow tears ran down her cheeks, leaving trails through the dirt on her face.

"Will you help us?" she asked. "My husband..." She paused as the tears began to fall harder. "He killed my husband. We were starving. Marcos lost his human job, and our house was taken from us. The children were so hungry. They have to eat so much to build their Drakán strength. We asked Alasdair for sanctuary, just until we could get back on our feet again, but he refused. He said real Drakán would go out and take what they wanted. Conquer the humans and feast on their flesh. Not try to be one."

"Yeah, that sounds like something Alasdair would say," I growled.

A small head popped out from behind Sarah's leg. A

towheaded boy who looked to be about four or five, but Drakán aging worked differently than it did for humans and I knew he had to be at least twenty. His pudgy face was covered with dirt and his amber eyes were filled with rage, the diamond pupils only pinpricks of black.

Another child held on to his hand, trying to pull him back out of the way. This one a girl and a few years older—maybe twenty-five. I remembered from our last gathering that I'd felt a sense of power from her. It hadn't manifested itself yet into something specific, but it would someday. Probably around the time she hit puberty. She'd be powerful like her father. The same rage that filled her brother's eyes filled her own, and I felt a stirring of pride at how strong-willed these newlings were. It was no secret that our clan was short on numbers and seemed to have issues with fertility, but these young Drakán were our future and should be treasured. Not turned out like garbage, which is what Alasdair had done. They had even less hope than before if they stayed trapped here. Alasdair would kill their mother if she didn't conceive, and the children would be turned out to fend for themselves.

"We must go quickly," I said, opening the cage and ushering them into the hall. I ran at full speed, the boy and girl sharing the weight of their mother as they used their dragon speed to follow me. I slowed down as we reached the door to Erik's lab. I closed my eyes and inhaled deeply. I felt the flutter of pulses—Erik's in the lab beating furiously as he tried to control his rage, and Cal's, barely stuttering every few seconds while he slept deeply. There was no sign of Alasdair.

"He'll find us," the little girl said wisely. "There's no place we can run that he can't hunt us down."

She was right, and there was only one way they would be able to survive once they left here. I just didn't know if they would agree to it, especially the children. We slipped through the door to Erik's lab, and I didn't bother to make eye contact with him as I brought the trio through. I was still too angry at his passivity to do nothing. At his ability to treat our people as lab rats instead of showing a little compassion.

I grabbed three clear vials from Erik's medicinal shelf and led Sarah and her children to freedom. Rain still fell in soft sheets and the wind had picked up so the cold pierced through layers straight to the bone. Sarah and her children were all dressed in no more than rags, and they shivered violently as I herded them inside the garage.

The garage that held our cars was the size of a large house, and each slot was filled with some mode of transportation—fast cars, rough terrain SUVs, motorcycles, and a sleek black helicopter that Cal had been begging me to fly. Every one of the toys in there was mine. I hoarded cars like other Drakán hoarded diamonds (though I had plenty of those too).

Most Ancients didn't like technology of any kind, and Alasdair was no different. He always flew in dragon form whenever he needed to go somewhere, but I didn't really have that option since I'd never acquired the ability. So I compensated with the high-powered rumble of an engine beneath the hood.

Sarah stumbled and leaned hard against the wall to get

her balance. She could barely stand, and her breath came in shallow pants. From the way she was hunched it looked as if she might have a couple of broken ribs.

"Drink this, Sarah," I said, holding out the vial.

"What is it?"

"Dragon tears. They have healing powers. You're barely conscious and you have a long way to go."

She unstopped the vial and drank it back, shuddering at the bitter taste, while I took a set of car keys off the wall and an emergency bag I'd stashed under the wheel well of an old Buick sedan. It was navy blue and rusted in places, but it ran like a top. I'd been able to hide the money from Alasdair because the smell of the rust overpowered the scent of the money.

"Thank you for helping us," she said.

"Don't thank me yet. You're not going to like what I have to tell you."

Sarah straightened slightly as her bruises started to fade. "What is it?" she asked. "We'll do whatever it takes to get out of here."

"You only have one option for survival," I said. "Alasdair can track you for as long as you belong to the clan. He'll be able to track your scents. It's one of the reasons for the yearly gathering. The only way you'll be able to escape him completely is if you let me erase your memories and give you new ones. You need to forget the Drakán, and we need to forget you. The dragon tears will cleanse you in every way, including your scent."

I was this family's only hope of survival. Only an Enforcer had the ability to take over another's mind so completely. I held the vials out to the two children, but the little boy shook his head no.

"I am Drakán," he said proudly. "I will not forget."

"I am Drakán," the little girl repeated.

Sarah's face was almost completely healed, but she was crying again. She would never separate herself from her children. If they chose not to have their memories wiped then she would make the same choice. And they would all likely die because of it.

I knelt down in front of the little boy and used his name, making his eyes grow round in his head with my knowledge. He was still too young to have developed the power of reading minds or blocking his own from intruders.

"Jacob, you will always be Drakán," I said. "No matter how many memories I replace, you'll still have dragon magic inside of you. Your body won't forget even if your mind does. You'll always be special. I'll make you a promise though if you'll let me help you escape."

"How can you make promises? You are not Archos."

"No, but one day someone will defeat Alasdair, and we will all be free. When that day comes I will find you and your sister and rejoin you with the clan. I give you my solemn oath."

Jacob grabbed his mother's hand and gave me a brisk nod. "If you do not, I will somehow remember my Drakán strength and hunt you down for revenge. I give *you* my solemn oath."

"I would expect no less," I said.

I wiped their minds quickly and gave them new ones— memories of a human life most Drakán never experienced.

They wouldn't remember the powerful father they'd once known or the horrors they'd seen in their young lives. It was for the best.

I implanted directions to a safe house I'd bought in Pennsylvania and gave them the bag of money. They had new names, and I took away the aggressive natures of both children so they could fit into human society easier. I'd have to follow up with them in a few days, find Sarah a job and a way to support her family, and get the children set up in schools. All Drakán children were homeschooled because of the violent tendencies that came with being Drakán and how slow they aged. It was especially hard for the very young to control such strong emotions.

But these children and their mother would be normal. And they would live. I'd make sure of it.

My heart and my conscience were both lighter as they drove away, but I knew my body would pay for the consequences of my actions later. I just hoped it didn't take me too long to heal. I had killers to catch.

THREE

My suite of rooms was in the east wing of the house. It was my escape from the heaviness of the rest of the place, and it was warded with what little magic I'd learned to wield over the centuries. I took my privacy seriously and had my own hoard to protect.

My part of the house was completely modern. Clean lines and sleek, black furniture. Low tables. Lots of mirrors and glass. Boldly printed art in bright colors that I'd never attempt to understand. I didn't particularly love the modern look. That wasn't the point. The point was that Alasdair hated it, so I'd learned to make do.

I took a shower and put the thought of rest out of my mind. I could go days without sleep if I needed to. I dressed in a pair of tan corduroy slacks, a black cashmere turtleneck, and black low-heeled boots. My long wool coat would hide my weapons.

A picture of my disfigured Land Rover came to mind, and I tried to think of a suitable replacement we might have in the garage. I'd need something that could handle the mud and the rough terrain of the roads. I'd bought a black H2 a few months ago and hadn't gotten a chance to use it yet. It would be perfect for the job. And if I was lucky, I'd even bring it back in one piece. Cal was right. I was hell on automobiles.

I'd stalled in my rooms as long as I could. I'd felt Alasdair's presence in the lair as soon as he'd flown back into his rooms, but I hadn't yet felt an elevation to his anger, which meant he didn't know I'd helped his prisoners escape. I needed to find him and tell him of Jillian's murder quickly, so I could leave the house for my hunting trip and hopefully avoid the confrontation to come.

I checked my appearance in the mirror that hung over my dresser. My hair framed my face, thick and black, and hung in waves to my lower back. My mother had been human—an Egyptian. And royalty of some sort, though my father refused to speak her name. I knew nothing about her other than what I saw in the mirror. My face was delicately angled with a square jaw and slashing cheekbones. My features were even and nondescript. All except my eyes. They were a touch too exotic, thickly lashed, and the color was purely Alasdair—a dark, stormy gray with streaks of silver so my eyes always looked like they flashed lightning.

I'd heard it mentioned once that I looked a great deal like my mother. It's only one of the reasons my father hated me so much. Dragons don't show affection in general—not to their mates and not to their offspring—it's the human mate's job to show love and affection, not the dragon's. It's seen as a weakness for us to show anything resembling love. Which is a hard concept to understand when most of us have human blood running through our veins, and the desire for such emotions is built in. I know I've never understood it. But I've learned to bury the need.

I checked the clock. Ten thirty. My stomach rumbled, but I pushed the thought of food away. I took a deep breath and headed downstairs to face my father.

The ring of chimes echoing through the house saved me from my task. I was grateful for the distraction, but in the back of my mind I thought it best to deal with the devil I already knew. We didn't get a lot of drive-by traffic in this area, and by not a lot, I meant none. The only thing that could bring someone to our door was trouble.

I picked up a modified weapon Erik had created that hung from a hook in the foyer. It was an air-compression chamber loaded with poisoned wooden spikes. It looked like a modernized crossbow. The poison would incapacitate a dragon long enough for me to snap the head away from the body and find a way to incinerate it. Sometimes I used them when I was hunting others of our race, but my ability to use compulsion was almost always sufficient.

I stopped at the arched front door and closed my eyes, searching for whoever stood on the other side. I smelled the musty scent of the ancient wood, the damp of the rain outside, and I heard the gusts of cold air whipping through the portico. And very faintly, I heard a heartbeat—a small flutter like butterfly wings that thumped steadily, and the rush of blood that fed it. But I couldn't grasp the person behind the heartbeat. Whoever it was had a solid wall built around their mind. I readied my weapon and opened the door, confident I could handle whatever or whoever it was on my own.

The man wasn't at all what I expected. I had the weapon pressed against his chest in a heartbeat, my hand steady even though my pulse raced.

"Are you going to pull the trigger?" he asked, somewhat amused. He towered over my five-foot-four frame, a few inches over six feet at least. His hair hung shaggily over his collar and ears, but the color was amazing—a rich auburn that glinted with shades of copper, russet, and gold. Rain dripped off the ends and rivulets disappeared into the collar of his shirt—a shirt that was plastered to a well-defined chest. His eyes were bluish green, like Caribbean waters, the expression in them good natured.

And they were human.

I lowered the weapon. "We don't get a lot of traffic out here. It never hurts to be careful."

"Fair enough, though maybe a No Trespassing sign would be a good idea so you don't give a Girl Scout a heart attack when she comes to sell you cookies."

"What fun would that be?"

He gave me the full force of his smile, and I almost backed up and slammed the door in his face. I didn't need a complication in my life right now, no matter how attractive.

"I'm Special Agent Noah Ford," he said, holding up a badge so I could see *FBI* printed in bold letters next to his photograph. "Do you mind if I ask you some questions?"

Instead of inviting him inside, I stepped out on the

porch and shut the door behind me. I didn't think it was a good idea to invite him in, considering Erik was probably up to his elbows in dragon ash.

Agent Ford raised an eyebrow, but didn't say anything as I joined him on the porch. If he really was human he wouldn't be there long. The temperature was in the lower single digits, and he was wet. I gave him two minutes before he started shivering.

I tried to read him again, but still got nothing, so I held out my hand. I'd never met anyone who could block my probes while I was touching them.

"I'm Rena," I said as he took my hand. "Rena Drake." His mind was like a hundred-foot cement wall. I got nothing. Not even the smallest impression. He smiled at me like he knew what I was trying to do, and my curiosity increased.

"Yes, Ms. Drake. I've read your file," he said. "You've been a lot of help to a lot of departments around the country."

"When they want the help, I don't mind giving it. For a price," I said, giving him a hard smile. "Is that why you're here, Agent Ford? Do you need my help?"

"In a manner of speaking." He still hadn't let go of my hand, so I pulled it back. "I work for the Paranormal Division of the FBI."

I snorted out a laugh before I could control it. As far as I knew, we were the only "paranormal" creatures who'd been banished to the Earth. It was weird to think the FBI had a division devoted solely to us. Basically, what he was telling me was that he did the same job I did, only not as well because he didn't really have a clue what or who he was dealing with.

"I get that a lot," he said. "But I figured you'd be more receptive."

"Oh, why's that?"

"Your file has some interesting theories. One of which is that you're one of the most powerful psychics in the world."

"Really?" That was something that was going to have to be remedied. I didn't like the idea of anyone keeping a file on me.

"Forgive me if I'm wrong," he said, though by his smirk he didn't particularly care if I forgave him or not.

"Why don't you tell me why you're here, so I can say no and go about my business," I said.

"I've been tracking a group of serial killers."

"Serial killers are, by definition, loners. They don't work in groups."

"You'd be right," he said. "Normally. But this is the same group, traveling from place to place, country to country. By my estimation, they've killed more than a hundred innocent people."

I knew all this already. And I kicked myself for not executing the contract on them sooner, but then I started rationalizing. *They were just humans.* I would never issue a warrant unless the Drakán who were killing were being careless and endangering our entire race. These Drakán had only recently been bolder in their killing, so I had a reason to issue the warrant. But I had a new problem on my hands since outsiders were knocking on the door, trying to take over my case. I couldn't help but question my judgment in delaying.

"What do you mean, by your estimation?" I asked. "Don't you know for sure?"

"Nope." His grin was easy going and self-deprecating, but I didn't fall for it for a second. Something in his eyes told me this man was dangerous. It was ridiculous that I found that attractive.

"No bodies were left behind," he said. "They've all mysteriously disappeared. And the crime scenes I've located have been swept clean. Unless you know what to look for, and I do. I've got missing persons that come across my desk weekly that I've been able to link to these monsters. I've spent the morning a few miles from here, just on the border. I was close this time. The body was gone and the place clean of evidence. But the smell was still there. It takes a long time for a smell like that to disappear."

He was right. The smell of burnt flesh wasn't something one would ever forget. I looked at the guy in front of me and knew he wasn't someone I should underestimate. He was smart. And as human as he seemed, he was something I'd never come across before.

"So if you have no proof and you have no bodies, how exactly are you tracking this band of serial killers? And why do you think it's something paranormal in nature?" I kept my tone disbelieving, though I was cold on the inside.

"Don't you believe in secrets, Ms. Drake?"

"Fair enough," I said. I had plenty of secrets of my own. "What do you want with me?"

"Like I said, just your help. You've made a lot of trips the past couple of months—Canada, New York, Florida, Texas, Washington, California, Mexico, Chile. Should I go on?"

"No," I said. If I'd known the FBI had a Paranormal Division and a guy who was tracking me, I'd have taken more care at hiding my tracks. I kept my eyes steady on his, not giving any of my thoughts away. He wasn't afraid to look me in the eyes. He somehow knew I couldn't read him.

"Coincidentally, these are some of the locations where I've gotten word of persons missing and found crime scenes like the one I just left. So I figure you're one of two things. A: You're either the killer, which I don't think you are. I'm not saying you haven't killed before, but not this time." He didn't wait to see if I'd react to him calling me a killer. "Or B: You're hunting them yourself, and cleaning up their messes behind them to keep local authorities from horning in on your own investigation. I figure this scenario is more likely."

"Prove it," I said.

"I wish I could."

"Then it seems like we're done here. Have a nice life, Agent Ford."

"Aren't you curious to hear what I want? Or do you want to try and read my mind again?"

I growled low in my throat before I could help it. "You're trying my patience. What do you want?"

"I'm proposing we combine forces and work together. For starters." His gaze was filled with desire and danger—two things that attracted me like a moth to a flame. "What do you say?"

It was unfortunate someone as sexy as Agent Ford had turned out to be such a pain in the neck. Now I was going to have to worry about stumbling across him when I finally fulfilled the warrant of execution. And with the way he'd protected himself against any mental invasions, it didn't look like I was going to have a lot of luck erasing his memories either.

"I'll pass," I said, holding out my hand once again so he'd get the point and get off my porch. "I don't think there's anything I can help you with."

He took his glove off this time before taking my hand, and when flesh touched flesh, the bottom dropped out of my stomach, my vision turned black, and my breath faltered. It was as if I was trapped in his body's embrace, and his mind didn't reveal anything he didn't want me to see. I knew he was attracted to me, and I knew by his shadows that violence and anger lurked behind his carefully built walls. I felt his touch over my body, whispering through my mind and caressing the deepest part of my soul. The sensation was incredible—addictive.

I remembered to breathe, and gray, hazy flecks floated in front of my eyes before my vision came back. He pulled me closer and rubbed his thumb in circles over the top of my hand.

"Let go of me." I looked into his eyes, using the strength of my power to get him to release his hold over me. But it was useless.

"You could change your mind," he said.

I wasn't sure if he was talking about working together or my request that he let me go. He was right, though. I could change my mind in either case.

"How about dinner?" he asked.

I was starting to think he was trying to compel me even

as I was him, but I knew my blocks were just as sturdy as his. "I don't think so. I think both of us would be better off if we never saw each other again."

"You might be right. What about breakfast?"

My mouth quirked in a smile before I could stop it. He was persistent, I'd give him that. I tugged my hand away from his and immediately felt an emptiness inside me that he'd somehow filled. Noah Ford was an unknown. And it probably wasn't wise to let him continue his investigation without keeping tabs on him. He might even be helpful some way.

"Let's start with dinner," I said. "We'll see where it goes."

Agent Ford smiled at me like he knew what I was thinking and walked back out in the rain to his car. "I'll pick you up at six," he called back.

I watched his taillights fade as he drove away. I looked at my watch and tried to estimate how far I could track and still get back in time to get ready for dinner. Far enough to know the next steps I'd need to take at least.

I turned to go back inside but the wind shifted and I stopped in my tracks. There was something in the air—a bitter smell of sweat and blood that clung to the body after a night of hunting. It looked like the killers had found me after all.

CHAPTER

FOUR

I lifted my nose a little higher, hoping to get another whiff. The atmosphere was thick with ozone and lightning raced horizontally across the sky. Mist crept in slowly, building in white waves so the ground below it was invisible to the eye. The rain fell harder, almost as if it was a sign of bad things to come. And then the mist grew thicker, taking the shape of a man—a mist dragon. I'd never seen one before, only heard the stories passed down through the generations.

He appeared to my left and wasn't large, maybe a few inches taller than me, but he was thick across the shoulders and chest—built like a brawler. His jeans were old and torn, his white T-shirt ragged and stained with blood. He gave me a feral grin as he stopped at the edge of the garden path.

I answered his smile with one of my own and leaned against one of the stone arches, enjoying the theatrics. His smile dimmed a little when he saw I wasn't as afraid of him as he'd hoped I'd be. I held the weapon I'd brought out with me in my left hand so it was hidden behind the railing.

It wasn't long before the others appeared out of the trees and joined the first. There were five in all. Maybe half of the original group who'd attacked the woman last night. I recognized their scent. There had been others with this group when they'd killed the woman, but those Drakán were no longer near.

I was looking specifically for one of my own clansmen. Each clan had a unique scent—ours smelled of clean rain and damp forest—and I'd recognized it immediately around Jillian's body. It was the reason I'd been able to see Jillian's death in my vision, even though she was from a different clan.

There was only one female in this group, but she was the one I focused on. I'd seen a little girl once holding a doll with blond curly hair, blue eyes, and rosy cheeks—the porcelain of her complexion so pale and flawless it seemed as if even the slightest touch would cause her to shatter. That's what this woman reminded me of.

Sapphires the color of the deepest part of the ocean were embedded in her human skin. This only happened to those dragons who slept on top of their hoard in human form. It's why we were never able to wear jewelry—our human forms absorbed the jewels just as our dragon forms did. It was just another way for us to keep our treasures close.

The female hoarder stood in the center of the group, slightly in front. Two other males—one as dark as onyx, the other as pale as buttermilk—flanked her left side. Their power was minimal. The last male was almost as old as the female. But not quite. The only difference was his clothes were pristine, his face calm, while dried blood and mud covered the others. This male stood in the rain eerily still, his dark hair plastered around his face and his eyes knowing. He gave me a slight bow with his head, and it was then I knew he had psychic abilities—pitiful as they were. He was practically an open book. But I could use him.

It was situations like this one where I thought our laws kind of sucked. I couldn't kill them just because I knew they'd killed one of our own. Legally, I had to file a warrant with the Council and wait for it to go through. The only way I could kill them today was if they moved to attack me first.

"You guys are pretty far from home," I called out.

"And your welcome is quite disappointing." It was the female who spoke. Her accent was thick and Slavic.

I cast my psychic power from my body and read them all quickly. The woman was obviously from the Russian clan, but what had me worried was that the other members of the ragtag group were representing three other clans—the Romanians, the Belgians, and the Irish. Our clans had been feuding since the Banishment, and I had no idea why they were working together without animosity now. They thought of themselves as a unit—a family. And for some reason, I couldn't siphon the reason they'd joined together from their minds. All I could read was that they needed me, and if I didn't cooperate, then I had to die.

"You made a mistake last night," I said. "You shouldn't have killed her. And you definitely shouldn't have been stupid enough to leave enough of her body behind so I could find her. Now I have to kill you."

The brawler to my left laughed thin and high, and the insanity of it raised chills on my arms. "You think you can kill us, Enforcer? You're outnumbered. And we have powers you could only dream of."

It was my turn to laugh. "I don't think so. You're the pawns. Who's your Master? None of you has the power to breathe fire."

The brawler took a step forward, his anger making him stupid.

"Bartolomé," the female said harshly. "Stand down and follow orders." Bartolomé stepped back, but he didn't like it.

"What do you want?" I asked.

"I'm here to ask you to join us," the female said. "When the time for battle comes, you don't want to be on the losing side."

"And let me guess, it would help to have a psychic with my abilities on your side to even the odds a little."

"It would," she acknowledged.

"You already have a psychic," I said, gesturing to the quiet male with them. "You don't need me."

"Christos' powers are dimmed in comparison to yours. Your mind is virtually untouched. Unexplored. Our Master can help you. You'll be one of the most powerful Drakán to walk the Earth."

"You still haven't told me your Master's name." I was stalling. It was hard to ignore the rush that the promise of so much power would bring me. My dragon nature wanted to take their offer and never look back. The human in me kept a more level head. "I'd like to know who I'm working for."

"His name is unimportant. You only need to know that there is no other of our kind who holds more power. He will be king."

"Tell your Master his arrogance looks like ignorance when he sends five children to the house of Alasdair. You are all foolish for following someone who holds so little value over your lives."

They all moved at once, closing the half circle they'd formed as they pressed in on me. My finger tightened on the weapon I held. I knew I'd get no help from my family for this battle. Erik wouldn't know we were under threat unless they broke into the house, Cal was probably asleep, and Alasdair would never help me. He would probably dance on my ashes if I died.

"Our Master will not like to hear your decision," the female said. "Maybe we can change your mind."

I waited patiently. All it would take was one of them to lose control. "You're all traitors to your Archos. No better than cowards."

Bartolomé growled low in his throat and rushed me, his hands shifting into sharp claws. It was all the excuse I needed. I pulled the trigger of the crossbow and watched as he crumpled to the ground with a howl of pain.

The cold numbness took over my mind as I faced Christos—the other psychic—and enveloped him in my power. The others didn't get a chance to react. Christos turned and faced the remaining three, his eyes wide with fear. The others looked at him in confusion. He wasn't in control of himself anymore. He belonged to me. He pushed his arms out into the empty air in front of him, and his friends went flying backward toward the trees. The dark-skinned male hit against a tree so hard that the base of it cracked in two, the echo deafening as it toppled to the ground.

"Kill them both," the female screamed.

I came at them with a vengeance. I was going to get hurt, but I was going to take as many as I could down with me. The female came up on me fast, her fists a blur as she struck at me, but I was able to dodge the blows. Something grabbed me from behind, and I struggled against the tight grasp fiercely. I didn't see the female strike, she was too quick, but I felt the sudden pain in my chest. Something inside me tore—muscle and cartilage that ripped away from bone. If someone hadn't been holding me in place I would have crashed into the side of the house. My vision grayed, and my heart stuttered.

Despite the damage to my body, I knew I had to think or die. A calm overtook me, and I sent waves of pain, as fierce as knives, into the one who had me trapped in his arms. He let go of me and dropped to the ground, clutching his head between his hands.

The rain sizzled off my skin so steam rose in a cloud around me. I was in a rage. And now I was through playing. Christos was no longer any use to me. His head lay detached from his body a few feet away, his eyes still panicked and his mouth opening and closing as he gasped for air that wasn't there. The two that were left moved closer together and turned to face me. I didn't have time to reload the crossbow, so I threw it to the ground.

I charged with a blur of speed at the dark-skinned male. My hand shot out, and I felt the give of flesh as I pierced through skin, muscle, and bone. My fingers ripped out his heart, and I held the pulsing organ in my hand and squeezed it to dust. He collapsed at my feet, but his friend took the opportunity to tackle me to the ground.

My hands were slicked with blood and kept slipping off his skin as I tried to find something to grab on to. We rolled through puddles and mud, exchanging blows, until I finally wiggled around and embraced his middle with my legs. I tore him in two with the strength of my thighs and tossed the pieces aside.

I was covered in blood from head to toe as I stood and faced the last dragon. The female.

"Tell your Master I refuse his offer to join him. I don't play with cowards. I kill them."

She nodded her head in submission and shifted into her dragon form, her clothes tearing at the seams as her body elongated and her bones seemed to turn to liquid. The sapphires encrusted in her human skin glittered across her pale belly like beautiful chain mail. She was icy blue, fragile, like spun glass. But the brief glance of teeth and talons I got before she flew away were anything but delicate.

I walked over to the one called Bartolomé. The stake in his chest protruded grotesquely. His eyes were open and confused, but the fear was there. I barely spared him a glance. I snapped his neck and took his head before he could draw any more strength to heal himself. We'd have to burn them all.

Drakán blood dripped from my body, and I stood in the rain for a few more minutes, my face tilted up toward the sky to let some of the blood wash away. I closed my eyes and pushed my senses outward, making sure everything was as it should be. My internal injuries were already healing, but my breath still came in shallow pants. I was going to be sore for a couple of days.

A colorful streak flew from the trees and over my shoulder, landing in front of me. She was long and sleek in her dragon form—one powerful muscle—her scales luminescent and pale pink. And familiar. It had been a long time since I'd seen her. More than fifty years.

The dragon slowly transformed until a woman stood before me. Her nakedness went unashamed, and her body was the palest of marble, the blue of her veins visible beneath the delicate skin. Her face was smooth and unlined, her hair so blond it was almost white. But her eyes were those of an Ancient—dark blue and clear like a deep lake.

"Hello, Aunt Calista," I said as the tension built between us.

"I thought you'd be dead by the time I got here," she said. "Your fighting skills have always been less than adequate."

"Apparently not this time," I said, moving to walk past her.

I barely saw the blur of her body as it hit me hard, the healing muscles and bones inside my body breaking once more.

"Don't speak to me that way. Rebellion does not become you, Rena. You disappoint me."

I'd been a disappointment to everyone in my family for my entire life, so I let the insult pass as I pushed myself off the ground. To say that most of my immediate family hated me would be an understatement. Calista resented me because she'd been forced to raise me. My father hated me not only because I was a constant reminder of my mother, but because I possessed the powers of an Enforcer. He didn't understand why I'd been blessed with such a gift, but not also been given the physical strength or other Drakán abilities to go along with it. He considered me weak, but at the same time he considered me a threat. And he was always watching me, afraid I'd take over his mind and claim his position as Archos.

An Ancient's shields were impenetrable to anyone, including me, but if he ever let them slip enough that I could sneak past his guards, I wouldn't hesitate to take control and free us all from his tyranny. So come to think of it, I guess he had a pretty good reason to want me dead. The only thing that was keeping me alive was my title as Enforcer. The gift was so rare that the Council had forbidden anyone from killing us.

There were only three who'd gained the power of Enforcer through the millennia since the human blood first tainted our race—Calista, me, and Cal. Alasdair was the Archos of our clan, a son of one of the original warriors, and the most powerful of our dwindling numbers, but the gift had passed him over.

Alasdair's feelings toward me were mutual, but we were

stuck with each other. I would have left long ago, and I'd tried on many occasions, but Alasdair always hunted me down and brought me back, usually broken and bloody. As Enforcer, I was a useful tool for Alasdair. When clan members became too powerful he liked for me to invade their minds and make them loyal to him, so they'd never try to challenge him for his position as Archos. I did it for him when I had no other choice, but I'd gotten pretty good over the last century or so of avoiding Alasdair whenever possible.

"Come inside," I told her. "I'll find you some clothes. Alasdair isn't going to be pleased to see you."

"He already knows I'm here. We've got trouble, Rena. I've seen it." Her voice was strong and made the hairs on my arms stand up. Calista was the most powerful psychic I'd ever known, so if she said we had trouble I believed her.

"What kind of trouble?"

"We're all going to die," she said, and then turned her back and walked calmly into the house, leaving me in the rain with my mouth hanging open in shock.

FIVE

After the initial surprise of Calista's bombshell, I disposed of the bodies on the front lawn. I didn't think Special Agent Ford would appreciate the carnage lying in the gardens. I tossed everything I could find into our incinerator—one of Erik's inventions whose temperature burned the same as a dragon's fire—and I twisted the dial to the highest setting, taking no chances that they might survive.

The day was starting to catch up with me and it felt as if bags of sand had replaced my bones. I went to check on Calista, the numbness in my legs growing so it was a struggle to put one foot in front of the other. I wasn't sure if it was because I was terrified of the vision she'd seen or because my body was more hurt than I'd thought. I looked down and saw the odd angle of my knee and figured that, at least, explained the numbness.

Calista lounged across the couch, the paleness of her

naked body a drastic contrast to the blood red of the sofa. Her body was eerily still, a Drakán trait that only the most Ancient of our race could truly master, and the only sign of life I could see was the tumbler of whiskey she held in a white-knuckled grip.

I went to my quarters and showered quickly, turning the water to blisteringly hot so my aches and pains would heal faster. I dressed quickly in jeans and a long-sleeved black T-shirt and pulled my wet hair back in a clip, not taking the time to dry it. I then went in search of clothes for Calista. I knew from experience if I didn't bring them to her she'd just walk around the house naked.

Calista used to live with us, and there was still a trunk of her things upstairs after her abrupt departure. She'd been the Enforcer for our clan before I took over the job. I'd been in the middle of my training when Alasdair had decided to propose a new law to the Council stating that as Archos and head of the family, he should receive a certain percentage of his clans' hoards. Calista didn't take the news well, because everyone knew that Calista's hoard was one to be envied— filled with gold and jewels and priceless artifacts.

Calista confronted Alasdair with his treachery and the ensuing fight left our lair in shambles. Some of the walls had been completely destroyed and all of the furniture had been turned to smoldering piles of ash. The floors had been slicked with blood for days. But what sent Calista over the edge was when Alasdair tried to breach her magic and break through the shields that surrounded her hoard.

She'd renounced her pledge to serve Alasdair as her Archos, breathed one last impressive stream of fire in his direction, and then flown off into the night. It became obvious pretty quickly that she wasn't ever coming back. Her hoard was suddenly gone the next day, and all that was left was a single trunk of her things. Erik and I were left to clean up the mess of our lair while Alasdair went on a hunting spree to quench his thirst for violence.

None of us knew where Calista had gone, and Alasdair and I couldn't track her because she knew how to hide her scent and guard her mind against us. The only contact I'd had from her had been a formal letter, giving up her title as Enforcer and passing it on to me. She said she no longer cared to protect her people from being discovered. She only cared to protect herself and her hoard. So I grudgingly stepped into the role of Enforcer, even though I was far from being ready. Cal had still been a child at that point, and I was the only other choice. Drakán law stated that as long as another Enforcer was available to take their predecessor's place, then an Enforcer could forfeit their position without punishment. And no one could find Calista to try to talk her into keeping the job.

Hell, sometimes I still thought I was far from being ready. My baser dragon powers never developed like they should have—the ability to shift, fly, or breathe fire. All I had was my strength and the ability to control minds—which granted, was a pretty powerful gift, but I'd always been a little upset that I couldn't breathe fire.

I grabbed a loose black caftan and a pair of matching slippers out of the trunk for Calista, and I used the intercom to contact Erik.

"Calista's here," I said.

51

"What?" Erik's voice held surprise and a little bit of suspicion. "Does Alasdair know?"

"She said he knows she's here, but I don't know if he was expecting her. She just kind of appeared out of nowhere."

Erik grunted. "Do you need me?"

"Yes. We're in the study. And on your way find Alasdair and bring him along." I disconnected and left the room so I wouldn't have to hear his response. I wasn't quite ready to deal with Alasdair, and Calista being here wasn't going to improve his mood.

Calista hadn't bothered to wrap herself in one of the numerous blankets that were placed around the room. She stood at the bar, naked as a baby, drinking another whiskey, and I rolled my eyes before I could control it. None of the Ancients had problems with nudity. I, however, still wasn't used to it, even at my age.

"I brought you some of your old things," I said.

She held out her hand without looking at me, and I placed the clothes in it. "This place hasn't changed much," she said. "I still hate it." She slipped the caftan over her head, and knocked back the rest of the whiskey like it was water. She walked over to a club chair angled next to the fireplace, sat down and pulled on the slippers. "Bring me another whiskey, Rena. It's cold out."

I did as I was told. I wasn't sure how I should act with Calista, or why she was even there. I felt a kind of responsibility toward her that people of my race don't often have —caused by the human in me, no doubt. We're predators by nature. Solitary creatures who stay within our immediate family circle forever. There's loyalty toward the clan, as long as it doesn't interfere with our basic wants or needs.

I never had a mother growing up. I didn't know my biological mother's name or what happened to her (though I'd always suspected Alasdair killed her), but I knew my earliest memories were of Calista. She was the one who raised me and schooled me. She and Erik had been the only two people I'd had much contact with when I was a newling —and Calista only spent the time with me because it was her duty to find and train the next Enforcer, just like I was doing with Cal. Since the ability of Enforcer was contained to only our clan, it wasn't difficult to find those who had the power. When we had our yearly gathering, everyone's powers were observed for any signs of rare Drakán abilities —especially the ability of mind control.

"Alasdair is angry with you," Calista said. "I can feel the heat of his rage at your defiance. You smell of human."

I kept my face blank of emotion as I reached out with my senses to see if she spoke the truth. It took all my control not to flinch at the scalding burn of his anger.

"I did what was right," I said. "The Drakán children were my concern, and they were being poorly treated. Our clan needs their strength."

"Don't lie to me, Rena. The pity you feel for all of them reeks from your pores. If you keep defying your father he will eventually let go of his control completely and convince the Council to lift the ban on our safety. If that happens, he will kill you. And he'll have just cause."

"I will continue to do what I see fit, Aunt Calista. I know exactly what I am, no thanks to you, and I'll keep damning you all to the Realm of the Dead until we change our ways and become a thriving society. We're as good as dead if we continue on the same path."

Her eyes darkened in anger, and I waited for her attack, but she stayed seated. There was no point at being angry at Calista. She'd dumped this job on me and left without a goodbye for her own self-preservation. I understood exactly how she'd felt. Living with Alasdair wasn't easy. Sometimes I wished I could move out and just disappear—live a life of solitude with the possessions I held most dear, much like Calista was doing—but until our antiquated laws were changed or Alasdair was killed, I was stuck here. Besides, my human conscience wouldn't let me leave Cal unprepared to face misbehaving dragons like Calista had done with me.

"Open the drapes. The rain soothes me," she said.

"What are you doing here, Calista?" I asked tiredly. "You know what? Never mind. I don't have time to deal with this. I've got to get out of here."

"You will deal with this. And you will listen carefully. Now open the drapes."

I fumed silently as I walked to the heavy red drapes and pulled them aside. Gray, watery morning light barely penetrated the gloom of the study. It wasn't a room I spent a lot of time in, being much more suited to Alasdair's tastes than mine—the furniture was large and ornate, the fabrics lush and expensive, the paintings fussy. A stone fireplace dominated one entire wall. There were no family heirlooms or mementos. Alasdair didn't believe in them.

In addition to the bloodshed that had happened between Alasdair and Calista, there had also been futures predicted.

She'd scared the hell out of Alasdair with her visions, even though he would never admit it, and he'd wounded her badly in retaliation. I knew her coming here meant circumstances were dire. And despite her proclamation of only caring about her hoard, she must still feel some loyalty to her clan or she wouldn't be here. I took a calming breath and prayed to the gods for patience.

Tension was high—mine and Calista's—with the promise of Alasdair's arrival. Awareness suddenly filled my body, and the fine hairs at the nape of my neck stood on end. The fire in the hearth disappeared to red embers, and the chill in the room was immediate. Alasdair always did like to make an entrance.

"Show yourself, Alasdair," I called out.

He appeared in the chair across from Calista. His legs were crossed and a tumbler of whiskey was held loosely in his hand—a man who looked to the world as if he didn't have a care. His expression was pleasant unless you looked in his eyes—they were red rimmed, his fire smoldering just behind them—a sure sign of his anger. And then he looked at me, and I knew I'd be lucky to leave the room in one piece.

Erik came into the room the normal way and bowed over Calista's hand before taking his place beside me at the hearth. He put himself between me and Alasdair and squeezed my hand in silent apology for his earlier behavior.

My father was a handsome man. To humans who could only see the surface he appeared to be in his early forties. His hair was jet black and silvered at the temples. His body was lean and muscled, and his eyes like gray storm clouds—

so much like mine it sometimes hurt to look at them. He never wanted for the attention of women, but despite the many who'd shared his bed, Erik and I were his only offspring.

"Why have you darkened my door, Calista?" he asked. "Shall I punish you for returning to my home at the same time I punish Rena for freeing my potential mate? I've always enjoyed spilling your blood, though not as much as I enjoy spilling Rena's."

I felt a hot breeze pass in front of my body and a quick slash of pain. The left sleeve of my shirt was in tatters and blood splattered steadily to the floor. Speed was one of Alasdair's gifts. He was impossible to visually track, and it was why no one had ever been able to defeat him in a duel. I could tell from the blood lust in his eyes that he was toying with me.

Calista ignored his taunt and licked her lips at the blood that pooled at my feet. My expression stayed blank, and I didn't move a muscle, not wanting to tempt the beasts in the room by showing weakness.

Alasdair stood against the far wall, his posture relaxed and his gaze taunting. His hand was transformed into sharp talons, and my blood coated the knifelike claws. The hot breeze passed by me again, and I couldn't help the growl of pain that escaped from my lips. I looked down my body and saw the damage at my thigh. The skin hung in tatters, and the sheen of bone glimmered white between the pink of useless muscles.

"Leave her be for now, Alasdair," Calista commanded. "There is time for play later. I am here for a purpose."

Alasdair didn't take his eyes off me. "We are not finished, Rena. You will pay for what you've done. And don't think to try and escape my wrath. I will just hunt you down, though the chase does make things more interesting," he said thoughtfully. He moved in the blink of an eye and sat back across from Calista. The tumbler of whiskey back in his now-human hand. "Tell us why the hell you're here, Calista, and then get out of my lair."

Calista kept her gaze steady on me. "I know who you're hunting, Rena. I've seen them," she said.

I raised my brow in confusion. "Yes, I believe I just dispatched some of them in the garden. What I need is their Master. I've already decided to ask the Council for a warrant of execution. They've killed too many humans. And if I keep hunting the minions, then there will only be more to take their place. The Master is my priority. But now I have a separate problem. The FBI has become suspicious. I was questioned this morning."

My arm was numb from the damage, and I was losing a lot of blood. I'd have to take at least a vial full of the dragon tears to heal enough to hunt.

"You have no idea what you've been dealing with," Calista said. "Your investigation has only skimmed the surface of what these Drakán are capable of. You've only been focusing on the humans they have butchered because those are the visions you've seen, and your humanity closes off your senses to the rest of it. But these Drakán have a vast hunger, and they'll keep hunting your humans and laughing at you as you continue to clean up their messes. It takes many victims to feed an army of this size."

"An army?" I asked as dread filled me.

"Yes, but the humans are inconsequential. This is what you always fail to remember. The Drakán remains you found last night are not the first to have been found. The ashes of dozens of our people have surfaced over the past two months—different clans from different parts of the world."

"I didn't know," I said.

"No, you wouldn't have seen as I have. Your powers are strong, but you're hampered by your lack of knowledge of the other clans, and your lack of connections to them. That is your father's fault for keeping you secluded here. He is the only one who could grant you permission to meet the other Archos. If you met them face-to-face your visions would encompass all of the Drakán and not just our clan. And then we wouldn't be in this mess."

Alasdair growled, but I could understand his anger at being provoked. I could also understand Calista's view. An Enforcer's powers had everything to do with connections. I had visions and was able to keep track of the members of our clan because I'd met them all—a little over two thousand at the last gathering. We'd be minus three at the next one since Alasdair had killed Marcos and I'd freed his children from the Drakán bond.

Calista went on. "It is also the fault of the Council that other clans are ignorant to what is happening. Not even they are fully aware of what is going on under their noses. The clans know only of their own losses. All the while, the Council sits in solitude and hoards its power, avoiding each other and the knowledge they could share because of the hatred that existed between their fathers."

I took a chance to look at my father. His face was hard and impassive, but his anger was growing hotter.

"So how do I find them?" I asked Calista. "I'm ready to begin hunting."

"Patience, Rena. I haven't told you the rest." The whiplash of her voice almost made me flinch, but I continued to hold myself still.

"I said remains had been found, but there are hundreds of our people who are simply missing. This is what I've seen in my vision. What I've come to tell you."

"Missing? I don't understand," I said.

Calista and Alasdair shared a look filled with knowledge —secret knowledge—and silent words passed between brother and sister I couldn't interpret. A warm wind rushed through the room. My father's rage was a palpable thing, thick and heavy as it lashed against my skin.

"Why didn't you tell me, Rena?" Alasdair asked. "I would have gone to the Council if you'd told me this group of Drakán was drawing attention to themselves sooner. Before they started kidnapping Drakán and killing them. It could be too late for us all now."

He had me by the throat before I could blink and pressed against the hard stone of the fireplace. "Answer me!" he roared. The stone crumbled beneath my back, and the heat of the flames licked against my legs. Blisters bubbled, but I ignored the discomfort. I had to focus on Alasdair—on living.

The room passed by me in a blur as my body was flung

in the opposite direction. Plaster and drywall turned to dust as my body went through the wall. I hit the marble floor with a jarring thud, but the momentum of his force pushed me another twenty feet or so, tunneling a path of crumbled stone in my wake.

I lay dazed for a minute before crawling to my hands and knees. The damage to my body was so severe the pain wasn't registering yet. I willed myself to my feet, and only had to steady myself against the wall for a moment. The bloody handprint I left on the wall was a stark reminder of the violence I came from. I was Drakán. Not human. And I needed to remember it.

A curl of smoke escaped Alasdair's nostrils as I faced him down. I couldn't defeat my father in strength. There was no point in trying. I'd been in this position before.

"That's enough, Alasdair. Don't damage her too much. She is of need to us," Calista said.

Alasdair broke eye contact and began pacing like a caged tiger. "Explain yourself, Rena," he demanded.

"I didn't tell you because I didn't see a need for it before now. You've never cared about what happens to the humans. You barely care and provide for your own people. Your father and the Council created the laws we live by. Even now that you and the other Archos make up the new Council, you still uphold the laws of old. And because of this, I've been doing my job half blind. I didn't know of the other Drakán being killed. And that oversight lies at your feet."

"Don't push me with accusations, Rena. You have an obligation to inform me when you feel we are in danger.

If Drakán are dying then we are most definitely in danger."

"I can't predict the future, Alasdair. That's Calista's talent. My visions have shown only the human kills, with the exception of the vision I had last night. And I have no idea why I saw her in my vision when we'd had no previous connection. The only conclusion I can come to is I saw her because one of our own was responsible for her death."

"I'd know if one of our own was the traitor," he hissed. "They are mine."

I didn't have to say the words, *"unless you're the one behind the attack,"* but by his darkening expression he was able to read the declaration quite clearly on my face. Alasdair and Calista were the only two Drakán I'd met who had that much power, but surely I would've recognized their scent at the kill sites.

"I've been tracking these Drakán the last two months," I said. "But their hunger hasn't dissipated. The kills are more violent. These predators play with their prey, using torture to prolong the death instead of showing mercy. They were close last night, only miles from here, but none of us sensed them. Not even you, Alasdair. I don't know how that's possible. The Master's power must be great to hide from us all."

The condescension dripped like syrup from my lips, and he absorbed the verbal accusation without flinching. Alasdair stared at me with hatred flashing in his eyes as he walked toward me. I prepared myself for another attack. I'd been goading him on purpose. I always did, looking for the slightest hesitation in the invisible protection around his mind. It would only take once for me to get inside and destroy him completely.

"I will call the Council together and share this news. Whoever is behind this must be stopped. And you must be the one to stop them, Rena."

I could tell by the gleam in Alasdair's eyes that he hoped the Master behind these Drakán murders would kill me as well. It would be a lot easier to have someone else to the dirty work for him.

"How is Rena to stop what she isn't allowed to see?" Erik asked boldly. "You are sending her to her death without the proper preparation. She needs to meet with the Council herself."

Before I could blink, Erik was on the floor of the study, his throat slashed to ribbons as his blood poured like thick wine onto the Persian rug. His eyes were wild with panic as the instinct to breathe like a human took over all logic and reason. But Erik calmed as he remembered he wasn't human, and therefore didn't need to breathe like one.

I knew better than to try to help him, or I'd end up back on the floor. The flesh at his throat was already knitting itself back together.

"You will get your wish, Alasdair," I said calmly. "I'll hunt for the Master until I find him. But I won't be tied down by Council laws once I have him in my grasp. The warrant of execution doesn't need a name attached to it. Only that I be able to kill any and all responsible for the death of the Drakán I found, and any other deaths that occur during my search. You and the other Archos can't hoard all of the power all the time. I have the right to kill just as you do.

More of a right, actually. And you never know, Alasdair. Whoever this Master is could be after you next."

Alasdair gave me a hard look. "I'll get your warrant on your terms this once, Rena. But you'd better be sure you have all the guilty parties responsible. I will not have any more shame brought to our clan. If there is, I will punish you until you're begging for death. Enforcer or no."

Alasdair's skin flowed like liquid and his muscles elongated as his dragon form fought to escape his human body. His blood-red scales rippled like rubies and his teeth gnashed together with enough force to bite a human in two. He launched himself in the air with his powerful haunches and flew through the front window into the rain. The house trembled with his rage and his roar rumbled across the sky like thunder.

CHAPTER

SIX

"Leave the boy alone, Rena," Calista said. "He'll be fine in a while. There's no need to waste the dragon tears. I never understood this need you have for compassion. No doubt the influence of your mother's blood."

I'd limped my way down to Erik's lab after Alasdair's dramatic departure. It had taken two vials of dragon tears to heal my body, and I'd grabbed a smaller vial for Erik's wounds.

"He's my brother. I'd do the same for you. Family should mean something."

I lifted Erik's head and poured the vial down his throat. The skin at his neck knitted itself together seamlessly.

"I've always told you that your need to have a connection to someone, to belong somewhere, is what is hindering your Drakán powers. You'll never be great unless you rid yourself of these useless feelings."

"I get by well enough the way I am."

Calista rose from the chair in an angry cloud of swirling silk and paced the length of the room. "Getting by is not going to be good enough," she finally said. "You're going to get yourself killed. You need to explore your other Drakán powers, see if you can waken them from dormancy. Otherwise, it's like going into a fight with only one good arm and leg. You have to be better. Your people need you to be better. Or we will all die."

"What are you not telling me?"

Calista hesitated and gave me a long look. I could feel her probes, though they were subtle, but she was unable to breach my shields.

I grasped Erik's arm to help him up, and I could see him fighting with his Drakán instincts to keep from attacking me. Erik might not have had any powers, but the thirst for violence was still there. It's what had made him such an impressive soldier.

We sat on the couch across from Calista. "Is this about the disappearances?" I prompted.

"Just listen," Calista commanded. Her body was rigid, her pale blue eyes intense. "These killings of our people are problematic, but it is something that happens from time to time. Usually when a Drakán grows tired of life and is looking for a way to die. What has me worried, and now has your father worried, are the disappearances. Drakán can't be kidnapped without some sign of a struggle. It's just not possible. But these Drakán were. Which leads me to believe that a member from one of the other clans has learned how to bend time and space to their will. There is a new *Viator* among us."

A *Viator* was a Drakán who could time travel. The only living Drakán I knew who could do such a thing was Alasdair. The evidence of who was behind these attacks was stacking itself against Alasdair very neatly.

"When the Atlanteans destroyed our homeland eleven thousand years ago, your grandfather Niklos was one of the five warriors who survived. Their strength was the only thing that kept them from being swept into the black hole the Drakán Realm became. The ability to travel through time was the only way to move from Realm to Realm. It's how we traveled to Earth to hunt. You know the history of the Banishment. Why the five warriors hated each other so much?"

I nodded in the affirmative as Calista went to the bar and poured herself another whiskey. She sipped it slowly as she walked back to the fireplace and stood there, staring into the flames.

"When the warriors couldn't decide who should be king, the gods cast them out of the lands forever and into the human world. The warriors, who'd once been friends, separated from each other and became enemies, forming the five clans. As my father and the others mated with humans and procreated, our powers began to diminish little by little, so that very few hold the abilities of long ago."

"I'm sorry, Calista, but what does our history have to do with what's happening now?" I finally asked. "I know all of this already. You speak to me of urgency, but I am spending my time here listening to stories instead of hunting."

"You're right. I'm stalling," she said. "This isn't a pleasant story. And there are parts of it you've never been told. Parts that very few of the younger Drakán are aware of. Alasdair spoke of shame brought down on our clan, and he was right. My mother was a traitor."

I sat up straighter in surprise and then looked at Erik. He sat very still beside me, and even though it was unconscionably rude, I read his mind to see if he'd known about Calista's mother. From what I gathered, he'd only overheard the rumors of the treachery, never the story itself. He gave me a long look, and I winced in apology at my rudeness.

"Niklos' lover, Maliah—my mother—was his human mate for a short time. I was only a child when she betrayed him, barely twenty, but I remember every detail. Dimitris, one of the other Archos, had seduced her and convinced her to kill Niklos and turn our clan archives over to him, promising her immortality if she agreed. All she had to do was bring him Niklos' ashes to show him the proof. She was a vain woman and she hated that she looked older than her lover, so she accepted his offer.

"Dimitris bespelled her so Niklos couldn't read the truth in her mind—only lies he'd planted there—and he kissed her, giving her one use of his dragon's fire so she could destroy Niklos. Maliah then went back to Niklos, claiming she was with child again, and he believed her because the lies had been planted. As you know, a pregnant woman is to be treasured above all else.

"Maliah had free rein over Niklos' private chambers and went to his bed boldly, wielding her axe with the rage of a woman who was losing her beauty, taking his head off in one fell swoop. She breathed out Dimitris' fire as he'd taught her, and watched her lover turn to ash.

"She wrapped his ashes in animal skin and stole the archives of our clan, leaving Niklos' lair to return to Dimitris. She traveled for two days and nights to reach his camp, and his victorious shout rang out across the Earth Realm, calling all the other Archos who had once been his friends. Dimitris thanked Maliah for killing his enemy and then fed her to his people.

"The other Archos came to Dimitris and agreed to join with him for a short time to declare war on our clan. Their sole purpose was to obliterate us entirely. We had no immediate leader and were considered weak, especially since Niklos had been destroyed by a mortal woman. The position of Archos couldn't be filled because our clan members began to vanish right in front of our eyes. There was no trace of them, as if they'd never existed. Much like the clan members who have recently disappeared."

A chill ran over my skin, but I held in the shudder.

"The loss of our archives is what gave the other clans our weaknesses. The archives held our entire history—the marvelous things our people had created, every documented power, every major event, births, deaths, and marriages. Our lair was impossible for outsiders to see in that time period, but with our archives in their hands we no longer had a safe haven. Our lair no longer had to be hunted for, and our scents no longer had to be tracked. All they had to do was travel to a specific place and time, at a specific moment in our history, and wipe us out one at a time.

"They assassinated the most powerful of our kind first.

Alasdair and I were the youngest of Niklos' children and the weakest. Niklos had sired twelve children in all. I waited in fear for the day of my disappearance, but it never came. And when our enemy clans traveled back in time to kill my brothers and sisters, it changed the course of history, so all of their children vanished as well—for they had never actually been born."

"How was it stopped?" I asked.

"Niklos and the other four warriors were the only ones who had the ability to open the portals to travel through time or between the other Realms. It was considered a lost power after the Banishment. But after decades of senseless killing, Alasdair's rage manifested into the ability to open portals just as Niklos had. His power to do so had only been lying dormant all that time."

She paused and gave me a meaningful look, and I remembered her earlier words about my lack of powers.

"Alasdair went back to a little-known time in our history, a time that was insignificant to our enemies," she said. "He moved the entire clan to a safe location, changing the course of our future. He saved hundreds of lives, and his heroism kept our clan from becoming extinct. His new powers gave him the right to be Archos."

"So you're saying the traveling power has manifested itself in others, and they're jumping time to kidnap other Drakán? To what purpose?" I asked.

"Unfortunately, not even I can see the enemy's thoughts or intentions. I have heard of only one other of our kind who possesses this power besides your father. And they are only rumors, whispered from fear, but I have heard them often during my travels through the other lands. There's a reason we consider the Belgian clan the most dangerous of all. It is their Archos, Julian, who is said to hold this power. Julian is the son of the original Archos, Dimitris, but there is a rumor that his mother was a Romanian Descendent. Which means that Julian has the blood of two lines in him, making him the most powerful of our kind."

I'd heard similar rumors over the centuries, but I never thought they were real. Stories of Julian of the Belgae were like human stories of the bogeyman. Complete fantasy.

"If he's as you say, wouldn't Julian fulfill the Prophecy?" Erik asked.

The Prophecy was the most important thing to the entire Drakán race. It was what gave us hope—a reason to follow the guidelines of human civilization. After the gods banished the five warriors to the Earth, one of the goddesses felt pity for the Drakán, and she came to them in human form. She called them to her and handed each of them a scroll, promising them a way to restore the Drakán Realm. She took one drop of their blood and put it on each scroll, and the words of our Prophecy appeared as if by magic.

"Not necessarily," Calista answered him. Her pupils grew large as she looked—present or past—I couldn't be sure. I felt the rush of her power tingle over my skin as she spoke the words.

There will be a child born of two Descendents, whose power is greater than all who have come before him. A child to rule all, to make peace with the gods as his forefathers failed to do, and return us to our homeland.

"But there are two sides to every prophecy, Rena—the light and the dark. One side gives us hope, but the other delivers despair."

Her words sank in and the blood drained from my head, leaving me light headed. "I swear I didn't know. I didn't realize." Panic tinged my voice, and the cold sweat of fear ran down my spine. I'd had no idea that what I was hunting for would be the one thing that was supposed to destroy us all. If I'd had all the pieces of the puzzle to begin with, I would have figured it out sooner.

"I know, Rena. But now the knowledge is yours. My visions have shown that the one responsible for these crimes is The Destroyer. And it is someone I've met in my time, otherwise the vision would not have come to me. I met Julian when he was just a boy. And I can still remember the strength of his power and his ability to make others want to follow him, even at such a young age. Remember what the second part of the Prophecy says about The Destroyer."

The Destroyer is a great pretender. His power is to be feared. He is seduction reincarnate, and all will follow him into battle without knowing the truth. He will destroy humanity, so the Drakán will starve and be forced to feed on the weakest of our own race. If The Destroyer comes to power, then this shall come to pass.

Calista looked straight at me—a piercing gaze right through to the depths of my soul. "If The Promised Child is yet to be, then Julian must be The Destroyer, also a child of two Descendents and whose powers are said to rival the gods themselves."

At the mention of The Destroyer, it was as if a lock snicked open somewhere inside of me. There was a connection—an invisible thread that tied us together. I didn't know why or how. I should have been afraid. But I wasn't. Anticipation coiled in my gut and held there, ready to spring loose at any moment.

"You must find The Destroyer, Rena. Seek him out. It is he who is behind these attacks on our people. It is your destiny to keep the balance in our world. But know this—in the end you must make a decision. A decision that will affect us all. For the dark side is temptation unto itself."

CHAPTER
SEVEN

I wasn't quite as convinced as Calista that this Julian was The Destroyer. Just because he was a *Viator* didn't make him the only suspect. There could be other *Viators* out there who had kept their powers hidden. Hell, right now all the signs seemed to be pointing to Alasdair, but somehow my gut was steering me away from him. I didn't know if it was because Alasdair was truly innocent or because the human in me found it distasteful to accuse my father of being the destroyer of the world. But whatever the case, it looked like Julian was as good of a place to start as any.

Erik's piercing gaze was almost enough to make me squirm in my seat. I knew he couldn't read me, but sometimes I thought his intuition was as good a strength as any dragon power. And somehow, after Calista's foresight about my destiny, it felt as if Erik found me lacking in some way, though he was too polite to say it.

"I must leave," Calista announced suddenly. She drank the rest of her whiskey and then threw the glass against the stone of the fireplace, shattering it into shards of glittering dust. "I really hate this house," she said, repeating her earlier sentiment. I wondered if it extended to the people who lived here.

Erik and I kept our seats on the couch, undisturbed by her theatrics, and watched as she exited the room with a swish of silk. I didn't hear the front door close behind her, but I knew she was gone for good. Again.

"What are you going to do?" Erik asked.

Nervous energy pulsed under my skin like small electrical shocks, and I got up to pace around the room while I thought about his question. I wished I knew the answer.

"I'm going to get your blood off my hands, and then I'm going to go to dinner with a man I can't read. A man, I might add, who has somehow managed to keep a file on me without my knowledge."

"And you let him live?" Erik asked.

"For now. He intrigues me."

Erik raised his brow in interest, but he didn't say anything. He'd always been good at passing judgment without having to utter a word. I could tell he didn't approve. Erik was fiercely loyal to our society, and in his opinion any threat must be eliminated immediately.

"I'll deal with him how I see fit," I said in answer to his silent question. "He could be of use to us."

Erik stood so we were face-to-face. The look in his eyes made it easy to see why so many Romans had cowered in his presence.

"You need to stay focused as Enforcer," he said. "Don't let a mere human distract you from your duty to your people. Whoever is Master over these killers is outsmarting you."

I stood straighter and moved in closer. "Since when have I ever done anything other than my duty to the clan? I said this human might be able to help me. My word is final on this matter. And since when have you ever shown any interest in my job as Enforcer?"

"Since your attempts at capturing these Drakán have proved unsuccessful."

"I've always done what I've had to do. I didn't wish for Calista to leave me to this job by myself. But I'm stuck with it, and I don't care if you or anyone else approves of my decisions. I'm only one Drakán."

I just didn't care anymore. I'd stopped trying to gain anyone's approval the night I had to fight Alasdair in a duel. He'd submitted my name under false pretenses as wanting to challenge him for Archos just so he could hurt me. I didn't have any choice but to fight, even though I knew he'd arranged the match, and what he'd done to me earlier in the study was nothing compared to the horrors I'd faced at the gathering. The only thing that kept me sane through the ordeal was the reminder that he couldn't kill me because I was an Enforcer. Lucky me. But the thick ridge of scars across my back was a daily reminder of what I was and where I came from.

"You're right," Erik said apologetically. "Yours is not a responsibility to be taken lightly. I just wish you'd take more care. You don't know who this man might be, and it sounds as if he knows too much about you."

"I'll be as careful as I can be under the circumstances."

"What are you going to do about The Destroyer?"

"My job. I'm going to have to travel to Julian's territory and speak to him. I have no other choice if I'm to decide if he really is The Destroyer."

"He'll try to kill you if you cross into his boundaries. Not even the law protects you if you go into enemy territory uninvited."

"No, but law says he has to wait until my investigation is completed and a verdict is passed before he challenges me. And only then if the verdict is not guilty."

"Do you think someone like The Destroyer is concerned with Council law? Julian of the Belgae *is* Council law. Even Alasdair fears him. He's always feared him."

"I have no choice, Erik. The entire Drakán race is in jeopardy."

"You must do your job. Just remember that it is better to die with honor than to live with shame." He gave me a shallow bow and exited the room.

I guessed by Erik's advice that he thought I would come out on the losing end of a battle with Julian. I had to admit, I was pretty worried about that too.

I'd talked myself out of meeting with Noah Ford more than a dozen times. But as the day grew longer, and the time for a decision grew closer, I found myself indulging in the female rituals of the mating game. I selected my clothing with care, something sleek and short and sexy, and I spent extra time on my hair and makeup, wanting the right combination of innocence and siren. Human men seemed to want both when they searched for mates. I'd never understood why.

If I was being completely honest with myself, there were two reasons for keeping my date with Noah. The first was he could potentially have enough information to help me catch The Destroyer and the army he'd created. The second reason was purely personal. I had to know why I couldn't breach his shields, and I wanted to know what I'd have to do to make his walls crumble.

I was pacing in the front entryway by six o'clock on the dot, stepping around the rubble of the marble floors. My stomach wasn't quite as settled as a woman's of my experience should have been. It had been a long time since anyone besides my family had made me uncomfortable, but there was something about Noah that was an unsettling mix of comfort and pure terror.

I heard the rumble of an engine approaching the house. I checked my lipstick one last time in the oval mirror to the left of the door and then slipped on my floor-length leather coat lined with fur. My toes would probably be frostbitten in the slinky black heels I'd decided to wear, but at least the rest of me would be warm. I shook off all my doubts, straightened my spine, and walked out the front door.

Night had already descended, and with it, the temperature. It wasn't the kind of cold that pierced the body with each whip of the wind, but the kind that was still and silent and crept through the marrow of your bones until it settled so deep you thought you'd never be warm again.

A black Jeep came into view. It was a sleek and sexy machine, with bulbous headlights and dark-tinted windows, and I had the feeling it represented its owner much better than the beige Taurus he'd driven earlier that morning. I pulled the passenger door open, before Noah had a chance to stop the car completely, and slid in.

"In a hurry to see me?" he said by way of greeting, his smile making me a lot warmer than it should have. "I knew you wouldn't be able to resist my charm."

I looked him over slowly from head to toe and saw his eyes darken with desire. He wore a charcoal suit and a crisp white shirt with no tie. His hair was just a little too shaggy for conventional standards, but it looked right on him.

"Maybe," I said and shrugged. "Or maybe it's the fact that my brother is looking out his window at you right now, debating whether or not he should come down and interrogate you. He's very protective."

"I suppose I should thank you for running interference. I'm not quite ready to meet your family yet. I think we need at least one more date first."

"Or a hundred," I said under my breath. The last thing I ever wanted was for Noah to be subjected to my family dynamics. I wouldn't wish that on my worst enemy.

"What was that?" he asked.

"Nothing. Listen, I don't want you to get the wrong idea here." I turned to face him in the seat, and my coat came open slightly, revealing the black dress. His eyes tracked the movement, but he had the decency to raise his gaze to my eyes before he turned his attention back to the road. "This isn't a date. The only reason I'm here right now is because there's something off about you, and I can't put my finger on it. Whatever it is, you won't be able to keep it from me for long."

"I think you're lying. That can't be the only reason you came," he said, eyebrows raised in disbelief, dimples winking.

"You're right," I agreed. "I'm attracted to you, I'll admit. But I have an agenda. I might also be able to use you." His satisfied smirk faded with my answer.

"At least you're honest."

"It's the exact reason you asked me to come in the first place, though I'm sure you felt the chemistry between us was a nice bonus. You must think I'm an idiot to not see through your charm and dimples to what you really want from me. This evening would probably go much smoother if we just cut the mating song and dance and got down to business."

His jaw clenched and his eyes narrowed, but he nodded. "I can certainly do that. As long as you're willing to cooperate."

"It depends on what you ask of me. I'm willing to hear you out. That should be enough to satisfy you for now."

"You know, I didn't have to extend the courtesy of giving you a choice in the matter. I could have come in with my badge and demanded you give me the information I wanted on these murders. Because I do have proof that you have information." He took his eyes off the road briefly to give me a hard stare, and I felt the first dregs of anger form inside the pit of my stomach. "I could take you to headquarters with me and keep you there. And there's nothing you could do about it."

"You could try to take me," I said softly, afraid if I raised my voice it would unleash the beast I was trying so hard to control. "Threatening me is not the way to gain my cooperation."

"I wouldn't dream of threatening you. I was just letting you know I could've handled things differently. Believe it or not, I have a great deal of respect for you, and I don't have any intention of making your life harder than it already is."

There was nothing else he might have said that could've deflated my anger as quickly as that. Respect was something I got precious little of in my life. I took a deep breath and relaxed in my seat. We rode in silence for almost an hour before I became curious enough to ask where we were going.

"There's a restaurant at one of the bed-and-breakfasts in Greenville that has excellent food," Noah finally said.

He shifted uncomfortably in his seat before speaking again. "Look, I want to apologize for starting things off on the wrong foot. I think if you'll give it a chance, you and I could benefit each other greatly."

"Why me?"

"Two reasons. First, because you've seen every one of the crime scenes, and I want you to help me piece things together and give closure to the families who are missing their loved ones."

I opened my mouth to speak, but he cut me off before I could get a word out.

"No, don't deny that you've seen the bodies. I thought you wanted to start off our relationship with honesty?"

I narrowed my eyes at him, but didn't bother to deny any longer.

"Don't you want to know the second reason?" he asked.

"Not if it's anything like the first reason." He stared at me patiently, his mouth quirked slightly at one corner. Sometimes my attitude was a little abrasive for humans. "Sorry. What's the second reason?"

He skimmed his finger down my cheek and I had to fight to keep the heat of my body from raging out of control. "I want you," he whispered. He moved his hand back to the steering wheel and turned his attention back to the road. The loss of his touch brought a moan just to the edge of my lips.

I couldn't control the longing that overtook my body. It had been so long since I'd been touched—since I'd wanted a man to touch me. I turned toward the window, deliberately slowing my pulse, and tried to figure out how I'd lost the upper hand.

The miles of nothing but road and trees finally merged into civilization, and Noah turned into a dimly lit parking lot. He parked the Jeep in front of a three-story log cabin that had a wide wraparound porch with an assortment of rocking chairs.

Noah came around to my side of the car and opened the door for me. He held out his hand, and I stared at it like it was a foreign object, trying to decide if I wanted to risk what seemed to happen to me every time we touched. He quirked a challenging brow at me and I made sure my shields were as strong as I was capable of before I touched my hand to his. Nothing. Thank gods.

I let go as soon as possible, and we walked side by side up a cobbled walkway that was lined with brass lanterns. They glowed a soft yellow against the dark, and cast odd shadows across our feet as we passed by them. The front door was painted bright red and flanked by two big urns, spilling over the edges with ivy. The boards of the porch creaked under our feet.

"Welcome," an older woman said as we entered the cabin. Her voice was brittle with age, and the lines on her face were etched deeply. Her eyes were a milky shade of blue and her shoulders were stooped with arthritis. I thought not for the first time that it must suck to be completely human.

A row of brass hooks lined the wall, and she took our coats and hung them there.

"Table for two, please," Noah said. "Somewhere private if there's room."

"Certainly. Right this way."

She led us to a table in the far corner. No one was seated around us, which I was grateful for, because I had a feeling dinner might get a little intense.

"I'll have a beer," Noah told our server. "Whatever you have on tap will be fine."

"The same for me," I said. Noah quirked his brow at my choice, but didn't say anything. I guess I didn't look like a beer drinker to him.

"So," he said once we were alone. "I want to get back to something you said earlier. Just how do you plan to use me?" The seductive glint was back in his eyes, and I laughed before I could control it. Noah Ford was different. I liked that in a man.

"What are you?" I'd caught him by surprise just as the server brought back our drinks.

"I beg your pardon?" he asked stiffly.

"Ooh, you're really good at that lord of the manor voice. But I think it's wasted on me. I want to know what you are," I repeated, more serious this time. "No one who can block me like you did today can be without power." I let the edge of violence I tried to keep contained around humans seep out, and he responded to it. Just not in the way I thought he would. His pupils grew large with desire and his foot bumped mine slightly under the table. Just the touch was as intense as any foreplay I'd ever experienced.

"I'll answer your question if you'll answer one of mine first."

"Fine. Ask it." He took my hand in his and held it loosely. I gasped in reaction to the touch, but it was purely physical this time.

"Did you ever know your mother?"

The feelings of pleasure died a swift death. I tried to pull my hand out of his grasp just out of reflex, but his fingers tightened around my wrist and kept me captive. I didn't know why, but my first instinct was to run and never look back.

My anger was swift, and I could feel my inner dragon fire building within me. I'd never been able to manifest physical fire like many other dragons, but when I became angry, intense heat suffused my skin and my eyes flamed bright red.

I looked down at the green trim of my napkin until I was sure the red was gone from my eyes. I listened closely to his heartbeat and slowed mine to match its pace. I stopped pulling against his hand and finally looked up at him, completely under control.

"No." I didn't explain further, and he let it go. "Now answer my question. What are you?"

"Much like you, I imagine."

"I doubt that."

"I've been known to see things. It's why I was asked to join the FBI."

"You're psychic," I said, feeling as if things were falling into place. It certainly made me feel better about why I couldn't read him. "You must be very powerful to be able to block me."

"I don't want to brag," he said.

We paused our conversation as the server took our order. Noah ordered lobster, and I ordered a steak—rare. No vegetables. No side dishes. Just meat. It was a point in his favor that he acted like my food choice was nothing out of the ordinary.

"I believe it's my turn to ask a question," Noah said. I was ready for more probes about my mother or childhood, but instead he turned my question back on me and asked, "What are you? And I don't mean psychic. I've been studying you a long time. And I mean a *long* time."

The implication wasn't lost on me. "I think this conversation is getting too personal for my tastes. Why don't we agree on a stalemate until we get to know one another a little better? I can't be out too late tonight. I've got a plane to catch tomorrow."

"To Belgium, isn't it?"

I felt the color drain from my face. I scooted my chair back out of reflex—whether to flee or fight yet, I didn't know. "How do you know that? I know you can't read me. Are you working for him?"

"For whom?" he asked. If Noah was pretending not to know who The Destroyer was then he was one hell of an actor.

"Answer my question."

"I've already told you I work for the FBI. And no, I can't read you, but your brother doesn't have the ability to keep me out."

I felt the lie roll off his tongue with a rush of warm breath. Something he'd just said wasn't the whole truth, but I wasn't sure which part. "You've never even met my brother. How can you possibly know his thoughts?"

"It's foolish, Rena, don't you think, to believe there aren't others out there who have a multitude of abilities just like you and your family? And it's ignorance to think there couldn't be other species living in hiding or trying to blend in just as you and your family do."

The sickly sweet scent of fear crept over my skin and clung to it like rancid honey. I knew there were other Realms out there, but as far as I knew the Drakán were the only ones inhabiting the Earth. If what he said was true then we might have a whole other battle on our hands.

"What do you want from me?" I asked.

Our food was delivered quickly and quietly, and our server scurried away. She'd have to be an idiot not to feel the undercurrents of violence at our table. My food sat in front of me, but I'd found I'd lost my appetite.

He gave me a look of what could almost be pity. "Believe it or not, Rena, I'm not here to hurt you. I'd like to help you. And I think you might be able to help me. Though we're approaching this from two different sides, we ultimately have the same goal."

"I don't like working with anyone. Just ask my assistant."

"You might not have a choice this once. There's always someone higher up on the food chain we have to answer to. I know that just as well as you do. If not better."

Boy, wasn't that the truth. I thought of Alasdair and of what my future held for me. My prospects were pretty bleak. And where did Noah fit in?

"Let's assume I could use your help," I said. "What are you going to contribute?"

"Two hunters are always better than one. And I'm a good hunter." He lowered his shields enough for me to see exactly what he wanted me to see. Violence lurked beneath his handsome exterior, and the thrill of the hunt and the pleasure it brought him rode on the crashing waves of death.

He rebuilt his shields quickly, and I hunched over the table, gasping for air. The need for flesh and blood was strong, and I had to close my eyes and focus with every power I had to keep the rush of fluttering heartbeats from the innocents around us from overpowering me.

Noah gave me a knowing look, and I realized he had hold of my hand once again, rubbing circles with his thumb over my tender flesh. I hated myself for wanting a man who seemed to know my secrets while I still knew nothing about him. Dragon lust was a powerful emotion. Almost as strong as the power of flesh and blood.

"I can also keep the FBI off our trails until these bastards are caught," he said as an afterthought.

"I don't even know what you really are. Why should I trust you enough to let you help me?" If he noticed that I'd said he'd be helping me instead of the other way around, he chose not to mention it.

"You've got good instincts," he said. "What does your gut tell you?"

I took a moment to look at him. Really look at him. Yes, he was handsome. As handsome as any man I'd ever seen, and in our race there wasn't a shortage of handsome men to choose from. Noah gave off pheromones that every woman in the near vicinity could pick up on. It didn't matter what age they were. They all watched him with hunger in their eyes.

He moved with a gracefulness that belied his size. Most large men didn't move like big dangerous cats. He was a predator, but there was something about him that was genuine. He obviously believed in justice, whether it came by human laws or his own sense of right and wrong, I didn't know. But I knew that like always recognized like, and I got the sense that Noah and I were very much alike in the ways that counted. This was more comforting to me than any of his other qualities.

"I need time to think about this," I finally said. "I'm

leaving tomorrow to get some answers. I'll contact you if I need help."

"Oh, you'll need help all right. I'm sure of it. Even you think you're going there to die."

"Stay out of my brother's head. Our lives are personal, and if I for one second believe you're a threat to my family, I'll kill you, no matter how much you intrigue me."

"You can certainly try." He got out his wallet and laid a bunch of bills on the table.

The tension between us was thick, and I was in tune to his every movement, just as I knew he was in tune with mine. My senses slowed and sharpened. The colors were brighter. The smell of danger, and to a lesser extent, want, was more potent. There had always been a fine line for me between danger and desire, and the dragon in me wanted so badly to conquer the male that dared to challenge me. But my human blood kept things more rational.

I felt my magic rise along my skin, tingling along my scalp and down my arms. I closed my eyes and called the power that brought my visions, searching for something that could give me hope for my future. A glimpse of what might become of me with the threat of The Destroyer hanging over my head. But for the first time in five hundred years, there was absolutely nothing to see. Just blackness. All of a sudden, it was just too much. Everything was too much.

I pushed back from the table and didn't care that I tipped the chair over, or that others were staring. I just had to get out. To breathe. I grabbed my coat from the rack but didn't put it on as I slammed out into the cold. It had started to sleet, and the white flecks of ice were bright against the blackness of the night. I ignored the icy wetness that pricked at my cheeks and trudged toward the car.

I heard Noah just behind me, but I didn't turn around to face him. Instead, I flicked my shoes off and threw my coat onto the hood of his Jeep. And then I ran. I ran fast and hard, the trees whipping by in a blur of speed, not caring as thin branches whipped at my body. The pain was welcome.

My feet barely touched the ground. I was faster than any human could ever hope to be, and for that moment I was free. Free from my family and my responsibilities to my people. I was free from the weight that Calista had placed on my shoulders. And I was free from The Destroyer and whatever the hell Noah Ford was.

I stopped when I reached the lake. My breathing wasn't labored, but my hands shook. I knew it was from fear. Not fear of Noah, though there was a part of me that respected the danger he could bring me. But it was fear of the unknown. I knew what it meant that I couldn't see myself in my visions. I was going to die, and no one was going to be able to stop it. Even worse, no one would care.

The Jeep crept to a stop behind me and the door opened. I kept my back turned, but I could feel Noah approaching from behind. He placed his hand on my shoulder, and I let out the breath I'd been holding. And when he wrapped his arms around me I knew I had nothing to lose and everything to gain. Loneliness overwhelmed me.

I turned in his arms and sought his mouth, avoiding his gaze at all cost. I didn't want to think. Only to feel. Liquid fire rolled in my belly as our mouths touched, and all I could think was I might have underestimated Noah Ford. My temperature spiked, and it wasn't until then I realized Noah couldn't possibly be human, or the heat from my flesh would have burned him.

I couldn't control the intensity of my inner dragon fire. It had never blazed so hot, and I thought I would die from the pressure of it building inside of me. I'd never felt this way with another man.

Noah either hadn't noticed the heat of my flesh or he just didn't care. I didn't know what to do, or how to make the fire stop, but the all-consuming pleasure was quickly turning to pain. Liquid fire burned down the right side of my body and I screamed.

"What's wrong?" Noah asked.

"God, it's like someone's taking a hot iron to my body." I broke free of him and writhed against the hood of the Jeep, rolling into the fetal position. I kept my eyes closed against the torture. I pushed Noah farther away from me, but he made a sound that made me open my eyes. His face was pinched in a grimace, and his eyes were clouded with pain. "You feel it too?"

He nodded and tried to get control of his breathing.

"What's happening to us?" I asked.

The naked surprise on his face was like a bucket of cold water over my head, and my curiosity intensified as he quickly blanked his expression. His voice was strangled with effort when he answered me. "Are you telling me you don't know?"

"Know what?" I looked frantically down my right side, positive I'd see burns along my skin, but there was nothing.

Just flesh that was quickly turning cold with goose bumps. "What aren't you telling me?"

He helped me off the hood and straightened my clothes like nothing more than anything platonic had just happened between us. "I'm sorry, but I need to take you home," he said softly.

I'd run the gamut of emotions for the night, and despite everything that had happened since I'd met Noah, my prevailing thought was one of disappointment. And shame. I was still woman enough to feel the sting of rejection.

It was followed closely by anger. The severity of my rage took me by surprise. My throat vibrated, and a roar erupted that I had no intention of stifling. I charged Noah with all the strength and speed I possessed.

He grunted as I tackled him to the ground, but he didn't cry out. The feel of flesh pounding flesh was fulfilling, and my body needed to be sated. If not by sex, then by violence.

"Dammit, Rena. I promise I'll tell you everything I can once I find out what the hell is going on. You have every right to be upset, but you have to trust me."

He captured my arms in an iron-clad grasp, so I butted him in the chin with my head and felt satisfaction at the crunch. He didn't retaliate against me. He only held me closer. In the back of my mind I knew he had every opportunity to fight back, and he was strong enough to injure me. But he didn't.

"Trust you?" I yelled. "You've done nothing but play with my emotions and evade my questions since I met you." We were tangled in a heap on the ground, arms and legs entwined. All my speed and strength was useless against him. *Definitely not human.* I kicked at the back of his leg, and he rolled with me until I was underneath him.

"Stop it, Rena. I'm sorry, okay. I'm sorry. Please listen to me."

I stopped struggling, not because I wanted to, but because we were at an impasse. We were evenly matched. Our faces were within inches of each other, and our breaths mingled as we gasped for air.

"Will you listen?" Noah whispered.

I nodded yes, but broke eye contact. I stared at his mouth instead.

"There are things you don't know that you should have been told before we move to the physical part of our relationship. Things that will affect your future. And mine. When I sought you out this morning, I fully expected for us to meet each other on a level playing field, but we can't when there's so much you don't know. It's not fair to you."

"What don't I know? Tell me."

There was regret in his eyes, and I knew it was hopeless for me to ask. He lowered his forehead to mine, and my breath caught in my chest at the sweetness of the gesture.

"I give you an oath on my life that I will tell you everything, but I must find out all I can first. I'll be betraying my people if I tell you this information, and I need to get permission. I need to find out why it was kept from you, and what will happen once you do know. There are those I can ask these questions and get the answers. And then I will come for you, Rena. There's nothing that could keep me away now that I've tasted you."

I didn't acknowledge his explanation one way or another. "Just take me home," I said.

He nodded and let me up. I got in the car with what was left of my dignity, and stared out the window the entire way, not bothering to reply to Noah's attempts at conversation.

It was late when we finally turned into the long drive that would bring me home. Noah slowed the Jeep before we got to the front of the house.

"Rena, look at me."

My pride wouldn't let me do anything but meet him eye to eye.

"No matter what you're feeling right now or what happens in the future I want you to know how much I want you. I've dreamed of you," he said, running his finger down the slope of my cheek. "And from now on you're mine."

"Excuse me?" I said, ire raised at his presumptuousness. "I don't belong to anyone but myself."

"Not anymore. And just as you belong to me, I belong to you as well. Your body burns for me just as mine burns for you. I know it goes against every part of your nature, but I want nothing more than to protect you. And to love you."

A fierce yearning rushed through my body at the mention of love, but I tamped it down. It was a human emotion, and I couldn't afford to let my humanness get in the way. "Why?" I asked.

"Because you need to be loved."

I leaned forward until the gear shift pressed against my hip bone and pulled at his jacket until his face was close to mine. I nipped at his lips and kissed my way down his neck until I could draw in the scent of him. He smelled of rain and wildness.

"You need to tell me what's going on here, Noah," I whispered in his ear. "You seem to know all the right buttons to push. The wants and needs I've kept hidden my entire life are like an open book for you. If you want those things from me, you're going to have to give me something in return."

He pulled back and a glimmer of humor shone in his eyes. I narrowed my own in return. Dragons were good at manipulation. We were hard to resist when we asked for something. It was a trait built in to assure the growth of our hoards. Most of the time we never had to steal. Items were just given to us willingly.

"I won't betray my people, Rena. You of all people should understand the honor in that."

I pulled back, feeling a prick of conscience that was rare with the Drakán. He was right. I couldn't ask him to betray his people.

"I'm sorry," I said. The words came out with difficulty. I wasn't sure I'd ever uttered them before.

"Give me your phone," he said.

I handed him my iPhone without a thought and watched with curiosity as he typed something into it. He handed it back and I stared at his information programmed into my address book.

"I don't know what's going to face you in Belgium, Rena, but I don't have a good feeling about it. No matter where you are. If you need me, I'll come."

"I appreciate the gesture, but I'd probably be dead by the time you got to me."

"I could be there faster than you think. Remember that and use the phone if you need me." He pushed down on the accelerator and drove to the front of the house.

I wondered what grand plans the gods had in store for me. They'd given me The Destroyer and a man who wanted to love me all in the same day.

When the car stopped, I pushed the door open, ready to flee and get control over my emotions once again. But Noah put his hand on my shoulder to stop me. My body turned toward him voluntarily, almost as if I couldn't help it.

"Rena." It was all he had to say, and I leaned in to kiss him goodbye. It was a soft kiss, with none of the explosive passion we'd shared earlier, but it was just as potent. His fingers were hot on my skin, and I could feel my own temperature rising. The unspent desire from earlier in the evening was rushing to the surface, and the liquid fire that had filled us both with pain was beginning to streak down my body. I pulled away before things could get out of hand and the pain became unbearable.

The blue of his eyes glowed eerily and his teeth were clenched together to fight the pain. His breathing was erratic.

"Have a safe trip," he said as he got himself under control.

I got out of the car on unsteady legs, and I didn't look back as Noah drove away. I knew Erik was waiting for me on the porch, but I pretended he wasn't there and opened the front door. I didn't feel like facing the inquisition or any more judgments.

Erik followed me inside and closed the door behind us.

"It must have been a hell of a date. You have sticks in your hair."

"It wasn't a date. It was business." I walked up the stairs with every intention of ignoring him. I had to pack for a trip, which led me to the question, what was the correct wardrobe when you were going to meet your potential death?

"I found your Jillian. I thought you'd want to know," Erik said, interrupting my thoughts.

It was the one thing he could have said that made me stop to pay attention. I turned around to face him, but he still stood at the bottom of the stairs.

"How did you find her?" I asked. "What clan is she?"

"She was in the database. She disappeared about two weeks ago, and her family put a notice up on one of the Drakán forums. She belongs to the Belgae."

"What?" This was not what I'd been expecting. She was one of Julian's. I wasn't a big believer in coincidence.

"This could work to your advantage," Erik said. "You now have a reason to show up in his lands unannounced without accusing him of anything and risking your death."

"Did you find out anything else?"

"Nothing that makes sense."

"What do you mean?"

"While you were gone I went to dispose of her ashes, and as I was sweeping them away I found two different places where silver had melted from her body and was re-hardening into discs. Each disc weighed exactly 5.995 grams."

"So she had coins embedded in her skin. That's not unusual for dragons who sleep on their hoards."

"No, but those were the only two pieces I found, and they just happen to be the exact weight of a silver half shekel—the silver coins that Judas Iscariot received to betray Jesus."

"So she was a traitor?"

"That's for you to find out. I'm just a scientist."

"You've never been just a scientist."

Erik's posture stiffened and he gave me a curt bow—every inch the Roman general he used to be—before turning on his heel and heading to his wing of the house. Erik's moods changed with the winds, and I never knew if the things I said hurt or helped the way he felt about being powerless.

I put Erik out of my mind and fled the rest of the way up the stairs, my thoughts racing with possibilities. I didn't know what Jillian had to do with The Destroyer, or what she'd done to deserve such a horrific death. But I knew I had to find him. And the best place to start was with Julian of the Belgae.

I had a plane to Belgium to catch. I just prayed to the gods that Julian gave me a chance to explain my reasons for crossing into his territory before he tried to turn me to ashes.

CHAPTER

EIGHT

When the plane landed in Brussels, I uncurled my cramped fingers from around the armrests and leaned my head back against the cool leather of my seat. The nausea was slowly fading. My skin was clammy with sweat and my legs were shaking. If an enemy wanted to kill me, now was the perfect time to do so. I hated to fly.

The only flight I could get on such short notice had three connections, so I got to experience the pure terror of takeoff and landing three times as much as normal. My connecting flight from Heathrow to Brussels had been the last one of the day. The flight attendant had announced—in a chirpy voice that made me want to vomit down the front of her crisp white blouse—that it was after ten o'clock in the evening when the wheels touched down. 10:07 to be exact.

I restrained myself from dropping to my knees and kissing the ground as I walked through the terminal with my small carry-on wheeled bag and my purse. The airport was all but deserted—the gray walls dingier than they would have seemed in daylight—the kiosks more pathetic as they stood abandoned. I was starving, but all of the food places were already closed. The only thing that was still open was a small bar, about a hundred square feet of long countertop and cramped tables. It was dark on the inside. A neon *OPEN* sign flickered in the front window, trying to decide if it wanted to go out completely. It looked like an oasis after the hell I'd just been through.

"Three fingers of whiskey, please. Neat," I told the bartender. She tore her gaze away from the book she was reading and looked me over from head to toe, obviously not impressed with what she saw. She handed me the drink and went back to her book. I knocked the whiskey back in two swallows, and finally felt warmth return to my body. The tension that squeezed along my spine and up to the base of my neck started to ease and I took my first deep breath.

I paid for my drink and turned to leave, but I caught a glimpse of my reflection in the front window. No wonder the bartender hadn't been impressed. I wore a black pencil skirt and white silk blouse. The skirt was wrinkled beyond repair and torn at the hem, and a man had spilled coffee down the front of my blouse during my connecting flight in Boston. I'd already thrown my jacket in a trash bin because the shoulder seam ripped when it got caught in the turnstile at Heathrow. Not to mention I'd been selected for a random security check at all three airports.

I had an extra change of clothes in my carry-on, so I headed toward the restrooms. It would be a few minutes before my checked luggage came through, so I'd have time. My heels clicked in rapid staccato against the tile floor and echoed against the space that surrounded me. Everything was too still. Warnings surged inside my mind, and the exhaustion that had taken over my body from the long trip flared into pure adrenaline.

My steps quickened, and I resisted the urge to rub warmth into the pebbled flesh on my arms. Power was a physical rush, and the greater a person's power, the larger the circle it cast out. The airport wasn't crowded, but the people who were there all began to slow. Their movements stilled completely until they all stood frozen in time—a life-like snapshot they'd never remember. It was surreal moving between the fleshy statues. I'd never before seen anything like it.

My dragon senses were rioting inside me, and I began to run.

Rena Drake. Come.

I looked over my shoulder. There was no one there. The voice wasn't low or high, but the language it was spoken in was unmistakable. Only the oldest of our kind still used the language of our lost civilization. My father and Calista both still used it. I knew how to speak it because it was required as Enforcer—just like it was required to speak the native languages of all five of the clans. But the old language was power in itself.

I'd never had the ability to change into a physical dragon form. It was an ability I'd always assumed had passed me by because of the human blood that ran through my veins, and I'd never questioned this lack because most of the younger generations couldn't transform.

But just because I couldn't transform on the outside didn't mean my dragon wasn't inside me. And she let herself be known with a vengeance as the old language was spoken. The words called her, and she writhed beneath my skin as she tried to follow orders like an obedient soldier. It took all my willpower to put one foot in front of the other and not succumb to the seduction of that immense power.

Julian had sent a telepath as strong as I was to greet me. Maybe even stronger. Other than Calista, I wasn't even aware that someone like this existed. *Is she an Enforcer?* These were questions I was definitely going to ask.

But for whatever reason, Julian had sent her for me. And it wasn't a good sign. Even in times of war there were rituals to be upheld, and I'd assumed Julian would follow tradition. I'd fully expected a ceremonial greeting as soon as I'd gotten off the plane. Stupid me.

Halt. And come to me.

My feet stopped moving before I could control myself, but I didn't turn around. I kept my breathing calm and slowed my heart rate so my powers would be more effective. I didn't know how the voice had penetrated my shield. No one had ever been able to breach it before. Not even Calista. I built the layers, brick by brick, in my mind so the wall was higher and stronger than ever. Chants for protection rolled off my tongue as I effectively shut out the voice. I gained control of my feet and broke into a run, veering my course from the restrooms to the outside of the airport. I needed to put as much distance between us as possible.

The walls of protection I'd built so carefully exploded behind my eyes. Shards of power stabbed at my skull like thousands of needles, and I hunched over, grasping the sides of my head with my hands to contain the pain. Nausea rolled in my stomach. My vision went black. I couldn't tell if I was still standing or if I was horizontal on the ground.

Come to me, Rena. I will not harm you. Yet.

I wanted to scream out, to fight back. To do something. But I couldn't. The power grew, and I knew whoever the voice belonged to was getting closer. My vision came back and the nausea ebbed. I was still standing. Yippee. My panic escalated as my feet refused to move. My heart pounded harshly in my chest until I thought it might explode from the exertion. I was a sitting target for whoever was coming my way, and no matter how I tried to escape the one controlling me, I couldn't budge.

I gathered my courage and turned to see who had enough power to render my body useless. I had to look up—way up—to see the face of the woman who had power over me. In her eyes I saw death. She was close to seven feet tall. Her skin was the darkest ebony and her eyes were as black as a starless sky. Skinny braids framed her face and trailed down her back. She was dressed in black leather—a three-button vest that displayed muscular shoulders, pants that looked as if they'd been sewn on like a second skin, and boots that laced in a crisscross pattern up the sides and ended just above the knee.

She was an Ancient, and her power was greater than mine. If Julian had clan members this strong then I was afraid to witness the power he possessed. I needed to get as much distance between us as possible and give myself time to think. Julian had obviously decided to dispense with all proprieties and call for all-out war. I'd be glad to accommodate him. Just as soon as I spoke to the remaining Council members to see how they wanted to proceed. It would probably take a small army for us to take someone of his abilities down.

But first things first. I had to break her hold over me.

What I planned to do wouldn't feel good. In fact, it would probably hurt worse than when she'd broken my shields earlier. But I was left without a choice. I slowed my breathing and drew in every ounce of power I had. It gathered in my stomach and pulsed in time with my dragon fire. This fire wasn't hot like it was when I was angry. This fire was cold—the color in my mind eerily green when I pictured it—and my flesh pebbled even as sweat gathered at my temples from the concentration it took to maintain it in such a focused space.

The warrior woman came closer and tried to speak to me again, but I didn't hear what she said. I couldn't wait any longer. With a scream of torment I shoved all my power and the hold she had over me back at her. I pushed it with a vengeance I didn't know I had. I stumbled as I felt it hit the solid wall of her body. She gasped in surprise, but she didn't falter. I'd done what I'd set out to do. I was free of her. For now.

I ran through the sliding glass doors of the airport, where the world was no longer frozen in time, and hopped in the back of a waiting taxicab. I shoved an undetermined amount of money at the driver who stared at me in horror.

"Step on it," I yelled. Blood dripped steadily from my nose and onto my silk blouse. My ears rang loud enough that I was partially deaf, and the inside of my mouth was dry with terror.

The driver floored it and I fell back into the seat, rapping my head against the side window. I turned around and watched her run outside and after the cab. She stopped and stared at me, her concentration fierce, but I was far enough from her circle of power that I could shield against her. The cab squealed around the corner, and all the aches and pains of using so much power at one time made their way known. The burning acid of bile rose up in my throat. I barely got the door open before I vomited all over the pavement.

CHAPTER

NINE

I needed to disappear for a while. I had the cab driver drop me at a small hotel that looked as if it had passed its heyday more than a century before. There weren't security cameras or nosy doormen. They took cash and didn't ask questions. I paid for the room, and the man behind the counter didn't even bother to look at my face as he took my money. Perfect.

I requested a room on one of the lower levels. I didn't want to be surprised in the middle of the night by a dragon entering through my balcony doors. I had no luggage. I'd dropped my carry-on with the extra change of clothes in it as soon as Julian's greeting committee had tried to mind rape me, and my luggage was probably still sitting on the conveyor belt at the airport. The only reason I still had my purse was because I'd put the strap across my body to free up my hands.

Alasdair should have already been with the Council,

getting the warrant I'd requested and informing the other Archos of what was happening. It was starting to look like Julian could be the guilty party in the murders after all. Why would he go to such trouble to try to control me if he wasn't?

My hotel room was tiny, but functional. Meaning it had a bed and a bathroom. The walls were exposed brick. The carpet a utilitarian gray. Hazy watercolors hung on the walls and a TV was bolted to a small stand. An exposed bulb in the center of the ceiling was the only source of light in the room. The bed was full size and covered in a wildly patterned quilt of pinks and greens. But the sheets looked clean. Unfortunately, I wasn't.

I went into the bathroom and stared at myself in the mirror. Dried blood covered my face and dark circles were shadowed under my eyes. My hair had come out of the clip I'd pulled it back with and hung limply in my face.

I washed the blood off my face and rinsed my mouth out, using the amenity mouthwash that was on the sink. I'd take time for a full shower once I finished calling the Council. Then I planned to fall face-first into the bed and sleep twelve hours straight.

I picked up the phone. My hand was steadier than it should have been as I dialed the number for this year's Council headquarters. It was an office building in Manhattan, fully staffed with secretaries and assistants to each Archos, with the exception of Julian, whose personal staff resided in his home. Because of the feud between each Archos, we also had office buildings in London and the Russian Federation. Headquarters for the Council rotated from year to year, so it wouldn't seem as if they were being called to meet with one specific Archos. They didn't want to give each other the opportunity to claim a false right as king.

If an emergency call came through to headquarters, then each Archos would be called and asked to meet about the situation. Only if they thought it was important enough. Most of the time, they didn't.

The Council should have already been in communication with each other, issuing the warrant for me to kill The Destroyer and all those who followed him. The fact that I suspected Julian was The Destroyer was going to make the Council extremely happy. Drakán in general would be terribly jealous of Julian's powers and see him as someone who could be a viable contender for the throne to rule all the clans. They'd want to see his power destroyed, and Julian obviously didn't have an equal in his own clan or they would have challenged him for the position of Archos.

Julian had already broken the law by threatening me when I'd come into the country. If he really was The Destroyer I wouldn't even have to wait on the warrant of execution from the Council to legally kill him. The problem was, I had no idea how to kill someone of his power. All I'd brought with me was the crossbow with poisoned spikes and the canisters of dragon's fire Erik had made for me. I'd gotten the weapons on the plane by controlling the minds of the TSA agents as I went through security. Usually the crossbow and the canister of dragon's fire was all I needed to kill a Drakán. Unfortunately, my tools of the trade were no longer in my possession.

Before I could finish dialing, electricity crackled across the room. The hairs on my arms stood on end. The temperature dropped to freezing and ice formed on the mirrors. I touched my finger to it and condensation snaked in different patterns until drops of water gathered in a puddle at the bottom. This was a kind of magic I'd never seen before. White puffs of air left my mouth with every exhale, and I found it hard to move my limbs. My blood slowed to a sluggish crawl under my skin. I was literally freezing to death.

Congratulations on your little victory today, Rena.

The voice in my head lay across my skin like a blanket, warming me and causing my body to convulse with shivers.

You outmaneuvered my Bellator. Not an easy task for anyone.

A Bellator was what my ancestors had called the warriors of the Drakán Realm—hulking beasts who protected our lands, whose talons were as long and sharp as cutlasses and whose teeth could shred thick dragon skin with one bite. They were defenders of our people. I'd not heard of any Bellators being born since the Banishment.

"Who are you?" It was hard to get the words past my lips. All I wanted to do was sleep. I collapsed to my knees on the threadbare carpet. I leaned my head against the dresser to keep from falling over, but it slumped at an odd angle. I didn't have the strength to move it.

Surely you know who I am, Rena Drake. You already have your perception of me formed in your mind. Do you not recognize the voice of the man you have already found guilty?

"Julian?"

Ahh, so you do know who I am. Then let me begin by

108

extending an invitation to stay with me at my home while you are in my territory. The offer will be my restitution for the lack of ceremony I gave you on your arrival.

I didn't have the ability to form words anymore, so I replied telepathically. "Thank you for your generous offer. There's no need to go to the trouble. I'm perfectly comfortable staying in a hotel during my stay. I'll call on you formally tomorrow."

His laughter rang in my ears. *I must insist on your staying with me while you're visiting. How would it look to your family if something untoward happened while you were here? You'd be under my protection. They'd blame me.*

"Sending your Bellator for me is an interesting way of showing your protection. It is an insult to me and my clan."

Perhaps. But I'm afraid I must insist on your coming to me. His voice held a thread of steel that couldn't be ignored. *Besides, I have your luggage, and your room has already been prepared. Xana is standing outside your door waiting to escort you.*

The chain on my door unlatched itself and the deadbolt turned with a decisive click. The door of my room opened soundlessly and the Bellator came inside, all seven leathered feet of her. I would have run or fought or—done something if I could have made my muscles move. Xana picked me up off the floor like a rag doll and slung me over her shoulder. The heat from her body warmed me immediately, and I moaned at the sudden flare of warmth, even as my teeth began to chatter.

I look forward to making your acquaintance in person, Rena

Drake. You intrigue me. There are so very few of my enemies I can say that about anymore. Adieu, for now.

His last words slithered silkily through my head. I felt strangely bereft as he left me.

Xana threw me in the back of a sleek black limousine and climbed in behind me. I sat stiffly on the soft leather seat as the numbness from the cold pricked like thousands of tiny needles across my skin. She sat across from me and stared out the window.

Almost as soon as the car left the hotel, we came to a stop. I was finally able to move my arms and legs, and I was determined to meet Julian standing on my own two feet. The driver opened the limo door. He extended his hand to help me out, keeping his eyes averted as I struggled to keep my skirt down. He was human. I wondered if he knew who he was working for.

I stood unsteadily and noticed I'd lost a shoe somewhere along the way.

"Come," Xana said.

I looked up and for the first time noticed where we'd stopped. "Julian lives at Chateau de Longévité?" I asked.

It was centuries old and built in the exact center of the city. I'd never seen it before in person, but I'd seen plenty of pictures of the famous landmark. It was as distinctive as the Taj Mahal or the Eiffel Tower, and decidedly French in its femininity. It was three stories of black stone and glass, surrounded by impressive towers of different sizes at each corner.

Xana's accent was thick. "It is the heart of our city. It is fitting for Julian to reside here, no?"

I decided to agree to disagree on this point. I figured anything I said would get me in nothing but more trouble.

The chateau was built on a hexagonal piece of lush green land that stood out amid the concrete of the city. It was protected on all sides by a twelve-foot iron-and-stone fence. Armed guards stood at attention by the front gates and at sporadic intervals around the palace. Again, the guards were human. I wondered why Julian used them at all. Maybe he just wanted to keep a steady food supply close at hand. I couldn't imagine he cared for them.

I happened to like working with the human authorities on occasion. I found their customs and beliefs intriguing and the simplicity of their minds refreshing. I also enjoyed watching the extremes of their emotions. They never did anything halfway, and were never afraid to let their feelings known. They weren't judged as weak if they fell in love or if they cried. They were just thought of as...human.

I looked for possible escape routes as I followed Xana past the security guards, through a well-tended garden of red roses and around an enormous fountain. The arched front doors were thick dark wood, and beveled glass curved fluidly around the arch. It would be impossible to get in or out of the palace without being seen. Cars drove at breakneck speeds each way on the roundabout that surrounded the chateau—each person behind the wheel completely oblivious to the horrors that lived inside such hallowed walls.

Xana pushed me in the back, and I stumbled forward. I straightened my spine and lifted my chin. No matter what happened, I wouldn't cower in front of Julian and shame my family. I was the daughter of an Archos after all, and I deserved a certain amount of respect. Julian didn't need to know that respect was the last thing I ever got from my own father. But I was here, and I was determined to see that I got it. For once.

CHAPTER

TEN

I'd been left waiting for almost an hour in Julian's great room. It was well past midnight, and I was going to need to sleep soon. It had been more than forty-eight hours. Normally I could go longer, but my body had taken a beating the last two days and needed the rest.

The great room was stark and cold. Black tiles of granite covered the floors and walls. Probably because it was the easiest way to hide blood. There were no windows. Gilded chandeliers hung from the ceilings. They were lit with actual candles. And there was only one set of very large double doors—one way in, one way out.

The room was completely empty except for a dark red velvet throne trimmed in gold. It sat high up on a platform. Whoever sat there would have a full view of the entire room. It was hard for me to keep from thinking that with a chair that big, Julian had to be compensating for something.

Laughter floated through my head like a silky caress, and the chamber doors opened with a resounding thud. I turned to face the man who I suspected to be The Destroyer. I didn't bother to smooth down my skirt or check my appearance when he walked in. I was past the point of caring what I looked like. The anger that had been lying dormant for the last hour surged violently at the sight of him.

The man who entered was huge, at least five inches over six feet, and built of solid muscle—built like the savage warrior his father had been. His chest and shoulders were broad. His waist trim. Hair as dark as midnight hung just past his shoulders in soft waves. The dark suit he wore fit him as if he'd been born in it.

But it was his eyes that held me captivated. A clear, pale blue that had no other color variations. There was something in their depths I couldn't describe. Something not quite safe. And as I looked deeper I saw a promise—a fulfillment I'd never known and could only wish for. I shook my head as if coming out of a trance and broke eye contact. I thought of Noah and had trouble remembering what he'd looked like. What it was I'd felt with him.

"It's rude to think of another man when you're with me, don't you think?" He spoke in the old tongue, so I answered him in kind.

"Stay out of my head. You haven't been invited." I drew strength from my anger and faced him down. "And don't presume that I'm with you in any way other than what I'm forced to be."

He bowed his head mockingly. "Understood. But just as I haven't been invited into your head, you were never invited into my lands."

"I don't have to be invited. I'm the Enforcer for the Drakán."

"Not my Drakán," he interrupted. "Only your clan."

"Nevertheless. Law states that if my investigations lead me to think another clan is the guilty party, then I have a right to cross into their territory for questioning."

"There's no need to quote the law to me. I helped write it." He glided closer to me as if he controlled gravity itself. His body flowed with the ethereal grace only the Ancients could achieve.

"You're right, of course. I have been quite remiss in my duties, Rena, daughter of Alasdair. I apologize."

His voice slid across my skin like liquid silk. His power nipped at the pulse points throughout my body. I shouldn't have let him use his powers on me like this, but I couldn't seem to help it. Were my own powers really so much less than I'd always thought?

"I am Julian, and I welcome you openly to my lands." He took my hand and bowed formally before me, kissing the back of my hand lightly. "And never doubt yourself, little one, for your powers are great indeed. You only need the proper guidance."

"I told you to stay out of my head." I jerked my hand away from his, and the moment our skin separated it was as if I could breathe on my own again. I couldn't seem to find my focus anywhere.

Julian laughed at the turmoil I was in, and I had a feeling he knew exactly what was happening to me. "Stop it." The words came out as a growl, and my fire brought everything back into focus. I embraced my anger. It was the only thing in my entire life that had never failed me. His eyes flared in response to the rush of my power, but he shut down his reaction almost as soon as it had begun.

"I apologize, but it's almost impossible not to hear them."

"Try harder."

"As you wish. Have you dined this evening?" he asked, changing the subject so quickly I had trouble following along. "I'd be pleased if you'd join me. We have much to discuss."

I didn't want to go anywhere with Julian. It was as if I was losing a piece of myself with every minute I spent in his presence. But I needed to follow protocol and accept his graciousness, such as it was. It would make things go smoother once the Council moved in to take over. I looked down at my ragged clothes and wished for nothing more than a hot bath and bed, but it would have to wait.

"If you'll give me a moment to change, I'll meet you in the dining room."

"I think you look lovely as you are. Blood looks good on you, but there's no need for you to change."

Something whispered across my skin, delicate and soft, and it felt like heaven. I looked down and my travel-worn clothes were gone, replaced by a sheer gown the color of rubies. Thin satin straps barely held up the soft material. It was gathered at the bodice and flowed softly all the way to the floor. Other than the color, it reminded me of the dresses of long ago. But it didn't seem at all appropriate now.

"That's much better," Julian said, huskily.

I ignored his offered hand, afraid of what his touch did to me. We walked side by side to the dining room. "Forgive me if I'm insulting you," I said, "but I find your change of heart on my arrival insincere. I was under the impression there would be no peace between us, since you sent your Bellator to greet me."

"Complete peace would make life quite boring. The Drakán have never been at peace. It's not in our nature. Besides, I already know why you've come. I know why you're here better than you do."

"I had a feeling you might," I said sarcastically.

"But I think we will speak of it later. Much later. Unpleasant talk disrupts the digestion."

He spoke as if that was the end of the conversation, but I wasn't ready to let my questions go unanswered. "You must understand my skepticism. There's no way I would trust you after the way I was treated at my arrival. I've heard you are a most—unaccommodating man." It was the nicest word I could think of to describe him.

"You speak the truth. My people learn quickly that I do not believe in forgiveness. My wrath is a powerful thing, but this is my right as Archos. My people do their best to never make mistakes, and my land flourishes because of it. We are stronger than all the others. Can you say the same of your people?"

The troubling thing was, I couldn't say the same about our clan. My father ruled with vengeance, much like Julian. But he ruled only when he was forced to—when a problem grew so out of hand extreme measures had to be taken. He usually called me in to handle those extremities. He chose to spend most of his time in seclusion, in his dragon form, ignoring the basic needs of his people and forcing them to make do on their own. If they weren't powerful, they were meaningless to him. If they were too powerful, he had me wipe their memories and make them malleable to his wishes.

In all honesty, our clan wasn't flourishing at all. We were slowly withering to death. My people had businesses and families, and once a year they came to our home and pledged their loyalty to my father at the gathering. But there were plenty of our people who didn't have families or businesses, who were forced to live on the streets and scrounge for food. These were usually the Drakán who hardly had any power at all, but whose savage beast was just prominent enough that they still had to feed their need to hunt and kill. My father ignored these Drakán and left them to their own devices until they started drawing attention to themselves and I had to kill them. I hated doing it, so I'd started making it a point to seek them out and use my powers of mind control to help them find jobs and lodging.

Julian interrupted my thoughts with his silver-tongued words. "There is a saying I'm sure you've heard, Rena. One that someone very wise once told me."

"What is it?"

"Keep your friends close, but your enemies closer."

118

Julian touched my hand and pushed his power into my body, and my inner dragon answered his call. She recognized his strength and wanted him. Ached for him. The human in me wanted to run screaming out the door.

I now understood my position perfectly. I was trapped in the enemy's hands with no way out but death.

ELEVEN

T he dining room was decorated much like the room I'd just left. Black surrounded us on all sides. A black lacquered table dominated almost the entire room. Yards of red velvet fabric ran down the length of it and pooled to the floor like blood. Heavy gold candlesticks sat at even intervals down the length of the table, and each one held slender white tapers.

I'd been brought a plate with a large cut of medium rare veal, topped with melted butter and garnished with parsley for color. Only good manners kept me from shoveling it in like an animal. The last time I'd eaten had been with Noah, and I'd hardly touched it.

Julian and I sat at each end of the long table, fully aware of each other and every little movement that was made, despite the distance that separated us. The silence was filled with tension.

"Are there other Bellators besides Xana?" I asked to fill the void.

"Xana is the only Bellator born of our people since the Banishment."

"You've done a good job hiding her." He didn't try to dispute the fact that he had, in fact, been hiding her all these centuries. "How could she control my mind? She's not an Enforcer."

His lips quirked in a smile. "That is a secret of my clan. But just know that Xana is under my protection. She is my sister."

I choked on a piece of veal, and took a long drink of wine to clear my throat. "Sorry, I missed the family resemblance."

Amusement crossed his face and he nodded. "Xana was the first of Dimitris' children. I was the last. There are hundreds who came between us. My father was quite proficient at populating our clan."

"What happened to the rest of them?"

"Most of them are still living. They are thriving members of my clan. Those I would call on if we faced war."

"You have that many Ancients in your clan?" I put down my fork in surprise. There were only four in my own. I couldn't imagine what Alasdair would have done if faced with that many other dragons of such significant power. "Do they challenge you for power often?"

"No, they all know they cannot defeat me. I've never had to fight for my position. When my father died, I stepped into his place without difficulty. The others sensed my power. And they feared it. You would be wise to follow in their footsteps."

He didn't have to worry about that. I had plenty of fear of his power. Julian was the son of Dimitris—one of the five Drakán survivors after our world was destroyed, and the Archos who masterminded my own grandfather's defeat at a human woman's hands. I couldn't help but wonder if Julian had also succeeded in populating his clan. The ability to procreate was considered a great gift from the gods, since it happened so infrequently.

"No, I have no children of my own," Julian said, reading my mind again. "Though I've certainly tried. But there is always the possibility it will happen someday soon."

The look he gave me was so blatantly full of desire I felt my own need rise up before I could control it. This was not happening. I didn't know what games Julian was playing, but I wanted no part of it. Anything that happened with Julian would just be a calculated maneuver in our own battle.

I deliberately slowed my heartbeat. I didn't like what was happening to my body. To my dragon. She recognized Julian for what he was—an alpha male—and she wanted him. To hell with any consequences or the fact we barely knew each other. It was at times like these when my human body and inner dragon fought the most.

Dessert was brought out by a well-dressed servant, his uniform black like everything else in the palace I'd seen so far. His skin was pale and his demeanor subservient as he bowed low before leaving. I was glad to see the diamond-shaped pupils in his amber eyes. I wouldn't think even

Julian could stand the temptation of having a human living with him.

Dessert was a delicate chocolate mousse served in a crystal goblet that melted on the tongue and succeeded in soothing my dragon. I'd done everything but pick up the goblet and lick the last dregs of chocolate from the bottom of the glass when Xana slammed into the room, knocking the heavy double doors against the walls with a crash.

She held a struggling young Drakán in her grasp. His nose was broken, and dried blood covered his mouth and down to his neck. One of his eyes was swollen completely shut. Xana picked him up and threw him onto the middle of the table. The table runner and candlesticks crashed to the floor, along with the crystal dessert goblets. Xana bowed before Julian then left the room.

Tension and the threat of violence filled the air as I waited for Julian to say something.

"What do you have to say for yourself, Petyr?" Julian asked.

Petyr spat at Julian and stared at him defiantly. He was a tall gangly man with thick, sandy blond hair. He probably would have been handsome if his face wasn't so swollen. I gauged his age to be no more than a couple of centuries at most, but I could sense his power and the hate that fed it. Petyr was strong—as strong as one of the Ancients in my own clan.

The silence was filled with energy, and I made sure to sit perfectly still so as not to draw any attention to myself. It would be interesting to observe how Julian handled his clan, and if he was really as powerful as he felt. Taking on Petyr wouldn't be a walk in the park.

Everything in the room was completely still. It didn't even seem as if we were breathing. Petyr's body suddenly flew across the room and hit with a painful thud against the black granite wall. The stone cracked behind him, but Petyr just grinned as blood stained his teeth and dripped from the corner of his mouth. His feet didn't touch the ground, and he was held spread-eagle against the wall. Hate shone like madness behind the green of his eyes.

Julian relaxed in his chair and stretched out his legs, crossing them at the ankles. It was as if he were lounging by the pool instead of holding a man's life in his hands. It didn't seem as if it took him any effort at all to control Petyr's body. I couldn't believe his indifference to what was happening.

Julian repeated his earlier statement. "I asked you a question, Petyr. I expect it to be answered."

"It doesn't matter what I say," Petyr hissed with pain. "My sentence is death either way."

"Yes, I know. But I like to give everyone a chance for redemption before facing the afterlife. I'd hate to travel to the Realm of the Dead with guilt on my shoulders. Nothing I can do to you here will compare with what you face there. It's best to clear your conscience."

Petyr's laugh was maniacal, but there was no repentance in his words. "She deserved everything she got from me—the human and her whelps that didn't have an ounce of power. I don't even think they were mine. You'll get everything you deserve one day. I curse you with my dying breath, Julian of the Belgae, for your time in power will soon end. I'll see you in the Realm of the Dead, Archos."

"Yes, you will," Julian said.

Petyr's body fell to the floor like a rag doll. There was a moment of silence before a great whoosh filled the room. Fire engulfed Petyr's body, and he turned to ashes in front of my eyes.

All I could do was stare in disbelief. I'd been witness to some horrible things in my line of work, but I'd never seen another Drakán with the ability to kill with just a thought. Dragon fire had to come from a dragon's breath. Didn't it?

Icy claws of terror scraped at my belly, and I stood up quickly, only thinking of the need to escape. To survive. I couldn't take my eyes from Petyr's ashes.

"I'm tired. I think I'll go to my room now," I said, backing slowly toward the doors.

"Come now, Rena, surely you're not so squeamish. I know your father, after all."

The way he'd said, "your father" was rather snide, and I wondered if there was something personal between Alasdair and Julian of which I wasn't aware.

"No, I'm not squeamish. I just wasn't expecting your methods. How do you manifest fire without your dragon form?"

He smiled, but didn't answer my question. "I don't delay justice when it is needed. A swift punishment is the best way to keep things in order."

"Unless he was innocent. But you only asked for his repentance, not if he was actually guilty."

"Your sense of fair play is very...human," Julian said with distaste.

I almost made a comment about how human blood also ran through his veins, but I remembered it didn't. Not really. His mother had been a Descendent from another clan and his father was one of the banished warriors, so Julian had very little human blood in him at all.

"What about the Council? You didn't ask their permission to kill."

"I don't need permission from the Council. As my power has grown, I've become my own Council. They can no longer defeat me and they know it."

Which meant Alasdair had known Julian couldn't be defeated, and he'd sent me to find him anyway. The evidence was stacking against Julian. He was the Descendent of two different lines of Drakán and his power was unmatched by even the Council. I couldn't imagine anyone else being more suited to the title of Destroyer.

I could tell he'd chosen that moment to read my mind again because his eyes turned to blue ice, and he stood slowly from his chair. I made a conscious effort not to take a step in retreat, but it was hard. Really hard.

"This is my clan, Rena Drake. And anyone who questions my authority is welcome to challenge me. My word is law and my decisions final."

"All societies thrive when there is true justice," I said, much more bravely than I felt. "For you to dole it out as you see fit simply makes you a tyrant, no better than the other Archos who mistreat their own clans."

"There is a difference in how I provide for my people

and how your father abuses your own. Do not get our ways confused because you were witness to the event. I could have tortured him, prolonged his pain. That's what your father would have done."

"And he listens no better than you do. No one wishes to live their lives in fear of being condemned to death before they ever have a chance to live. I know the people who live with this fear. And making them live that way is its own cruelty."

"You know nothing, Enforcer. Petyr brutally murdered his human mate and left their two children to starve—twin boys nearing puberty who have shown great promise in their powers. There were witnesses to her murder, but it doesn't matter. I am linked to all my people, even the human mates, through a blood oath. I know every thought and deed that crosses their minds. I know when they feel joy. And I know when they suffer. Does a man like Petyr deserve for me to draw out his death just so I can hear his endless excuses? I would never show such weakness."

His explanation caught me by surprise. When he put things in that perspective I could understand his reasoning. I'd never heard of an Archos tying himself to his people through a blood oath. And I wondered why Alasdair didn't do it with our people. I wondered if he even knew he could.

"What happens when someone in your clan merely disagrees with your methods or your rules? Is it instant death or are they allowed to voice their opinions? All of our people should have a choice in how they live. And if they make the wrong choice there should be consequences, but the choice should be theirs."

"But we aren't people, are we, Rena? We're monsters with the instincts of an animal, even though we have many human traits. And what you might think are simple choices could possibly affect our entire race. I am their executioner, just as you have come to be mine, but I am also their greatest protector."

He looked at me with an intensity I couldn't decipher, as if he wanted me to understand something I wasn't quite grasping. I couldn't think of anything to say. It was a rare moment for me to be rendered speechless.

"Xana," he called out.

Xana appeared once again in the doorway of the dining room in her black leather, only this time there was a whip coiled at her side. She stood silently, waiting for instructions.

"Please show Ms. Drake to her room. I believe she's feeling the jet lag from her trip."

I had no choice but to follow Xana deeper into the dragon's lair.

CHAPTER
TWELVE

Xana led me down a long hallway. The black granite was a familiar motif. Enormous gold-leafed mirrors flanked each wall, and I watched my many reflections, fascinated how the red of my dress stood out like a flame against the gold of my skin. My slippered feet made no sound against the hard floor.

We came to a curved staircase at the end of a hallway. The steps were so opaque you could barely see where one began and the next ended. The handrails were columns of twisted black iron that spiraled to the upper floors. Xana led me up three flights and down another long hallway before stopping in front of a heavy oak door. She left me there without so much as a goodbye.

I was truly alone. I opened the door to my new prison and was pleased to find it was more than accommodating. The bed was large—lush with a red satin comforter and sheets. Sheer drapes in a matching shade were tied back to the corners of a massive four-poster bed.

Thick black carpeting had replaced the granite and was soft under my feet. The walls and ceiling were painted a flat black to match. Red satin curtains hung from the windows. I was relieved to see there was actual electricity in the room instead of the candles that seemed prevalent throughout the rest of the palace. Gleaming gold sconces flanked the doors and windows and a fluidly curved chandelier hung from the ceiling.

The luggage I'd left at the airport was neatly stacked in the closet. My clothes had been unpacked and put away by some unknown servant. Not that I needed the clothes I'd brought. A look through the wardrobe and drawers showed a full selection of clothing for every occasion. A look at the exclusive tags showed they just happened to be in my size. Hanging face front on the door of the wardrobe was a peignoir of the sheerest silk. I rubbed the fabric between my fingers, and my dragon sighed in envy. My dragon *loved* expensive clothing. I closed the door before I could think better of putting it on, and put myself out of temptation's way.

A lady's writing desk sat in the corner, complete with stationery and a gold pen. And on top of the desk sat my purse. Before I could think better of it, I rushed to it and pulled out my cell phone. I automatically dialed Noah's number and held my breath until I heard his voice on the other end.

"Rena," he said on a whoosh of relief as soon as he picked

up. "I'm glad you called. I've had a terrible feeling all day, but I haven't been able to see anything."

Just hearing his voice released the tension I'd been holding in my shoulders. "That's not unusual. You've never been able to read me. My shields are too strong."

"No, I mean I can't see anything. Not your brother. Not the average person walking past me on the street. My visions are completely gone. Someone has me blocked. I can feel the guards they're forcing down on me. I don't know how they're doing it, but it's really ticking me off. Are you okay?"

After the power I'd just seen Julian wield, I wouldn't be at all surprised if he could control another psychic across an entire continent.

"I'm fine," I said, deciding to keep Julian's power to myself for now. "I'm in one piece at least."

"Do you need me? I can be there in a heartbeat."

"You'll have to tell me how you'd accomplish that before I let you. You have too many secrets, Noah."

I had so many emotions fighting for space within me. I didn't know Noah well, but I was drawn to him. Not the dragon in me. But the *human* me. He made me nervous with his mysterious answers and his need to protect me with his life. His need to love me. Even thinking about his words from the night before gave me chills. Love was foreign to me. But there was something comforting about it at the same time. I didn't know how to deal with these emotions. But I knew I needed normalcy in my life. I wanted normalcy. What made me even more nervous was the chance that I might get Noah killed by bringing him into Julian's territory. It would put an end to normal, that's for sure. I couldn't risk his life by exposing him to Drakán business. No matter how strong his own abilities.

"Rena..." He hesitated. "My people are looking over our situation. They'll eventually give in and let me tell you what I know. Just be patient."

"Yeah, that's really not one of my better personality traits." I rubbed at my gritty eyes with my fingers. "Just stay put for now, Noah. I don't think this is a mess you want to get in the middle of."

I could practically hear his silent struggle to argue on the other end of the phone, before the struggle eased and his breathing changed.

"What's really bothering you?" I asked. "Besides me being here."

"Don't ever doubt that I want you, Rena," he said, his voice tight with frustration. "I'm worried about you because I care about you. That's how relationships work. And I don't know how to warn you to be careful without spilling the secrets I'm oathbound to keep."

"I'm not asking you to break your oath. I understand secrets better than anyone."

"Just know that you're special—in different ways than you think. And I think you might be in greater danger than you realize. Just know there are others outside your own race who might wish to do you harm. You have to keep your senses open and your guard up all the time. They'll strike when you're weak."

"Believe me. I'm used to that concept."

"Just promise me you'll be careful. And watch your back

around the man you've decided to hunt. He's dangerous. I don't know what it is about him, but he's more than you think he is. And you'll be blinded by his strength and drawn to his power." The bitterness in Noah's voice rang out loud and clear.

"What is it you're trying to tell me?" I asked.

"Yesterday, before my visions were blocked, I kept seeing you with someone. The same scene played over and over again. His hair was as dark as yours, and his hands were pale against the gold of your skin. Your lives are entwined somehow. But so are ours, Rena. Remember that when you're with him."

"You have no say in my life," I said. "You've known me a day."

"It only took me a minute."

We were both breathing heavy and something that felt suspiciously like tears gathered behind my eyelids. I didn't know how to deal with this. I was tired of everyone in my life playing me to their own tune.

"It seems like things would be a lot easier if I just walked away from you both."

"You'll want to before this is finished. But there are some things you can't control the outcome of. Prophecies are like that."

"Wait, what do you know of prophecies?"

"Enough. They're not unique to your people, you know. Just take my advice and be careful. You won't forget me when you're with him."

Noah was already talking like Julian's claim on me was a done deal. I belonged to no man, and hormones were the last thing I wanted to add into the mix of this disaster. I had to stay away from Julian, plain and simple. My thoughts were so deep I didn't catch all of Noah's words, but I managed to mutter a goodbye before I hung up.

I still held the cell phone to my ear, listening to the empty distance between us. I turned it off completely and dropped it back in my purse. My life had taken a decidedly weird turn somewhere along the way, and Noah was a distraction I didn't need.

What I needed was to clear my mind, to think of some way I could defeat Julian and get what I wanted without dying in the process. I opened the dresser drawer and grabbed one of the nightgowns I'd brought with me and headed into the bathroom. I laid my clothes on the counter and piled my hair up on the top of my head and secured it with a clip.

The bathroom mirrored the bedroom in decoration. Black marble veined with streaks of white dominated the room. The faucets were gold and delicately curved—the towels blood red as they draped over the towel rods like a sacrifice.

Hot water poured from the faucet as it filled the tub, and I added perfumed bath salts into the water, watching them dissolve into cloudy bubbles. I slid into decadence as the steam rose around me and fogged all of the mirrors. The heat felt like heaven against my weary body, and my inner dragon writhed with pleasure against my skin.

I nodded off a couple of times before I realized the water had turned cold. I pulled the drain and climbed limply out of the tub, my bones practically liquid with exhaustion. I dried off quickly and rubbed scented cream over my body. I slipped a thin nightgown the color of violets over my head and shivered at the coolness of the silk.

I'd only been thinking of falling face-first into the bed when I walked back into the bedroom, so it took me a minute to realize something wasn't quite right. Dozens of tapered candles glowed from candelabra around the room. Champagne chilled in a bucket next to the bed. A glass flute sat on the nightstand, filled with a liquid full of fresh bubbles. I looked at the door and saw it was still locked. Not that something as flimsy as a lock could keep Julian out. I'd learned that lesson at the hotel.

The black peignoir I'd admired lay across the bed, and my pulse sped with yearning. It was all but transparent with straps that tied into bows at each shoulder and a plunging neckline. On top of the nightgown lay a single red rose.

My breath exhaled nervously as I thought of Noah's vision. *Willpower.* I was here to do a job. Not to fall prey to a powerful dragon. I was determined for Noah to be wrong. He had to be wrong.

I grabbed Julian's not so subtle gift and took it to the window. The material was impossibly soft and delicate as I clutched it between my fingers. I opened the window, relishing the icy cold wind that allowed my mind to snap out of its haze. I let go. The gown fluttered down three stories onto the garden below.

I snapped the window closed and walked over to my dresser, stripping off the nightie I'd put on after my bath. I dug through the drawer until I found the most chaste gown I'd packed—a high-collared, white nightgown that fell all the way to my ankles. I was going to be hot as hell all night long, but at least I felt a little more protected from Julian's gaze.

I turned around and spoke to the room at large. "I am not one of your 'monsters' to command, Julian. I am the Enforcer, and it would do you well to remember it. You will answer all of my questions eventually. And so help you gods if you really are The Destroyer. Because I will kill you."

The laughter in my mind slithered up my spine like a caress.

Sweet dreams.

And then the voice was gone, and I knew I was alone again.

I was far from tired, but I went over to the bed and pulled back the covers, knowing I was going to be sweltering under so many layers all night. I got into bed and punched my pillow a couple of times for good measure before closing my eyes and ordering my body to relax. I realized I hadn't bothered to blow out the candles as soon as I saw the soft flicker of lights behind my eyelids.

I said a few choice words and pulled back the covers, getting out of bed to blow out the candles when the room went dark. The smell of wax and smoke lay heavy in the air. I waited to feel Julian's presence, but there was nothing.

I closed my eyes and tried my hardest to think of anything but Julian.

THIRTEEN

I finally found sleep as the gray light of dawn began to creep through the windows. It wasn't long after when the dream began.

The blood-red throne at the head of the great room was still impressive in size. The chandeliers weren't lit, but there was light coming from somewhere because I could see the throne clearly, even though the rest of the room tapered off into nothingness.

My dreams were always real, but something about this one was even more so.

I wore my white nightgown, and the black granite was cold beneath my bare feet as I walked into the room. I practically floated up the small set of stairs that led to the throne, and I ran my fingers across the soft red velvet.

They came away smeared with blood. Hot, like only freshly spilled blood could be. Now that I'd touched it, the sweet coppery smell was unmistakable, and my mouth watered with need. I jerked my hand away and wiped my fingers on my gown—the stain bright crimson against the snowy white fabric.

"Your true powers are alive in your dreams. Why would you not make them just as potent while you are awake?" a seductive voice asked from the shadows. "Your humanness stifles your dragon. Your need to feel all the things they do is making you weak."

I searched for the voice. Julian walked straight out of the wall—more than a shadow, more than a man. Just his presence awakened things inside me I wasn't aware of. The need to run my fingers across the blood once more and rub them across my lips was as tempting as any aphrodisiac. I could see my wants mirrored in Julian's eyes.

"Denying your beast will eventually wither every part of you, human and dragon. Open yourself and accept what you really are. Leave your humanity behind and let your dragon take control. You've been fighting her when she should be your greatest ally. What does your beast want?"

I screamed inside my head. I didn't want to be more monster than human. I didn't want to be like Alasdair or Calista. Or like Julian. The added power of leaving my humanity behind wasn't worth the price I'd have to pay.

As far as what my beast wanted, I didn't have an answer. I could feel her thoughts as if they were mine, and I was terrified because at the center of everything she coveted, there was only Julian. My beast wanted him.

I shoved my dragon away and got myself under control. I changed the subject and asked, "What are you doing here?"

"This is my dream. I can go where I please," he said arrogantly. "I invited you, and you accepted my invitation. There is something between us, Rena. A connection. I knew you wouldn't be able to resist me for long."

I shivered at the thought of how closely Julian's words had mirrored Noah's. "Your ego leaves something to be desired. I still have my free will, no matter how much you wish it otherwise in your dream."

"I like to believe that the gods have brought you here for a reason. It's up to you whether or not you seek the reason out. Now, I asked you a question. You have halted the growth of your powers by closing off your natural-born instincts in your need to feel more human. Your emotional state when awake is what holds you back. Only in your dreams can you truly be the dragon you were meant to be. Why would you make yourself less, when you could be so much more?"

"There's nothing wrong with wanting to have human emotions," I said before I could stop myself. "And when I'm awake, I'm the one who's in control of them. I like being in control."

"Ahh, yes, I've noticed this about you. Like this ugly nightgown you are wearing. It is just to prove a point, no? To prove that you have the strength to stand against me?"

"You seem to be missing the point of how my decisions have nothing to do with you."

"Hmm," he said, circling around me. "I think you must not realize your appeal. All of that sexy hair. Skin the color of gold dust. And a stubborn chin that had rather take a punch than back down. And then there's your eyes. They're like black fire."

Dragons weren't self-conscious by nature and we never backed away from desire as long as the feelings were mutual. But I felt the urge to cover myself, even though I knew I was perfectly decent.

"Ahh, but you aren't, my sweet. That chaste gown is as transparent as the naughtiest lingerie. But still, I believe I prefer my choice. Don't you?"

I felt the whisper against my skin, just as when he'd changed my clothes before dinner. Only this time I was afraid to look down. I could already tell there was much less there than had been before.

"You're wasting time with parlor tricks, Julian. We have many things to talk about."

I walked over to the throne with purpose and sat down. The blood was gone, and only the softness of the velvet touched my skin. I noticed the wisp of smoke curl out of Julian's nostrils and knew he was irritated that I'd taken his place of power. Good. That made us even. Because I was furious with him.

I crossed my legs. He took a step toward me before he could stop himself.

"I don't think my throne suits you, Rena. I had something a little more...primitive in mind for you."

"Chains in the dungeon, no doubt."

"Never. I was thinking more along the lines of this."

He nodded his head to the space next to me and another throne appeared out of thin air. A smaller version of his, just as plush and ornate. Just as ancient. But a lady's chair.

"I would have you rule at my side," he said. "Think of how powerful we could be."

"I don't know, Julian. I don't think you'll be very comfortable there. It looks a bit small."

He threw his head back and laughed, a full-bellied laugh that echoed off the walls and sent tingles low in my stomach. He looked surprised at the sound.

"You're right," he said. "This is much more suitable to us."

He snapped his fingers and both thrones were gone. In their place was a bed the size of a lake. I was lying in the middle of it.

This was not like any bed I'd ever seen. It put the one in my room to shame. This was a carnal bed, a bed for vices and wicked things. Things I was desperately trying not to think of.

"You're a bad man, Julian. How are we supposed to speak of important matters when it is obvious your mind is elsewhere?"

He gave me a smoldering look, and I felt his power slowly creep around my body so it held me in a loose embrace. His dark hair was unbound around his shoulders and his clothes changed before my eyes. Gone was the suit he'd been wearing at dinner and in its place was a pair of black lounging pajamas. His chest was bared, so I had a beautiful view of hard ridges of muscles that rippled across his chest and down his stomach. He was broad and smooth, and I longed to run my hands over him. My hand moved toward him instinctively, but I jerked it back just in time.

"You look good for your age," I said with false bravado. I was losing the battle and he knew it.

His eyes crinkled at the corners in silent laughter, and he stalked toward the bed—a dragon on the hunt.

"So what should I get for answering your questions?" he asked. "I'm an expert at negotiations." His accent was thick and his breathing heavy.

"You've had many years of practice." I closed my eyes against the onslaught of his power. It felt as though his hands were already touching me. They started at the pulse in my neck and slowly skimmed downward toward my waist. A moan escaped my lips.

"What do you propose?" he asked, reverting to the old tongue.

The bed dipped down and I opened my eyes. He crawled toward me, and his muscles flexed with every movement that brought him closer. I couldn't remember my own name, much less think of why I'd gotten on a plane and ended up in Belgium.

"Come now, *chérie*, surely you can think of something worthwhile."

He was too close. I couldn't breathe. He reached down to touch me just as I got my brain back under control. I knew I wasn't ready for any kind of contact. Just our hands touching was enough to make me lose control of every power I had. I scrambled off the bed in a hurry, all sense of decorum forgotten, and left him lounging in satisfied male pride.

"I want to know where the missing Drakán are," I blurted out.

"Ahh, you wish to ask me questions? Is this correct?"

"Yes."

"And what shall I get in return? These are negotiations after all."

"What do you want?"

His gaze left my face and traveled slowly, sensually, down my body, and I knew instinctively I was blushing everywhere.

"That is a dangerous question," he said. "What would you say if I asked for your body in return for these answers I'm supposed to give?"

"I'd say, no."

"Very well, then. I suppose I will have to settle for a kiss."

"Just a kiss?" I asked, not trusting the gleam in his eyes.

"Of course. You doubt my word?"

"Absolutely. I don't trust you, Julian."

"Wise beyond your years as well as beautiful. But yes, this time I promise nothing more than a kiss. The rest will be up to you."

"Agreed," I said before I could change my mind. "But I want my questions answered first."

"Yes, yes," he said. "Ask."

He flicked his wrist and the bed was gone. In its place was a chaise longue in the same red velvet and gold trim as his throne.

"Please get on with these questions. I am most eager to get to my part of the negotiations."

"I don't suppose you can change my clothes to something a little more appropriate for a business meeting?" I asked.

"Of course, but why would I do that when I can see all of your lovely body the way it is displayed now?"

"Never mind," I said.

143

I took a deep breath and tried to think of a good place to start without giving away too much information.

"If you're tied to your clan members as you say, then you know Jillian is dead," I said.

He grew solemn at the mention of his fallen clan member. "Yes. It is why I knew you'd be coming to me. I saw you in her last moments. I saw what you did for her. I'm grateful for the mercy you showed her."

"There have been more like her. Dozens more. And humans as well."

"I am also aware of this."

I was surprised to hear this. I knew of no other Drakán who could see things as clearly as Calista did. Julian either had much better connections across clan lines or his psychic ability rivaled Calista's.

"And do you know about the ones who have disappeared altogether? The ones who have vanished from the Earth Realm completely?"

I paced back and forth in front of the chaise, my agitation growing the more I learned about Julian. He lounged lazily, waiting for me to come to my own conclusions.

"Of course you know," I said. "You seem to know everything. Were you alive during the slaughter of my family? When Niklos was betrayed?"

"Yes, but I was just a boy," he said. "My father got great enjoyment out of defeating Niklos because of his stupidity."

"Because he trusted his mate?" I asked.

"Because he trusted anyone. Especially with clan secrets."

I was disturbed by his answer, though I didn't know

why. "Then you are aware that Niklos was killed because of the other warriors' ability to travel through time?" I asked.

He nodded once, his eyes a little more wary.

"I'm told that you have the ability to travel. That you're a *Viator*. Is this true?"

He gave me a blank look and raised an eyebrow. "If you have already heard such things about me then you know the answer. At least you think you do. Now, if you've finished can we please get on with my part of the negotiations?"

"I'm not finished," I growled. "If you can travel then you must realize that the disappearances of these people could be laid at your feet. The list of those who can do so is rather short."

"Ahh, and I suppose you've already crossed your own father off the list of suspects. The last I checked he also had this ability."

"Did you kill your own clansman? Are you The Destroyer?" I yelled, a billow of black smoke curling out of my mouth and nostrils. I closed my mouth in surprise. I'd never had that happen before.

"Ahh, you have such passion. Such hidden depths," he said, inhaling the slightly sulfuric scent. "And since I told you I would answer your question, then I will tell you the answer is no. I am not the one you're hunting. I am not The Destroyer."

"Oh," I said. "Of course, I'm sure the real Destroyer would tell me that as well."

"I'm sure you're right. I can't prove it to you. Both of my parents were Descendents, just as the Prophecy says. But if you search harder, you'll find there are others like me. It is rare for different clans to meet and procreate, but it does happen."

"If you are not The Destroyer, then who is?"

"I cannot tell you."

"Can't or won't?"

"I don't know who The Destroyer is. But he is someone very powerful. Someone with Ancient blood."

"Will you help me search for him? The Council is supposed to deliver a warrant of execution for me to kill anyone who has become involved with The Destroyer. Contact them and let them know they have your support. The warrant will come through faster."

"No," Julian said. His answer was definite.

"I beg your pardon? How can you just say no? The Destroyer could affect what's left of our entire civilization. Not to mention all of these deaths are bound to draw attention to us from the humans. If he lives, then the Prophecy can never be fulfilled."

"Do you think the Prophecy matters to me? I am king in my own right here among my people. Why would I give it up to see The Promised Child rise to power? I agree that The Destroyer must be stopped, and if I stumble across him, I will kill him simply because he dared to harm one of my own. But that is as far as I'll go."

"Fine. I'll do it without you. I'll leave first thing in the morning to go hunting."

"No. You will stay here until I say you can leave."

"You're welcome to say no for yourself, Julian. You are not allowed to say no for me. I am the Enforcer. It is my job to kill those who break our laws, and I will see this through."

"Then you will die."

"So be it. At least I'll die with honor instead of cowering in a corner protecting my hoard."

I knew I'd gone too far. The pale blue of his eyes turned red around the rims and black smoke curled out his nostrils.

"No, you will not die a coward. But you will die a fool. I've heard enough of this talk."

Julian had moved closer without me realizing it. Before I could issue a protest, he touched the back of his hand to my neck. The gentleness of the touch was completely at odds with his obvious anger. And then the bottom dropped out of my world.

His lips found mine in a scorching kiss that left no doubt of the power that raged through him. My eyes closed, and colors swirled behind my eyelids. My power sought his and embraced it. The two magics melded together, so I couldn't tell where mine began and his ended. I went blind with the intensity, so my other senses took over—touch and texture the only things that were important.

His mouth was open and hot on mine, as hot as any fire I'd ever created. A moan came from somewhere, and I assumed it was mine when Julian gave a triumphant laugh and changed the angle of the kiss.

When our tongues touched a blue flame erupted around us—a swirling flame of such intense heat it should have burned us to ash. But we sustained the heat and fed its hunger, both of us desperate to merge and make the fire whole—a living, breathing power that would have been ours to control. I needed to be a part of him more than I needed to breathe, more than I needed to be.

"No," I said, and tore myself away. I thought of Noah and his vision. What was I doing?

"Not exactly what a man wants to hear when making love to a woman."

The blue flame began to ebb as I broke our connection, but I could still see the inferno blazing in his eyes and knew that if I were to look in a mirror I would see a matching gaze. I watched in awe as the flame snuffed itself out and left me cold.

"Get away from me," I said as I scrambled back as far as the chaise would allow. "What do you think you're doing?" My breath was unsteady, heaving in and out rapidly from my lungs. "What was that? What just happened?"

"I kept my end of the bargain," he said much more steadily. "We agreed on a kiss."

I was angry because he was obviously not as affected by the results of the kiss as I was. Before I could stop myself tears came to my eyes. I couldn't remember the last time I cried, and I wasn't about to start now. I blinked rapidly to stop the tears from falling.

I looked down and noticed for the first time we were both naked, our clothes disintegrated by the flame.

"That was more than just a kiss," I said, struggling to breathe.

"Perhaps," he said arrogantly, his face giving away nothing.

"It will not happen again."

"Perhaps not."

"I came here to find out what's happened to our people. And I will do whatever it takes to see that whoever is involved is stopped. No matter what you say, I don't believe you are completely innocent in all this. You know too much and are sharing too little. Petyr might have been right when he said your time of power was coming to an end."

"And who's going to defeat me, Rena? You? A Drakán so desperate to turn her back on her dragon that she doesn't recognize a mating fire when she sees one?"

He was right. I had no idea what had just happened between us other than the fact it scared me. "Stay away from me, or I'll kill you."

"Would the human in you allow you to kill a man who was your lover?" he asked smugly.

"You've already made it very clear that you're a monster, not a man. I won't forget it next time."

I turned and walked away, my anger so great I didn't realize I was trapped in Julian's dream world. I ignored his taunting laughter, but against my better judgment I turned and looked at him when he called my name.

"I've changed my mind about the nightgown," he said. "I've decided I don't prefer my choice after all."

The words hit me like a slap to the face. My pride was already damaged and now my self-esteem and ego were following close behind it. I held my chin up and began to turn around again, not bothering to reply.

You are splendid just as you are, he whispered in my mind. *And next time, lifemate, your cowardice will not stop me from taking what's mine. You are bone of my bone, and flesh of my flesh, and you are a worthy opponent. Run while you can.*

I followed his advice. I ran until I couldn't any longer—until the walls of Julian's dream world disappeared, and I was left running through the thick blackness of night itself, alone in a place between this world and the next.

I woke in my bed, the stitch in my side a not so gentle reminder of where I'd been. My body was unclothed, and the white nightgown I'd gone to bed in was tossed in a heap on the floor. My heart pounded violently in my chest, and when I got shakily out of bed, I saw the sheets had been scorched by fire.

CHAPTER

FOURTEEN

There was no way I'd be able to go back to sleep, so I splashed cold water on my face and dressed in a pair of jeans and a long-sleeved black T-shirt. I slipped on a pair of black ankle boots, and left my hair loose around my shoulders.

It was still shy of noon and my stomach rumbled loudly, but I wasn't ready to face Julian just yet. Where had the blue fire come from? As soon as I got home I was going to do some digging in our archives. I'd never seen it mentioned in anything I'd ever read, and with my luck any mention of the mating fire was probably in the archives that had been stolen by Dimitris. But if the mating fire meant what I thought it meant, I knew I wanted to take no part.

I picked up the black cell phone from the desk, and turned it over and over again in my hands. The temptation to call Noah was overwhelming. I wondered what he'd say if

I told him pursuing me was pointless because I was already mated to a dragon. Nothing good, that's for sure. I put down the phone and picked up the gold pen and a piece of stationery instead. I needed a plan, a visible list of goals to help me stay on track.

The number one thing on my list was to get out of Belgium, but I crossed it off and deemed it impossible for the time being. With the power Julian wielded, it would be impossible to leave without his permission.

The second thing on my list was to stay away from Julian. I also crossed that one off the list. As much as I wanted to keep my distance from the man who could literally become "the old ball and chain," I still needed to ask him a few pertinent questions. Our discussion during the dream had been interrupted much too soon.

I was finally headed in the right direction with my next idea. The best thing I could do with my forced time in Belgium was to talk to Julian's clan. They'd give me a little insight into their leader, and one of them might know something about the disappearances. Gossip was rampant among the Drakán, especially with the use of the internet. There was a good chance somebody had overheard something about the missing Drakán.

Satisfied with the idea, I left the privacy of my room in search of food. I jogged down the three flights of stairs, lost in my own thoughts, so I was taken by surprise when I almost ran into a child no taller than my shoulders and dressed like a gypsy. I did a double take when I realized it wasn't a child after all, but a woman.

Her pale skin was smooth and flawless, her hair as red as

flame and her eyes emerald green. She wore a skirt of filmy layers in shades of red and a white peasant blouse that hung off her shoulders. Her feet were bare, her toenails painted a wicked red, and a silver toe ring wrapped around her pinkie. There was a wisdom of age behind her pleasant expression. I knew at once she was an Ancient.

"You're quite right," she said. Her teeth were small and square and very white. "I'm terribly old and quite set in my ways." Her voice was husky and smooth like fine cognac and her power felt me out, testing my strengths and weaknesses automatically.

I ground my own teeth together in frustration. It was starting to get on my nerves how easily my enemies read my mind. I'd never faced anything like it before, and I was starting to wonder if my own clan was really that much weaker than Julian's or if something else entirely was going on.

"You've always been very critical of yourself. But don't worry. I have an unfair advantage over you. My mother was Faerie and my father was Drakán. Faeries are impervious to dragon magic, so you're an open book to me. And before you ask, Julian sent me to keep you company over breakfast and answer any questions you might have about our clan. We'll have a nice chat, and then you can go prepare for tonight's *sfara*. He feels badly that you were not given the proper ceremony for your arrival last evening."

"I just bet he does," I growled.

"He also requests that you wear black, as is our tradition at such gatherings."

"Black is not the color of my clan. He presumes too much."

It wasn't unusual for *sfaras* to be color mandatory. But I wasn't a member of Julian's clan, and it was an insult for him to request that I wear his colors. Each clan was recognized by the color of their dragon scales. Alasdair's was red, which worked out well because he thought it appropriate for his clan to represent the blood of the hunt. I knew from experience that fresh blood was almost black and dried dark brown. It was my firsthand experience that made the upcoming *sfara* the last place I wanted to be.

"He wants you to feel at ease. Wearing your own colors will only bring animosity toward you from the others."

"It doesn't matter. Everyone will know who I am. They'll smell my clan on my skin. I will always be the daughter of Alasdair, and wearing Julian's colors won't stop their hatred or their curiosity. I'll not bend to Julian's will. Red is the color of my clan, and that is what I'll wear."

"So be it," she said, a measure of respect in her eyes and an odd smile. "Now, let's see about getting you something to eat. We've got many things to do. My name is Esmerelda, by the way".

She took my arm and led me to the solarium. It was the only room on the main floor I'd seen that wasn't black. Watery light filtered through the large expanse of windows that overlooked a lush garden. There was green as far as the eye could see, and no sign of the city traffic that bustled just outside the gates. The rain fell hard, and I watched as fat leaves bounced rhythmically beneath the assault of water.

The tile in the solarium was textured and the color of sand. The walls a buttery yellow. An oblong table made of dark wood sat in the middle of the room and was already laid out with food. Esmerelda gestured to a seat, and I gladly sat down to satisfy my hunger.

"I don't mean to be rude," I said, lifting the lid on one of the silver platters, "but there are some things I need to see to today. I don't know what Julian has put you up to, but I believe whatever it is, is probably unnecessary. I don't need a babysitter." I heaped my plate full of bacon and sausage. I sniffed at the scrambled eggs and curled my lip, but I put some on my plate anyway. I needed the extra protein.

"Don't worry. You'll have plenty of time to speak to other members of our clan. They wouldn't talk to you anyway without Julian's permission."

I narrowed my eyes as she read my mind again. My shields didn't seem to work with Fae magic, no matter how high I built them. I'd never had anyone break my shields before I came to Belgium, so it was a new experience for me.

"I understand why you can read me," I said. "Fae magic is not something I understand. But why can Julian and Xana read me? I know my abilities are strong."

"I'm afraid they've got you at somewhat of a disadvantage. Julian is a very powerful Ancient. His father was a pure blood and his mother was a Drakán Descendent. One of the lost powers from our Realm was the ability to absorb another's powers. It was a trait of only those of royal blood. So he uses my Fae magic whenever he feels it's necessary."

"So my powers are useless here?" My mind was screaming in revolt at this revelation. No wonder the Council was afraid of him and didn't like to meet. They ran the risk of Julian absorbing their powers.

"Not completely. You need a mentor. Julian is concerned by your lack of power. He does not wish to have a mate who turns her back on her dragon and therefore closes off the potential to further her powers. And he's right. You'll eventually end up dead."

"I have no intention of becoming Julian's mate."

"Your refusal lacks conviction. There's no use lying to yourself."

"I'd prefer if we just didn't speak of Julian at all. Would you mind answering some questions? I could use an Ancient's insight."

She nodded her head, and it was then I noticed her ears were slightly pointed at the tips.

"Is it possible for the Prophecy to be wrong? Or, I don't know—" I shrugged, "—maybe even possible to change the outcome of the Prophecy?"

"The first thing you must realize about prophecies is that they are female in nature, which means they are reliable to a certain extent. The goddesses are fickle creatures and can stab you in the back just as they hold out their arms to catch you when you fall. Prophecies also hold a vagueness about them that could allow free will to interfere if necessary."

That sounded just crazy enough to be something the goddesses would do. I'd always secretly wondered if our lives were so long because it took an eternity for the gods and goddesses to decide what they wanted to do with us.

Esmerelda chuckled, a high-pitched laugh that sounded like bells ringing. "You know the story of how the gods Banished the five warriors to this Realm because they couldn't decide which of them would be king."

I nodded in agreement.

"I can see from your memories that the new archives of your clan are lacking some of the knowledge of the original archives that were stolen. Allow me to illuminate you a few things that were missed. The goddess gave each warrior— Niklos, Gregori, Dimitris, Lucian, and Thelos—a scroll containing the Prophecy after the Banishment. These five were the last pure bloods our race has known, and they each did their best to create as many offspring as possible. Once the clans were plentiful in number, the five Archos set out to discover each other's lairs so they could kidnap the female Drakán and try to mate with them. It was the only way to ensure The Promised Child would be born since both parents had to have Drakán blood."

"But the five pure bloods didn't succeed in creating The Promised Child," I said. "You'd think it would only be their power that was strong enough to ensure the salvation of our race."

"The Prophecy says The Promised Child shares the blood of two Descendents. It could be anyone. Anywhere. The five pure bloods had their chance, but they all met with untimely deaths before they could breed with other Drakán females."

"You were alive when this happened?" I asked. If this was true than Esmerelda could very well be the oldest Drakán in existence.

"Yes, though I was still a newling. As you know, Niklos was beheaded by his wife and torched. But the others shared a similar fate. Lucian was poisoned by an enemy and then turned to ash. Dimitris was killed in a terrible battle. Gregori was killed by another Drakán in a duel over a woman. And Thelos was captured by the Faeries and tortured before he was burned. The Faeries' magic was powerful enough that they could emulate the heat of dragon fire and turn a Drakán to ash."

"I didn't know that." I filed the information away. It gave me a new respect for Esmerelda's powers.

"I wouldn't expect you to know, but it's not a secret. Just as it's not a secret that Thelos was my father. But my mother was Faerie and her people didn't care to have their royal princess stolen and impregnated by a dragon."

"I can imagine. What about Julian's parents? They were both Drakán. This is one of the things that led me here. You have to admit that there are aspects of Julian's powers, combined with his parentage, that give me good reason to suspect him of being The Destroyer," I said.

"Maybe you should ask yourself if *you* think he is The Destroyer. Mates should know each other better than themselves. What does your heart tell you?"

"To stay away. And I've already told you, I have no plans of becoming Julian's mate. No matter what he says."

Esmerelda sat there and stared at me patiently until I felt I had to explain.

"I know that there's an attraction between us. A need comes over me whenever he's near. I won't belong to anyone, and I'd never let him have that much control over me. It's best I leave before things get too far out of hand."

I realized I was moving the cooling eggs around on my plate instead of eating them, and I set my fork down deliberately on the table. I needed to get back in control and not let Esmerelda distract me from my goal.

"I also don't trust Julian," I said. "His psychic power makes mine look inconsequential."

"Julian is unique in many ways, but he is not who you are seeking," she said. "The human world is vast, and the Drakán are not the only race to have lost their homeland. It would benefit you to remember that in your search for The Destroyer."

"What is that supposed to mean? Does that mean The Destroyer isn't Drakán? I couldn't care less about any other creatures or what has happened to them at this point. No offense."

"None taken," she said, her smile genuine. "And yes, The Destroyer is most definitely Drakán. Julian's parentage has never been a secret among our own clan, or a secret from the other Archos. I can't say that is always the case for other Drakán who share similar parentage. Many of them relish their privacy.

"You know that Julian's father was Dimitris. But did you know that Dimitris was the most feared of the five warriors? He was of royal blood, a prince of the Realm, and the true heir to the throne. He was the cruelest of all the Drakán, and he was very angry the gods didn't choose him as king just because he was the next in line."

"Then Julian should have the right to call himself king

until The Promised Child is found," I said, surprised by this information.

"I agree, but Julian is not his father and he wouldn't presume to second-guess the gods as Dimitris would. Julian knows well how cruel his father was. Dimitris was a warrior so fierce it was said no woman would bed him voluntarily for fear of being torn in two with his ferocity. He saw all things in terms of battle, and he constantly schemed to eliminate the offspring of the other Archos so they could not produce The Promised Child."

"What happened?"

"Dimitris set out to find Gregori's clan first. This was long after he created his plan to kill your own grandfather. It took Dimitris more than two hundred years to track them down, and by then Gregori had hundreds of children and human mates in his clan. I was a newling when this happened, barely a hundred myself, but I remember the stories of destruction as if it were yesterday.

"Dimitris tore through Gregori's compound with a vengeance, destroying all that was in his path, until he came upon Ileana in her bathing chamber. He was lovestruck— the beauty of her body and the fire in her eyes an aphrodisiac he couldn't resist. He changed to dragon form and took her. He flew her to a place no one could find—a place on the other side of the world just on the edge of this Realm and the next. They were surrounded by water and couldn't be tracked. Not by her family. Not by his.

"Dimitris' clan thought he was dead and roamed aimlessly waiting to see if another Archos would rise to power. But Dimitris was still very much alive. He bedded

Ileana every night for a century against her will until she bore him a son. When Julian was born, Dimitris wrapped him tightly in the stars and sent him to me to care for. He knew I held no allegiance to my father Thelos, and that I'd chosen to live with the Faeries. Ileana was so enraged that he took her child—because she truly did love Julian—that she challenged Dimitris in battle.

"It is said their battle lasted years. Julian heard the stories of his parents' war even among my people. But by the end, both of their wounds were so severe that Ileana finally set flame to them both, just to end the misery. They cursed each other as they turned to ash."

I was horrified for the child. Drakán children were our most precious possessions because they were our future. For Julian to be thrown into the middle of a battle at conception was beyond reprehensible. It certainly explained a lot about his personality.

"So Julian was raised with the Faeries?" I asked.

"Yes, after Thelos kidnapped my mother and she bore me, she gave her own life to send me to live with her family in the Realm of the Fae. I don't remember her, but I thank the gods daily that she sacrificed her life so I could know the other half of my heritage. Because I wouldn't have gotten to raise Julian if she hadn't. He is like my own son."

The affection in her voice was obvious, and her Fae heritage couldn't have been more pronounced than when she spoke of him. Affection was not a Drakán trait.

"Julian learned how to rule from my maternal grandfather, the King of the Faeries. It is why he knows so much of other cultures. I could tell Julian was destined to be special from the first moment I held him. I knew he was not The Promised Child as the gods had foretold. But I also knew he was not The Destroyer. Julian is greatness itself. And his destiny is still untold. The question is, Rena Drake, will you be a part of his destiny?"

"That's a decision that will be between him and me." An image of the blue fire that had enveloped us only a few hours before went through my mind.

"Can you tell me what a mating fire is?" I asked.

Esmerelda gasped and looked at me in surprise. "Have you seen such a thing? Have you experienced it with Julian?" I felt her rifle through my mind like the rapid flipping of book pages. "You have. You are true lifemates."

"Please. Could you just tell me what it means?" I asked.

"The mating fire dates back to the time before the Banishment. Drakán were blessed by having one true mate to call their own—a single mate for all of eternity. The mating fire only occurs if you have found the other half of your true self. Your soulmate."

"No," I whispered, terrified of what this meant for me.

"You should be ecstatic, my dear. There hasn't been a sign of the mating fire since the pure bloods set foot on the Earth Realm. It was considered one of the lost powers, and many assumed the mating fire died because of the mix of human blood in our systems, but clearly that isn't the case. It's also been speculated that the lack of mating fire is the reason behind our infertility problems."

An image of a child came to mind so powerfully that I gasped for air. Black hair curled around an angelic face as he smiled, and blue eyes, the exact shade of Julian's, stared back at me. I viciously wiped the vision away and felt Esmerelda grab my hand.

"You are destined. You cannot fight it. The mating fire is so intense it will devour anyone or anything who comes near it. You can only have each other now. This is a gift from the gods. And if you've experienced it, you should treat it as such."

I didn't respond. A rush of emotions came over me—caused by my human blood, no doubt—and none of which I understood. I felt an elation that made me want to scream with joy. But there, just behind it, was sorrow and the ever-present anger I knew as my only friend. The gods couldn't be so cruel as to bind me to a man like Julian for all eternity. And what would happen to me if I chose not to accept him? I was going to take as much time as I wanted to think it through. Eternity was a long time to spend in misery.

"Do you know the names of the others like Julian?" I asked, my throat raw. "The ones who are children of two Descendents? The list can't be long. One of them will have to be The Destroyer."

"Unfortunately, I don't. Julian's story is not a secret, but there are many who are caught in the middle of two clans because of their parentage. Some choose to live their lives in solitude, and that must be respected."

"How do I draw him out?"

"You don't have to. He already knows you're looking for him. I can see from your memories that you believe he's taunting you with his kills. He likes the chase. He wants you to belong to him."

Esmerelda's dark eyes became unfocused, and I knew

she was probing deeper. I embraced my anger at the intrusion, but kept it contained. There wasn't anything I could do to stop her from looking, and I couldn't defeat her in a fight. Her face took on a pensive look, soon replaced by one of shock. Her gasp made the hairs on the nape of my neck stand on end, and the gold of her skin turned pale.

"What?" I asked. There wasn't anything in my life I thought was worth that reaction.

Her face cleared and she gave me a long look, choosing to ignore my question. She returned to our earlier conversation as if nothing strange had just happened. "The Destroyer is an arrogant man. He is playing a game, and it is only a matter of time before he gets bolder in his attempts. The Prophecy says that The Destroyer will be defeated by a fearsome warrior. A child blessed by the gods and of mixed heritage. A leader who has no people, but who is followed despite the fact."

"Which could be anyone. We're all of mixed heritage. These prophecies are really starting to irritate me."

Esmerelda giggled. "Oh, I promise, they get much worse. The goddesses are often vague." She smiled serenely at me and said, "I'm going to give you some advice, Rena. You're approaching all of this as a human would. Stop. Don't fight your dragon. Embrace her. She wants to be free. Julian was right about your powers. They're only waiting on you to use them. As much as you want your human half to rule your emotions, you cannot allow it. Our kind needs soldiers like you. Because there will be a great battle. The Destroyer will not go down without a fight. And you'll die if you go in as you are. Your humanity will kill you."

The heat of my anger swelled outward. "I have tried countless times to increase my powers, and what all of you choose to conveniently overlook is that human blood *does* run through my veins. And it's obviously weakened my dragon abilities. Other than the strength of my psychic visions and my Enforcer powers of compulsion over other Drakán, there just isn't anything else inside of me. Believe me, I've looked. I can only use the powers I was taught. The ones I was born with. How can anyone expect more from me?"

My rage was to the boiling point, and I hated feeling cornered. Esmerelda had voiced aloud what I'd refused to admit to myself. There was a part of me that envied the humans and their lives of complete ignorance. I envied their capability for love, and their desire to care for others. I wanted those things. I was torn between two worlds, trying to ride the fence and get the best out of both of them. Instead, I was living a half truth. I loved what my Drakán powers brought me, but I was scared of losing my human self completely to the dragon, so I held back. I didn't want to be like Alasdair.

"To feel greatness, you have to achieve greatness," she said. "You have many fears inside of you. Fear is an emotion almost unknown to our kind. But you hold it. And you nurture it."

"You're forgetting about my human blood again. I can't just cut those emotions off completely. Julian said I needed to open my senses, to feed on the anger of my dragon, to use my full powers."

"He's right. Our senses are a large part of our powers.

But unfortunately genetics play just as big a part. Your blood is more than you think, and you come from the line of a great warrior. The power is in you if you wish it to be."

I knew a gift of good genetics did make a difference. I thought of Erik and what it must feel like to live forever and have nothing. To watch others grow and do amazing things and have to stand by and be an observer.

"There are many others like your brother," Esmerelda said. "There are so many of our people who are nothing more than long-lived humans. And often they choose to live the life span of a mortal. The powerless lead a solitary existence because Drakán are drawn to power. Many cause their own deaths to keep from having to live an eternity alone. But you are different. Your power is inside you, lying dormant and waiting for you to release it."

"I don't know how," I confessed. The breakfast I'd eaten was like lead in my stomach.

"But you do know how. Can you not visualize yourself as a dragon? Can you not feel the pull and tug of her wanting to escape your fragile shell?"

Of course I could feel her. She'd been a part of me my entire life.

"Our powers are very basic, fed by heat and fire." Esmerelda said, "What color is your dragon?"

I didn't know. Whenever my dragon nudged me too hard, whenever our thoughts were too aligned, I always did my best to push her away—to reject that part of me. I refused to see her. Dragon color was hereditary. My father was red—a red so dark it was almost black, and the members of our clan who could transform were all shades of the color.

I very tentatively called to my dragon. She was already close because she'd felt my turmoil, and I shivered as she rubbed against the inside of my skin. For the first time I looked at her clearly. She shimmered silver, almost the exact shade of my eyes, and I gasped in surprise. She was beautiful and tears sprang to my eyes.

"Very good, my dear. You're a fast learner."

"What?" I asked, opening my eyes in confusion.

She nodded toward me and I looked down. My neck and chest were covered in silvery scales, iridescent in the light. I lifted my shirt and saw my stomach was the same. But I wasn't fully transformed, my legs and hands were normal. I started to panic and the flesh of my human body came back into sight.

"Why am I silver? This can't be right." Horror pierced my chest as scenarios went through my mind. Was it possible Alasdair wasn't really my father after all? No wonder he hated me. Did I belong to anyone? There were no silver dragons in any clans that I knew of.

"You are exactly as you are supposed to be," Esmerelda soothed. "And Alasdair is your father. But you know as well as I do that genetics are a fickle thing. Sometimes they dredge up the unexpected."

"I don't think I want this," I said.

"You will. It's really very simple," Esmerelda assured me. "If you can close your eyes and see your true self, then the change will happen. You must embrace it, Rena. Don't turn your back on what you are. You need to practice transform-ing, and when you're comfortable I'll teach you how to fly."

I wasn't anywhere near ready to take that step. As much as I hated to fly in airplanes, I couldn't imagine flying without one. But I was curious enough about the change that I'd try to transform again once I got back to my room. Maybe I'd just imagined the color of my scales. I prayed to the gods that Alasdair never saw the true color of my dragon form, because he'd kill me on sight.

FIFTEEN

I searched through the clothes Julian had stocked in the wardrobe for something appropriate to wear to the *sfara*. There wasn't a single color other than black, not that I expected there to be. I knew without looking that there wasn't anything in the suitcases I'd brought. I hadn't planned on attending any formal events while searching for The Destroyer.

My choice of clothing would be important. I had to dress to impress Julian—to impress his people—but at the same time I needed something functional and easy to maneuver in if things became violent.

I paced restlessly around the confines of my room and watched the minutes tick by on the clock. I still had three hours before the *sfara* began, and I was sick of my own company. I had to get out of this place. I was under the impression Julian wanted me to think I was a guest. That I was welcome to come and go as I pleased. But in reality I knew that was an illusion. I'd have to find a way out on my own.

I'd never doubted my compulsion ability before, but Julian and Xana had certainly made me a little self-conscious. I didn't bother to try to sneak out of the chateau. In my experience, people were more likely to question you if you looked guilty. I grabbed a light jacket and closed the door to my room behind me. I headed down the stairs as if I owned the place.

There were two guards at the front door, both Drakán and both with average powers. I could have taken them, but I didn't want to if I could help it. Security cameras sat unobtrusively in each corner of the foyer. I turned in the opposite direction and headed toward the back of the house. I figured going through the back garden and over the fence was my best bet for escape.

I hadn't taken the time to explore the chateau during my short stay, so my knowledge of the floor plan was minimal. I finally came to a small room, something similar to a den, with plush leather couches and a large-screen TV that took up almost an entire wall. It was all black of course, but it also had a set of French doors that led out into the garden. Perfect.

The rain had stopped and the sun was finally peeking out from the clouds. I reached the French doors and had my hand on the silver handle when I felt an ominous presence behind me. One I wasn't familiar with. I whirled around and ducked low into a fighting stance. I swept my leg out and hit what felt like a block of cement. Something cracked in my ankle, but I ignored the pain. The man didn't fall flat on his back as I had planned. I hadn't budged him an inch.

I moved to attack again, but he held up his hands to stop me and backed out of reach.

"You shouldn't sneak up behind me if you want to live," I said. I finally looked him over from head to toe. He was intimidating—the size of a small tree and bald as a billiard. The dragon tattoo on his skull moved when his facial expressions changed, making it look alive.

"I am Olaf," he said.

"Of course you are. Why were you sneaking up on me, Olaf?"

"I was not. I swear on my oath to my Master. I was sent to give you a message."

"Let's hear it."

I put a few more steps between us just in case, but never took my eyes off his. I didn't trust Olaf.

"Julian wanted me to remind you that he prefers you stay on the grounds. He says it isn't safe for you to wander about the city until he has introduced you at the party tonight. There are still many of our people who do not know of your arrival."

"Sure, no problem." I waited until Olaf left the room, and then escaped out the French doors.

The wind cut through me like a knife, and I wished I'd worn a heavier jacket. The gardens were massive and lush with winter greenery. A bricked path snaked throughout, and I followed it until I came to the last row of hedges. The stone fence that surrounded the chateau was probably twelve feet high, and it was hard to ignore the cameras perched in various locations. At least there was no barbed wire.

I took a running start and felt the muscles in my legs stretch as I pushed off the ground and jumped straight over the obstacle. I couldn't help but give the cameras a little finger wave as I landed on the other side.

Freedom had never felt so good.

I started up the street at a jog, intending to catch a cab into the city, but as I got to the corner a car I'd never seen before screeched to a stop inches from me. Like everything of Julian's it was black and sexy as hell.

But it wasn't Julian who rolled down the passenger-side window. "You don't think I'd let you go shopping without me, do you?"

I sighed in irritation. Of course Esmerelda would know exactly what my plans were. I opened the door and slid across the buttery leather seat.

"What kind of car is this?" I asked.

"A Bugatti Veyron. And there's not another one like it in the entire world."

"That figures. I wouldn't expect Julian to be like anyone else."

She smiled and said, "Come, one of our clan members owns an exclusive shop close by. I know he has something that will render Julian speechless."

"Well, that would certainly be a nice change."

I held on to the door handle as she pushed her tiny foot to the floor. The car took off with a squeal, and the scent of burnt rubber permeated the air. I prayed to the gods the people of Belgium had enough sense to stay out of her way. She weaved through traffic like a maniac, and when the street became too congested, she moved to the sidewalk. If Cal thought my driving was bad, he'd better hope he never had the chance to ride in a car with Esmerelda.

I added this car ride to my list of things I hated, right under flying and Julian.

She screeched to a stop in front of a small store on Avenue Louise—a long street filled with exclusive shops in the middle of Belgium. My body slammed against the seat belt and then back into the seat again.

"I'm going to have to get one of these someday. There's nothing like it. I'll let you drive on the way home if you'd like."

"Thank gods," I muttered under my breath.

"Let's get you something to wear and get back. Julian doesn't want you out of his sight for long."

I decided right then I was going to take my sweet time. The dress shop was squeezed between a pâtisserie and a store that made handmade leather items. Discreet gold lettering on the front window labeled the store in Bulgarian as Бърлога—The Lair. Cute.

And in the front window was the exact dress I wanted. I couldn't imagine anything more perfect.

"I knew it would be just right for you," Esmerelda said. "Let's go in. I want you to meet Luuk and his family."

I felt terribly underdressed in my jeans and T-shirt once we walked through the front doors of the sophisticated dress shop. I'd been to Versace in Rome and Chanel in Paris, and neither of those stores held a candle to this one. And neither did their clothes. Whoever designed these was a true artisan.

"Out! Get out of my shop," an angry voice screamed in Belgian before my eyes could locate where it was coming from.

A mountain of a man, probably a full foot taller than me, whirled like a tornado to the front of the shop to keep me from progressing any farther. His dark hair was slicked back from a high forehead, and square glasses framed menacing black eyes rimmed with red fire. His slacks were gray silk and fit perfectly and his white dress shirt was unbuttoned at the throat and rolled up to the elbows. He had a tape measure draped across his shoulders and a pencil stuck behind one ear.

"I could smell your peasant stench a block away, dragon. You are not welcome here."

He pushed at me with his power, and I absorbed it, rolling the intricacies of his magic through my body like an undulating wave. My dragon turned her back on his scent. He wasn't the dragon she wanted.

The man I assumed was Luuk grabbed my arm, and I let my power unleash. I hit him with a wall of psychic power that made him gasp and brought him to his knees.

"Don't touch me," I said, no louder than a whisper. Luuk dropped his hand away from my arm obediently, and stayed in a submissive position on the ground.

"Now, Luuk," Esmerelda said, coming around from behind me. "You know better than to touch a strange dragon. Someday you'll let your brain make decisions rather than your temper."

"I apologize, Esmerelda." Luuk glanced at Esmerelda, and I felt the relief move through him at the sight of her. "I will take responsibility for my mistake, but I ask that you spare my daughter. She is in the sewing room today."

I opened my mouth to assure him that he'd done nothing wrong, but Esmerelda touched my hand slightly and I let her handle it.

Esmerelda moved with the startling speed of an Ancient. She grabbed Luuk by the throat and raised him above her head so she had to look up to see his eyes. Luuk's skin mottled and flames danced in his eyes. I could smell the sulfur of his fire as he fought to control it. Fighting Esmerelda was futile, and he knew it. She was much too strong.

"You have done Julian's honored guest a great disservice," she said. Her voice wasn't full of rage like I expected it to be. It was the same smooth croon that she'd used when she'd first greeted me earlier that morning. My dragon responded to its power and nudged impatiently against me.

"She is welcome in our lands, and you will treat her as you would treat your Master. Have I made myself clear?"

Luuk nodded since he was unable to speak, and Esmerelda released her hold on him. He fell to the ground and composed himself before he stood up to face me again. He made eye contact, which surprised me, and it was obvious by his smoldering eyes that he was less than happy at having to follow her orders.

"What do you want?" he asked.

"I'll take the dress in the window." I took a step forward, and found satisfaction as he stepped back. I had to show my dominance now, or he would test me every time we ran across one another. "And you'll answer my questions."

He nodded and went to retrieve the dress for me. Esmerelda was on the other side of the shop, looking at a black dress that would barely cover the pertinent parts of her body. I knew she would be able to hear the questions I asked, but I didn't have much choice in having an audience.

"Do you know what I am, Luuk?" I asked.

"You are of Alasdair's clan."

"Yes, but I am also an Enforcer. *The* Enforcer." He paled at the title, and I moved closer to him, circling him like prey. "Drakán law states you must answer my questions under penalty of death."

He swallowed and nodded as he carefully took the dress and laid it out on black-and-white-striped tissue paper.

"Have you heard of the Drakán who have gone missing?"

His hands faltered as he folded the tissue over and moved the dress to a long white box. "Yes, my cousin is one of the ones missing. He's been gone almost two weeks."

"Do you know how he disappeared? How it happened?"

"All I know is that we went hunting one night, twelve of us from my family. There was a great pop in the sky and Eliyan disappeared in front of our eyes. There was nothing left of him. No sign he'd ever been there at all. All his belongings were still at the house, and there was nothing we could do except put the problem in Julian's hands. He promised he would find him, and I know he will. Julian always keeps his word."

Luuk's faith in Julian was absolute. There was no doubt in his mind that Julian wouldn't do what he'd promised.

KINGDOM OF FIRE AND ASH

"Do you know of any others?" I asked.

He put the lid on the white box and wrapped black ribbon around the corners. He stuck a card with the name of the shop in bold letters under the ribbon.

"I've heard rumors that the ashes of many Drakán have been found. More of my clansmen, and a few of the Russians and Irish. It's strange I haven't heard of any American Drakán who have disappeared. Maybe you should be asking your own clansmen these questions, yes?"

I let the insult pass as he wrote the amount I owed for the dress on a ticket and pushed it across the counter at me. The price was outrageous. Probably ten times the amount of its actual cost. But a dragon was never one to let such a one-of-a-kind item pass by. I pulled out my credit card and had just handed it over when Esmerelda snatched it from his fingers.

"Luuk," she said, her voice filled with warning. "You will be properly compensated for your cooperation. She is the mate of your Archos, and this is your gift to welcome her to your clan. Tell our people of this news, and make sure they welcome her warmly tonight at the *sfara*."

Luuk's mouth dropped open in surprise at the exact moment mine did. I started to stutter a protest, but she grabbed the box and my elbow and ushered us out the door. I was still speechless as she shoved me back into the front seat of the Bugatti Veyron, peeled out with a U-turn in the middle of the street, and scared a bunch of tourists on our way back through the city.

SIXTEEN

T he dress on the mannequin in the window looked vastly different than it did on me as I stood in front of a floor-length mirror and cringed at the sight of exposed flesh. I wasn't an exhibitionist on my best day. I'd never really been comfortable in my own skin like others of our race. And this dress definitely qualified me for exhibitionist status. The only good thing about it was there wasn't a lot of extra material to get in my way if there was a fight.

The top half was blood-red leather and fit like a glove— better than a glove. The straps were finger width and hooked at the back of the neck in a halter style. The neck-line plunged, terrifyingly so, and I knew the only reason my breasts didn't spill out was because they had no place to go. The back was open to my waist and showed the multitude of scars that crisscrossed on my lower back. The red skirt was gauzy and flowed to the floor, and the red satin of my underwear could be seen through it. The ice pick heels that finished the outfit made me a full four inches taller.

I grabbed the cell phone on my desk and hit speed dial before I could talk myself out of it. I felt the need to hear Noah's voice. I needed an anchor: someone who could keep me grounded in reality and remind me who I really was. Or at least the person I wanted to be. My dragon didn't like the idea and nudged against me hard.

But the phone rang and rang and finally went to voicemail. I didn't leave a message.

Tsk, tsk, Rena. You fool yourself if you believe he has the power to help you. I am your true lifemate. You should come to me with your needs.

"Stay out of my head. And I wouldn't go to you for my needs if you were the last dragon on Earth."

You'll regret those words. Your fire is already burning for me, just with the sound of my voice. Your passion speaks the truth, while your brain tells you lies.

"Leave me alone."

You know I cannot. The party has started and we are without a guest of honor. Olaf will escort you down.

A soft knock sounded at the door. I checked myself in the mirror one last time before going to answer it. I'd left my hair down, so it covered my shoulders and helped alleviate the nakedness I felt. I opened the door, and just as Julian said, Olaf was waiting for me. He followed closely behind me as I maneuvered down the stairs in my heels.

Julian stood at the bottom, and the look of possession in

his eyes made me want to turn around and run back to my room. The black tuxedo fit him to perfection and he looked even more devastatingly handsome than the last time I'd seen him. Lack of attraction between us definitely wasn't the problem. His hair hung long and loose against his shoulders and his eyes were fierce and penetrating as they looked me over from head to toe. I stopped where I stood.

You're not a coward, Rena. Come to me. He took a step forward and held out a single red rose.

"Stay out of my head," I said again. I accepted the rose with a gracious nod. Tonight wasn't the time for pettiness.

"I see your disobedience this afternoon was well warranted if this is what you escaped my walls to buy." His gaze was enough to start the glow of blue fire just under my skin.

"Stop it," I hissed. My own angry fire ate at the gentle blue flames until they were completely gone. "I'd prefer to meet your people without my clothes turning to ashes."

"Very well," he said, obviously disappointed. "Has anyone ever told you how magnificent you are when you're angry?"

I growled and my anger escalated. But then something incredible happened. My rage physically jumped from my body to Julian's. It then dissipated and fizzled into nothingness. I felt as calm as I ever had.

"Relax, little one," he said.

My mouth hung open from how easily he'd taken away my anger. There was a link between the two of us, almost like an invisible thread that attached our emotions. I thought back to what Esmerelda had said about absorbing others' powers, but I hadn't realized he could do the same with emotions. He leaned down as if he were going to kiss me.

"No, absolutely not." I put my hands against his chest to push him away. Big mistake. The planes of muscle under his shirt were solid beneath my fingers, and I found myself grasping hold instead of pushing away.

"Why?" I asked, though it sounded more like pleading.

He knew what I was asking even though I wasn't sure I knew myself. "Because we are meant for each other. Stop fighting it."

"I don't want this."

"You lie." His voice whispered across my skin. "Your resistance wears thin. I know you want me. I can smell your desire. You won't be able to fight me much longer, Rena. Now come, we have guests to greet."

I followed him into the throne room where we'd shared our dream. I looked around the room. Long trestle tables filled every space. A head table sat upon the platform where the thrones had been the day before. There were no decorations on the black granite walls or rugs scattered on the floor to give the room color. The candles in the chandeliers had been changed from white to black, giving off an eerie glow. Black velvet tablecloths draped across each table.

More than a thousand Drakán milled around the large room, and others were still arriving. "I didn't expect for so many to come."

"All my people are here. I demanded it. This will be a night of celebration, a time of judgment and sentencing for those who need it, and a time for all to renew their oaths to me. This will also give them the opportunity to meet my lifemate."

"I am not your lifemate."

"A technicality, one which I will thoroughly enjoy rectifying. I find it quite a coincidence that after all these centuries of spending our lives apart, you were forced to darken my doorstep as Enforcer. And then only to find yourself mated. Just think, Rena, if we'd come across each other centuries ago you'd already belong to me. You wouldn't have put up the fight you are now."

He brushed my hair back in an oddly intimate gesture so my shoulders were exposed. "Maybe you should ask yourself what the real reason is for denying me."

"I don't believe in coincidences."

"No, neither do I. So I wonder what steps have really brought you here to me. Is the search for The Destroyer truly your idea? A simple step in your investigation? Or has someone manipulated events so you are here as a pawn in someone else's game?"

I didn't know the answer. All I knew was my clan would try to kill me if I became Julian's lifemate. They probably would anyway once they found out my dragon wasn't the same color as the rest of them.

I looked back toward the double doors as he led me farther and farther into the room. My only chance of escape disappeared with every step. As we made our way toward the table, I noticed a short podium with what looked like a kneeler attached to it.

"What is that?" I asked.

"It is where my people come to voice their grievances or

where an accused party must kneel before me to hear his sentence. It was my father's and one of his greatest treasures. I keep it as a reminder."

"A reminder of what?"

"That I am not my father."

He pulled out a chair for me, and I sat down cautiously. My eyes kept glancing at the doors, so I noticed as two children walked into the room. A boy, somewhere in his mid-teens, who was stiffly pressed into a black suit. In human years he was probably closer to sixty. He was on the brink of manhood. His pale skin shone like a beacon against the dark fabric of his clothing, and I could practically feel the excitement coming off of him.

A little girl walked stiffly beside him. She was still child-like, and looked eight or nine rather than the thirty years of age she was closer to. Her black hair was braided into pigtails and her small hand was grasped tightly in her brother's.

"You allow children to come to the *sfara?*" I asked surprised.

"Of course. They are our people too and must also be allowed to have a voice. It is a weakness of the other clans that they think adults are the only ones who can have valid ideas. Children think in simplistic terms, and sometimes that is what we need to better our society. How can anyone know their own worth if they must be an adult before they find it?"

It was a good point. The only problem I had was that they might be too close to the action if things got violent. And with this many dragons in the room, things were bound to get violent. I'd no sooner had the thought than an argument broke out in the corner. The heat spiked in the room as two dragons faced each other, already half transformed.

Julian stood and did exactly what he'd done with me earlier. The heat left the room, and the anger that was beginning to call to everyone's beast evaporated. It was as if Julian were a vacuum for our emotions. A nifty trick. Everyone quickly took their seats as if nothing had happened.

I sat through what seemed like an endless evening. A seven-course meal, followed by what must have been thousands of people swearing their oaths, one by one, to Julian. Twelve marriage proposals were approved, to much rejoicing. And to everyone's great disappointment, including my own, there were no pregnancies to announce. The punishment portion of the evening came last, and a man was sentenced to forty lashes for owing back child support.

It had to be past midnight, and I was about to fall asleep in my dessert when Xana burst into the room with Olaf and several other guards at her back. Xana was in the center and the other guards fanned out to make a V shape behind her.

All talk and clatter from the tables ceased, and everyone's attention was focused on the warriors approaching us. The temperature in the room dropped and puffs of air came out of my mouth as I breathed.

Julian stood slowly beside me. I felt the arctic blast of his anger whip through the room hard enough for his people to flinch. I wasn't sure exactly where it was directed.

"What's going on?" I whispered to Esmerelda.

She was seated on my other side, anciently regal in her petite body and skimpy dress. The only sign that she was bothered by what she saw was the white-knuckled grip she held on her dessert fork.

"Something terrible," she said, her face ashen and aged by some unseen thought. "Something tragic."

SEVENTEEN

Esmerelda turned her head and looked at me. Her dark eyes went completely opaque, much like Calista's did whenever a vision came upon her. I was told mine did the same. Esmerelda smiled and I knew she was back with me.

"You'll be okay," she whispered. "Though I don't completely understand why you'll be okay. Just remember that you have great power hidden within you. And try to stay out of the line of fire. I have some salve in my rooms to help with the burns if you need it."

"That doesn't sound promising," I said, already dreading what was to come. How could I be burned bad enough to need salve, but not burned bad enough to turn to ash? I was afraid to find out.

The deep timbre of Julian's voice resonated through the hall and snapped me back to reality.

"What did you find, Xana?"

"It is as you claimed, my lord. They are all gone. There is no trace that we can find."

I was beginning to get the picture, and I could feel the swell of Julian's heat replace the cold and wrap itself around his body like a cloak.

The silence in the hall was deafening, and Drakán throughout the room reached for their mates as their worst nightmares became a reality.

"What happened? Were there any witnesses?" Julian asked.

"It is just as you saw. A group of our clansmen were on their way here tonight, from different locations, using different modes of transportation—none of them were connected in any way other than their destination. They all had their mates with them, and then somewhere between where they began and here, the Drakán just disappeared into nothingness. By my estimation, including the other clans' losses, the total of missing Drakán is now close to a thousand."

Anger vibrated around the room as outraged beasts railed against their human counterparts. These were their own brethren, and they wanted to hunt for who'd done this to them.

"They are not dead," Julian said to calm the dragons. "I would feel it if they were. Someone is taking them and transporting them to another Realm where I cannot pinpoint their location."

Xana nodded her head. "I've collected all the human mates of the missing and put them in the front parlor." She waved her hand and the large doors to the gathering hall opened by an unseen force. It was then I could hear the low, keening wails of the grief-stricken. It was a sound I'd never heard before, and one I hoped to never hear again. Maybe human emotions weren't so great after all.

Julian's face was a mask, but I could feel his pain at the loss and heartbreak of his people as if it were my own. Then something crossed my mind. Maybe all of this could have been prevented if Julian had actually put some effort into finding The Destroyer when this all started. He'd obviously known about it from the start, and more extensively than I did, since I didn't have complete access to other clan information like Julian. He could have at least gone to meet with the other Council members to determine The Destroyer's true identity instead of ignoring him. There must have been something he could have done to prevent this.

The thought passed through my mind like a gentle breeze through a windstorm of emotions before I could stop it, and Julian's anger shifted to me. I was in exactly the place that I didn't want to be. Right in the line of fire. Literally.

There was a swift decompression of air around my body that made my ears pop audibly. My body flew across the room like a rag doll, and I landed with a thud on my hands and knees in front of Xana. The air closed in around me and it felt like cinder blocks were pressed against my chest. My hair hung limply in my face and sweat beaded on my brow.

"Who are you to pass judgment on me, Enforcer?" Julian said.

I couldn't get a deep enough breath to bother wasting the oxygen to refute him, so I stayed silent.

"You are the one who speaks of the law and your rights as Enforcer. This is your responsibility, but you've done nothing. Maybe you're the one responsible. Is this your way of proving a point? Is your power so great that I've been deceived into thinking you were merely untrained? It was foolishness on my part not to keep you under a more watchful eye, but I was somewhat distracted by our chemistry. It's the oldest trick in the book, no? Did The Destroyer tempt you? Do you already belong to him?"

I shook my head no. It was all I could do. The rage of his words lashed out at me like a whip, though his voice never escalated in volume. Then it was over as quickly as it had begun, my body frozen in terror in the eye of the storm. I somehow got the courage to look up and realized that Julian's anger hadn't diminished—only his target. Xana stood in front of me, taking the full force of his power.

"You protect her?" Julian asked, surprised.

"No, my brother," Xana said, bowing her head in submission, "but I'm protecting you. She is your lifemate and the daughter of another Archos. You would bring war to all the clans and your own death."

I thought Xana was wise for reminding Julian that they were indeed family—their father the same cruel man who begot them both, though I was afraid Julian was past the point of caring.

"You need not remind me of who she is," Julian spat. "And you need not remind me of who I am, Xana. We are already at war."

"Fine," Xana said. She stepped aside and the pain hit me

full force. It was a good thing I was still on my knees. I didn't have far to fall.

Xana continued in her mocking tone. "I defer to your wishes, my Lord. You are correct that it is your decision as to whether or not you sacrifice your true lifemate, though it seems a shame to ignore the mating fire when a child might be the result. I'm sure Dimitris would approve if he were alive."

The entire room gasped at the mention of the mating fire and silence reigned. I hadn't noticed until that moment how Julian's power affected his people. His anger intensified their own, and already some of them had shifted to their dragon form, ready to tear me to shreds as soon as he gave the word. Julian's own fire engulfed him and swelled with his anger. The little girl with pigtails I'd noticed earlier had shifted completely, her scales gunmetal gray and her body no bigger than a baby cub. She wiggled for freedom against her father, her talons clamping tightly around his forearms, wanting to take part in the possible carnage.

Xana bowed low before Julian, her braids brushing the floor, and the sarcasm was thick enough to cut with a knife. I couldn't decide whether or not she was the bravest woman I'd ever met or the stupidest for provoking his attention back on her.

The temperature in the room increased until beads of sweat dripped down my face and body like a river. I looked around the room through a fiery haze and realized the other Drakán were feeding off his fire, though they all stood back far enough to not get trapped in its flame.

A towering inferno of the brightest orange swirled

around Julian in a rage and licked at anyone who stood too close. This was not the gentle blue mating fire I'd experienced earlier. This was a fire meant to destroy, and if he unleashed it, Xana would be dead. And I'd probably be caught in the aftermath, though I was pretty sure I'd much rather be incinerated alive than eaten first.

I could understand Julian's anger at the disappearance of his people. I could even understand the need to punish Xana for her insubordination, but I knew if Julian destroyed Xana he'd never forgive himself. She'd been his protector for most of his life, and she was his family.

The force of Julian's power brought Xana to her knees. Blood dripped slowly from her nostrils and plopped to the black granite. His fire grew, and if he wasn't careful it would consume the entire room.

The human mates in the room had all been shuffled out the doors at the first sign of fire. I had to do something. I couldn't let any more deaths happen on my watch. I was already guilty of losing too many. I prayed to the gods for a strength I knew I didn't possess.

I hadn't appreciated until that moment what great control Julian had over his powers. If Julian wasn't really The Destroyer and he wielded this much power, I was afraid to run into the real thing.

I stood up slowly, fighting against the waves of heat that pressed against me. My eyes burned with the intensity of Julian's flame, and I felt a moment of such despair that I almost sunk back to my knees and let the fire destroy us all.

And then I remembered, and I realized what I had to do. I took a deep breath and felt for the tug of familiarity between myself and Julian that we'd shared earlier. It was there, though hidden partially by the strength of his power. As I focused on it, I felt the thread strengthen and grow until I could grasp on to it with my own power. As his flame swelled, I opened myself further, until his fire was part of me.

I took a deep breath and absorbed as much of the volcanic heat as I could into my own body. When I could take no more of its intensity, I blew gently from my mouth until his flame was snuffed out completely. It flickered and dissipated as if it were no more than a candle.

I collapsed on the ground from exhaustion, but I knew I'd succeeded. Everyone was still alive. The room swelled with voices and drowned out the pounding of my heart. My brain was in better shape than my body, and I knew I needed to find the energy to get away. I was easy prey.

I looked up and watched as Esmerelda began running in my direction. I turned to Xana and saw an identical expression of horror on her face. Everything moved in slow motion, but their warning was clear.

Run.

I needed to run.

I found the energy from some reserves I had no idea I possessed. I got up off my knees and sprinted for the doors. I knew mentally I would never be able to escape Julian, but the reflex was instinctive. I made the mistake of looking back over my shoulder before I reached the exit, and I saw the most magnificent sight I'd ever experienced. Julian's piercing blue eyes were staring straight at me as his body changed form. Scales the color of the most precious black diamonds rippled over his body like liquid silk and covered the pale flesh of his human form.

His dragon was a beautiful machine, his body sleek and lithe—one solid muscle that would have enough strength to propel him through the air. His claws and teeth were vicious, both in sharpness and length, and his tail was thick and could be wielded so it broke every bone in the body.

His body flexed once and then he came after me in a blur of speed. His scales pressed against the back of my body and I screamed. My feet left the floor in a wave of vertigo, and we catapulted out of the chateau and into the night.

EIGHTEEN

M y stomach roiled and pitched as we spiraled into the sky. The temperature of the air was a cold shock against my bare skin. We soared higher and higher, and I grew dizzy as he circled with me in his arms—a dance he was leading and I was forced to follow.

He flew us toward the tallest turret of the chateau, and I squeezed my eyes shut as he headed straight for the arched window that seemed impossibly small for a full-grown dragon to fit through.

The cold stone around the open window grazed my skin as we glided into the room. Julian released me with something less than a gentle touch. I stumbled to my knees and crawled across the hard floor as I tried to put as much distance between us as possible. That wasn't easy to do in a room that was completely round and had no doors and only one small window for means of an escape.

Julian shifted from his dragon form back to his human one, but the expression on his face didn't make me feel any safer. He was naked, but I stood slowly and faced him defiantly. If I was going to die, it wasn't going to be on my hands and knees like a weakling.

"I can't say I'm surprised to see another room that's full of black marble," I said to fill the silence.

"It makes it easier to hide any messes," he said. His accent was much thicker than normal. "You're a brave woman, Rena Drake. There aren't many who would publicly defy me. Xana is one, and her betrayal, though understandable, won't go without punishment. And then there's you," he said moving closer. "Do you still deny our connection, Rena?"

He circled around me, but I kept my gaze straight ahead. Fear sliced its way through me, but my dragon writhed in triumph. Julian was calling to her. And she wanted him.

"I felt what you did to me," he said. "It is a powerful weapon you wield. One that could be my downfall. And if I was more like my father your death would be unavoidable. But I'm not my father. Nor am I naïve in my experience of the female mind and the perception of love. Those are not things I understand completely, but I do understand loyalty.

"I am giving you a choice, Rena, since you are so fond of them. If you wish to keep your life, then you will complete the mating ritual with me and share my fire. You will belong to me, and my family will be your family. I will be your protector. And I will want only you for the rest of eternity as is the magic of true lifemates. And if it appeases your human side, we can say the traditional vows of husband and wife. But if you wish to die, then I swear I will send you to the Realm of the Dead with the honor a true mate deserves. What do you choose?"

I honestly had no idea. Was death better than being mated to Julian? I did know my family was not going to be happy to lose the potential heir to lead our clan to our most hated rival.

"Being mated to me will not be the misery you seem to think." I felt his breath on the nape of my neck and my flesh pebbled. His human form was glorious.

His expression was arrogant and pleased by my obvious approval of his body.

"All right," I agreed. "But I have a condition to add to the agreement before we're bonded."

This was the strangest business meeting I'd ever been to, and I had the sudden urge to laugh hysterically. I was afraid if I started, I'd never want to stop.

"I can't promise anything, but I will at least listen."

I nodded and fought the urge to crack my knuckles nervously. "I will mate with you, but if I'm unhappy here or if my clan needs me, I want the option to return home."

"As long as you give me the opportunity to talk you out of it."

"You must also remember that I am the Enforcer. I must fulfill my duties."

"Rena, my love, how could I ever forget what you are?"

I instinctively took a step back when he reached for me, and then I realized what I was doing and forced myself to stop.

"Then it's settled," I said and closed my eyes to accept my fate.

"Not quite." The sound of his soft chuckle made me open my eyes.

"What else?" I barely managed to ask.

"I have two more conditions. As your mate I will help you search for The Destroyer, but when the time comes it is I who will kill him. Not you. I will take revenge for what he has done to my people."

"Agreed."

"The second condition is that I want you to give your body to me voluntarily, of your own free will, for this first mating. I want the human in you to want me as much as your dragon. Bring your fire to me and I will embrace it."

This request was more difficult than I thought it would be. Noah's vision had been right. I did feel conflicted, but my body would belong to him of my own free will. Because when I answered myself truthfully, the human in me wanted Julian as much as my dragon. We had just met, but our souls had known each other for centuries. He was a piece of me that had been missing, and he was right—he wasn't his father. Julian actually had the capability to love, though I wasn't sure he knew it. He loved his people very much. Some day he might even love me. At least that's what the human in me hoped for. I could be his wife—his lifemate.

Julian stood still as a statue while I tried to talk my feet into moving forward. My body was stiff and my muscles sore from the events that took place at the *sfara*, and I knew there'd be bruises on my skin. As soon as I had the thought my muscles relaxed and a soothing heat passed over my body. I knew it was Julian's doing, and I appreciated his consideration. He didn't have to make this easy on me. Many in his position wouldn't have.

I walked closer, one step in front of the other, until I was just a breath away from a man I wasn't sure I should fear or try to love.

"Both," he whispered.

The blue flame erupted around my body and leapt for Julian as if it were starving for contact. Our fire recognized each other and engulfed us, though the flames were quite cool. They rose higher and higher in intensity, but still Julian waited for me to be the aggressor.

I moved closer until our bodies touched, and I felt raw power run through my veins. A growl of pleasure erupted from his throat and the fire spread in a whoosh around us, swirling and sparking in an intimate dance. I leaned in and touched my lips softly to his.

"Wait," he said. I moaned in protest as he pulled away from me. "I've thought of one more condition."

"What?" I growled impatiently. "You can't add conditions now. That's cheating. I just agreed to become your wife? Doesn't that count for something?"

"Don't ever try to control me in front of my people again," he said, holding the back of my head firmly so I had no choice but to meet his gaze.

"Or what?" I dared to ask.

"Or you'll regret it."

And then he kissed me again. My dragon bumped against me, eager to feel her mate skin to skin. My shoe fell off and hit the hard floor with a thud that echoed through the room like a shot, and I realized we were no longer on solid ground.

"Julian," I said, eyes wide.

"Yes, love?"

"Why are we on the ceiling?" I finally asked.

"Because there's no bed in here."

"Oh." The blue fire that surrounded us was so intense in brightness that I had to close my eyes. But as soon as I closed them I realized I could see better with my senses than with regular sight anyway. He was using his power to hold my hands captive, to keep from touching him. It was obvious he wanted our magic to mate first.

"Relax," he whispered.

"Easy for you to say."

"If you'll quit thinking so much and open yourself to the possibilities, the ritual will happen as it is supposed to."

I kissed him again because it was easy to lose myself when I did. His teeth were sharp as they scraped over the skin at my neck—sharper than they'd been the last time he'd kissed my mouth. My eyes widened in surprise as I realized what he was going to do, but by then it was too late. He bit down on the pulse point in my neck. Colors swirled behind my eyelids as my powers erupted from somewhere inside of me.

My mind opened with the pleasure, and I knew instinctively that the Drakán mating ritual called for the sharing of not only flesh, but also blood. Something shifted in my mouth, gums tearing and the taste of my own blood against my tongue. My teeth elongated and became impossibly sharp.

The urge to bite into flesh became need. It was the most overwhelming sensation I'd ever experienced—more consuming than the instinct to kill when on the hunt. I knew I could lose control very easily in my current state, the inborn violence of my being so closely entwined with the pleasure.

I didn't want to hurt Julian, and my mind didn't want to love him. My body, on the other hand, needed his flesh between my teeth more than I needed to breathe. And as much as I tried to fight it, I knew that loving Julian would be inevitable. We were the definition of true soulmates, our connection created by the gods—closer than two people could ever hope to be.

I knew what I had to do to complete the ritual, but I wanted full control over my body. I was incapable of speech, so I had to speak mind to mind.

Release my hands.

My hands fell from the ceiling as if the invisible cord had suddenly been cut. I wrapped my arms around Julian's neck. I bit down gently and felt the give of his flesh. My thoughts and feelings were his just as his were mine.

The pleasure was quickly overwhelmed by the most severe agony imaginable. It was familiar agony, and the last time I'd experienced it I'd been with Noah.

"Don't think of him," Julian said through gritted teeth and I knew that he shared the same excruciating pain.

A searing agony burned down the entire left side of my torso. Julian tensed in my arms. I opened my eyes to see what was wrong. Patterns of gold fire curled around one side of his body, and the smell of burnt flesh—his and mine —mingled with the scent of blood, magic, and desire.

We were being branded—branded by the gods to spend eternity together. It was more binding than any wedding band.

The pleasure and the pain interchanged until I was delirious with exhaustion. I was no longer whole but a part of someone else. And when the blue fire around us turned white I fell into unconsciousness until everything went dark.

NINETEEN

I awoke lazily, disoriented until the details of the round room came into focus. The night before played over and over in my mind. I stretched and winced as my muscles protested. I was sore everywhere.

The only light in the room was from the small window we'd flown through the night before. It looked to be just after dawn by the hazy, gray hue that teased the window with its light. I could smell the rain in the air and knew we'd get a downpour by midmorning.

I sat up slowly and realized I lay dead center of the big black bed from my dream. Julian's bed. The satin sheets were twisted around my body and the pillows were strewn on the floor. Julian was nowhere in sight.

I was relieved not to have to face him just yet. We'd done things that even now brought a blush to my face, and I laughed at the irony of what a human bride must feel after her wedding night. I pulled the sheets up higher around me.

I looked at the ceiling and then back down at the bed. I'd thought Julian had said he couldn't get a bed into the tower.

No, Rena. I never said I couldn't bring a bed to our tower. I simply told you the truth, that there was no bed. I felt we should not use such conventional means the first time. It should be different between us, no? We have a lifetime to try out all the beds you want.

I slammed my mind shut, cutting Julian off before he could say any more. I really wasn't ready to talk to him yet. I sat there a few seconds longer before I realized how easy it had been to get Julian out of my head. I wondered if this was one of the advantages of being true lifemates.

My neck burned fiercely, and I touched a finger to the ragged skin there. It was healing slower than a normal wound would have, but at least it was healing. I looked down at the rest of my body, afraid of what I'd see. A beautiful tattoo scrolled down the side of my body—henna in color. It was written in the old tongue, but I couldn't make out the words from this angle. I needed a mirror. The burns were still tender to the touch, and I remembered that Esmerelda had told me she would give me some salve for them.

I gingerly got out of the bed and made my way over to the window. It didn't take long to realize I had a problem. How was I going to get down from this tower?

A good question indeed, Julian said.

"You did this on purpose."

Of course. It is now my job to teach you how to survive as I have.

"Well, great master, what do you suggest?"

You must fly, of course. And if I were you I'd do it quickly. It will be full daylight shortly. I'm not sure the good citizens of my country are ready to see a dragon over their morning commute.

"What if I can't do it?"

Then you will have a long, lonely day spent in the dark.

"Hell."

Indeed.

I looked out the window at the threatening light of day and then down to the gardens. It was a long—long—way down from where I stood. A knot formed in the pit of my stomach. I tried to swallow past the lump in my throat. I was going to have to change into my dragon form. I'd never heard of a Drakán being able to fly without it. The problem was, other than the morning I'd eaten breakfast with Esmerelda, I hadn't been able to shift into my dragon.

Just thinking of my dragon brought her to the surface. Her joy was contagious as she moved inside me. She'd gotten what she'd wanted the night before, and now she was up for anything. She wanted to fly, to feel the wind beneath her scales. I closed my eyes and fought against the nausea. I could see her clearly. Her silver eyes were pleading. She gave me a final nudge and then disappeared.

Bones and cartilage slid and re-slid inside of me. It didn't hurt, but it wasn't exactly comfortable. I was cold. A clear fluid burst from my skin and was replaced by silvery scales. But the scales were dry and cool to the touch when I felt them. Smoother than I thought they'd be. My teeth were sharp. My vision extraordinary. Every particle that floated across the air was crystal clear. Every color vividly bright.

The change brought a rush of power I never could have imagined.

I was stronger. Everything about me was stronger—including my magic. But with the change came an overwhelming need for violence. My dragon was in charge now, and just as she'd been trapped inside me, writhing to get out, the same was now true for my human self. My sense of smell was powerful—gasoline, coffee, dirt, pastries—they were each defined and tickled my snout. But there was something else that was stronger. Meat. Flesh and blood. I wanted to fight. And I wanted to hunt.

But first I needed to get out of my prison. Even my dragon looked down from the window with trepidation. She wasn't sure what she was meant to do.

It will all happen as it is meant. Success and failure are up to you.

You're not helping, I answered.

I looked out the window once again at the plunging depths that awaited me and closed my eyes. My dragon didn't know the mechanics of flying. But she wanted to jump. Instinct took over. I took a last deep breath and plunged over the edge.

The wind rose beneath me, and for a short moment I soared. But the ground grew closer and panic clouded my mind. Dragon and human both screamed as I sank like a stone several hundred feet. I lost control of my dragon form, and I shifted back into myself. I opened my mind and pleaded for help.

A black dragon swooped in from out of nowhere and caught me in a rush of speed just before I hit the ground. He set me down a few feet away and quickly transformed back to his human form. I dropped to my knees and closed my eyes, willing my heart to slow and the nausea to go away. Julian conjured clothes for both of us, and then helped me to stand.

"Th...thank you," I said.

He ran his hands down the length of my arms and stepped away from me quickly, as if he was afraid to touch me.

"That was less than impressive, Rena. You'll have to do better next time."

I snarled in his direction. I was itching for a fight and Julian was as good of a target as any, but he turned and walked away, leaving me impotent in my rage. As if I weren't there. As if the two of us hadn't spent the most incredible night of our lives together.

"Come, Rena. Esmerelda will tend to your burns and then we must talk."

I'd had enough. I was just to the edge of the breaking point, and I couldn't be responsible for what I might do if anything else traumatic happened to me.

"I'm not going anywhere," I said.

Julian turned around and arched an eyebrow. "We do not have time for you to play games, Rena."

"I'm not playing. If you'd like me to go somewhere with you then you might try asking. You might try even saying good morning first."

He looked at me strangely. "You are displeased with me."

"You're very astute, lifemate."

His expression turned hard, and I knew that I'd

somehow hurt his feelings. It would be wise to remember that Julian was as new to being a lifemate as I was.

"I'm not displeased," I corrected. "I wanted you to kiss me. To speak with me as if what we shared mattered to you. But you didn't. You just walked away and acted as if I didn't matter in the least."

"I saved your body from considerable damage. If you hadn't meant anything to me, I would have let you fall."

He moved closer to me until he stood less than a breath away. I could barely see the edge of his own tattoos over the collar of his shirt. "And the reason I do not kiss you is because once I start, I will not want to stop."

I put my hands against his chest and leaned into him, daring him to kiss me anyway. His eyes darkened with desire. And then we vanished. One moment I was about to be kissed in the garden. The next I was gone into nothingness.

CHAPTER
TWENTY

My body was weightless, and it floated across a great void in millions of tiny little pieces. My atoms fizzled back together, and when I was able to get my bearings, I noticed we were somewhere back inside the chateau. Julian backed away from me and headed toward the door.

"Wait, what was that?" I asked.

"It speeds up travel time tremendously, yes?"

"If you like your insides to feel like scrambled eggs."

I now had proof to the rumors that Julian could travel through time. I wasn't sure I'd believed him yesterday, even when he'd admitted he could. I'd never seen—or felt—anything like it before. But Julian wasn't The Destroyer. He couldn't be. Because a lifemate would know something like that. Right?

"Where are we?" I asked. "I take it these aren't your private quarters?"

The room was wholly feminine in its décor—Queen Anne furniture, lace curtains, crystal candlesticks. Knick-knacks and photographs covered every surface, and a fire blazed in the hearth, making the room toasty warm.

I wondered if I'd ever get to see Julian's private space. I'd slept in his bed, and I knew what every part of his body felt like against my skin, but I really didn't know anything about *him*. And I found it a little surprising that I very much wanted to know.

"These are Esmerelda's rooms," he said. "She will treat your burns, and then you and I must talk." He turned his back and left me standing alone in the middle of the unfamiliar rooms. I guessed Julian wasn't very knowledgeable about morning-after etiquette.

A throat cleared behind me and I turned to see Esmerelda giving me a steady, serious look. It wasn't one I'd seen before on her good-humored face.

I almost didn't recognize her. She wasn't dressed as a gypsy today. Instead, she wore black leather pants and a matching halter top that showed a surprising amount of cleavage for a woman so small. Her red hair curled riotously around her pixie-like face, and large gold hoops hung from her pointed ears. She looked like Bondage Barbie.

"Come," Esmerelda said. "Let me treat your burns. They must be stinging."

"They're not too bad. Just a little tender."

"Have a seat and take off your blouse. This won't take long. Julian is quite anxious to speak with you."

"I noticed," I said dryly. There was something unfamiliar inside of me. The feelings bombarded me—anticipation, rage, sadness. I knew they were Julian's emotions, now a part of me forever.

I took a seat on a small chair and unbuttoned the blue silk blouse. I slipped it from my shoulders and draped it over the back of the chair before unsnapping the front clasp of the black bra Julian had dressed me in. Esmerelda removed a small silver dish from the mantel of her fireplace. It was octagonal in shape, and the engravings around it were beautiful. It looked incredibly old, but the silver wasn't tarnished.

"It belonged to the Fae side of my family. It was my grandmother's. She was a great healer."

We were both silent as she lifted the silver lid and touched her finger at each point of the octagon. Her lips moved and her eyes were closed, and the sheen of the silver grew brighter. I couldn't help but let my thoughts wander to Julian. I hated being apart from him now, and I needed the reassurance of his touch.

I shook my head, hoping some common sense would rattle loose. I didn't like the feel of neediness that came over me since we'd become lifemates. The worst part of it was that Julian obviously wasn't as affected. He'd been able to walk away without any problems at all.

"You should be more understanding," Esmerelda said. "His path is a hard one, filled with obstacles and tragedy. You could be a light to his darkness. Rule beside him as an equal. But your own demons are swallowing you whole."

"What demons?"

"Everyone's are different. But we all have them. You

know what you struggle with. And though you and Julian have mated, your path is not forged yet. There are forks in your road that lead in many directions. You'll have choices to make."

I looked down at the tattoo that was supposed to represent everything Julian and I meant to each other. The writings were there, but the meaning was empty. Though the gods outdid themselves with the artistry. The scrollwork truly was a masterpiece.

"It is, isn't it," Esmerelda said. She pulled up a padded footstool and sat across from me. "This is the first time I've seen the writing of the old lands outside of the ancient Drakán scrolls."

"Do you think it is written the same for everyone?" I asked.

"I don't know, but I would think so. These are the sacred vows of our people, much like the vows in a human marriage ceremony. But these vows are more precious because they are bound by magic, not just words. It is tradition for mated Drakán to read the inscription to each other on their first mating anniversary, or the *Yiun*."

I wasn't sure that Julian and I would be together in a year. Or if we were I wasn't sure we'd have anything to celebrate. We'd had a pretty rocky beginning so far. Not to mention I wasn't sure I'd be alive in a year if The Destroyer had his way.

Esmerelda rubbed the salve between her fingers, and the sharp scent of eucalyptus leaves and something else permeated the air.

"This is also magic," she said. "When you heat the salve with your dragon fire it releases the magic, and the healing can begin. When I enchant it with the words of Faerie, it will also help prevent future injury. I find being a half-breed Fae Drakán has its uses every now and then."

I smiled and then hissed between my teeth as the salve touched the burn. It seemed to get hotter, and the tattoo came to life. The scrolls undulated and moved like waves down the entire left side of my body. The scrolls glowed from beneath the skin with golden light.

"The sting will only last for a moment," Esmerelda soothed. "It's drawing the heat out of your skin."

The scrolls stopped moving and the glow dimmed. The heat of the salve dissipated and left my skin cool to the touch. It was over. The pain was gone. Not only from the burns, but also the bite mark on my neck and all the aches, pains, and bruises I'd suffered from making love on ceilings and hard floors all night.

I put my shirt back on and thanked Esmerelda for the salve. "Do you know where I can find Julian?"

"I do not. But you are his lifemate. Your souls are tied together. If you open yourself to him, you will always be able to find one another."

"Keeping myself open to anyone seems like a good way to get hurt."

"Perhaps," she said, smiling. "Good luck with your demons, Rena." She turned around and went through a door I assumed led to her bedroom and left me standing there alone.

I didn't have a choice but to do as she suggested. I lowered my walls, and the thread I'd used to put out Julian's fire the night before was even stronger, no longer a thread but a rope. I closed my eyes and my dragon came into view. She was always happy when I thought of Julian, and she rubbed against me approvingly. I pushed her back and followed my instincts.

I could see him clearly in my mind. He sat behind a massive black desk, carved with Drakán images. His face was serious, and at first I thought he must be terribly sad, but the clenching of his fists made me rethink my assessment. Angry fire burned just beneath his skin.

I followed my vision and our invisible link down the stairs, all the way to the bottom floor of the chateau. I ignored the guards and their curious stares, my focus absolute, as if I were in a trance.

When I walked through the double doors of the great room, I had no idea what had led me there. It had been cleared of the tables from the night before. The blood had been cleaned from the floor. There was nothing in the room. It was completely empty. Yet I didn't turn around and walk out. I dropped my shields all the way this time. His emotions were raw and hit me with a force that made me stagger. The tug between us grew stronger—the invisible rope thicker.

I remembered back to the first night—the night I had met Julian in his dream. He'd appeared from the shadows against the wall. But it hadn't really been shadows. It had been a door.

I walked across the room, one foot in front of the other, and placed my hand against the cold wall. I didn't know what compelled me to push my magic into the black marble. I just knew I had to get to Julian, and that he was on the other side of this wall.

The door opened soundlessly—seamlessly—and I walked through. It closed behind me, and I was left in darkness. I could see the faint glow of fire somewhere in front of me and I headed toward it.

The heat was intense inside the hidden room, and my dragon did lazy somersaults inside me, loving the feel of the warmth. I knew that this heat was created by Julian. I could sense his presence, his magic, everywhere around me. I also knew that anyone else who tried to find their way down these secret halls would be crushed under the force of his magic and reduced to ash where they stood.

But not me. I was his lifemate, and his fire was mine.

I followed the curve of a staircase deeper into the ground. It smelled of earth and dust, and I could feel the rush of water from somewhere nearby.

It also smelled of gold. My dragon began to move faster and faster, anticipating the treasure that surely awaited her.

I reached a point where I couldn't go down any deeper. A metal door stood in front of me. It was warded by magic, and I automatically took a step back when I felt it strike out against my power.

But I stopped my retreat. It wasn't striking out at me. It was trying to grab hold and pull me closer. With my shields down I was aware of Julian as I never had been before.

There was something wrong. I'd known it since we'd

first spoken this morning. And I knew without a shadow of a doubt that he needed me.

I breathed in his magic that warded the door. It tingled along my spine and caused my dragon to growl with pleasure. The tie between us was still strong and pulsing, so I pulled his magic into my body and absorbed it.

I touched my hand to the metal door and met no resistance. The metal was like liquid mercury beneath my fingertips, and I slid my hand through easily. I pulled back and stared at my hand. It looked just as it should have. And when I looked back at the door it was already whole again. Amazing.

Are you going to stand out there all day? Julian asked.

I pushed my hand through the metal once again, but this time followed it with the rest of my body. I was blinded for a few short seconds, and then I was on the other side of the door. Julian stood close in front of me and looked rather pleased with himself.

"Very good, Rena. You are becoming more receptive to using your Drakán powers since the mating ritual."

His voice caressed across my skin like a whisper, and chills raced along my skin. My shields were still open, and my dragon responded to his call. She would always want him. She belonged to him now. As he belonged to her.

I slammed my shields tightly closed and breathed deeply. My dragon might be good at many things, but common sense was not one of them. Now was not the time to get distracted by mating.

I moved away from Julian and turned my back to him, trying to gain focus. I looked around the spacious cavern. It was larger than the great room above us, and to my amazement, it wasn't filled with black marble. This room was old. Very old. And it held everything Julian valued most in his life.

"Oh, my," I said.

My dragon was envious of his hoard. She wanted it fiercely, and if she could have gotten away with it, she'd have taken every last thing in the room for her own. Mounds of gold were piled into big, heaping hills. There were diamonds and sapphires and rubies. There were sculptures and paintings from every era of time. Rare books and artifacts lined shelf after shelf as far as the eye could see.

And at the center of his hoard was the big black bed I'd woken up in. Lust slammed into me like a wrecking ball. It consumed me. My breathing changed and my dragon fought to get free. She wanted to make love with Julian in the middle of such wonderful treasure. I wanted it too.

I turned to find him, to seek him out and claim him for my own. He was suddenly there in my sight and I rushed toward him with a speed I'd never possessed, hitting his body hard with my own. I clamped myself around him, but as I raised my mouth to his, I realized the hands that squeezed my waist were pushing me away. Not pulling me closer.

"Rena. Look at me." His face was shuttered, and he was saying my name over and over again, trying to break though the lust that controlled me.

I didn't want to be stopped and anger replaced the lust, my fire igniting just beneath my skin. I roared and sulfur and smoke escaped from my mouth and nose.

"Rena, stop!" he commanded.

But he no longer had the control over me he'd had before we were mated. I pushed against him hard, and we both ended up in a heap on the floor. We rolled over and over across the floor, arms and legs tangled. It was obvious his body wanted me, but he was still trying to stop me.

"Rena, you are the Enforcer. You must get yourself under control. Our people need you."

His words slowly started to penetrate the fog of lust that had consumed me. I was the Enforcer. I had a duty to my people. Not just a duty to my own people, but to Julian's now as well.

My eyes cleared and I looked up at Julian. His eyes were wild with need, but they also held caution and regret. His breath heaved in and out of his chest. There was blood on his cheek from where I'd clawed him, though the wound had already healed. His hardness still pressed against me, but my body belonged to me now.

"What was that?" I asked. "I don't know what came over me. I'm sorry. I didn't mean—"

"Don't apologize for wanting me. This is what we are supposed to feel for each other. And if our people didn't need us, I would have matched your desire with my own. Stopping you was one of the hardest things I've ever had to do."

He meant it. His honesty rushed through me and joy filled my soul at his words. He leaned down and kissed me softly—with a gentleness I didn't know either of us possessed.

"We will come back here later and finish what we

started, no?" He shifted off me and rose smoothly to his feet before helping me to stand. I stumbled against him and realized I was still a little unsteady on my feet.

"What's happened?" I asked.

"The remains of some of my people were found a little while ago."

"The ones who went missing before the *sfara* last night?"

"Yes, but not all of them. Only four are dead. The others are still missing."

"You're tied to your people by blood. You said last night that you felt when they were taken."

"Yes, but I lost all ties to them when they were taken to another Realm. I cannot feel the bond of my people across time and space."

I wondered if the same would be true for me now that we were joined.

"I do not know," he answered without me having to ask aloud. "I hope we never have to find out."

I ran my hand down his arm and then squeezed his fingers. I had to touch him. And the ferocity of the need scared me. I released him and paced back and forth in front of his desk so I could think.

"How did you find the remains?" I asked.

"Their bodies entered back into this Realm shortly before dawn. I felt the tie immediately, but it was short lived. They'd been dropped into a densely wooded area far away from any civilization, Drakán or otherwise. Their hands and feet were bound. And then they were torched by the flame of another dragon while they lay there helpless. It had to be The Destroyer. I could feel the strength of his power through my people. But I could not see his face."

"Take me to them," I said, no longer thinking of myself as his lifemate, but as the Enforcer. I wasn't sure I liked it that the title I'd always associated myself with was now over-shadowed by another.

TWENTY-ONE

J
ulian drove us to the crime scene in a mean-looking SUV that had tires the size of small elephants. I'd convinced him it would be better to drive instead of dematerializing, since I needed some way to transport the remains back to the chateau once I was done inspecting the ashes.

The rain was a light drizzle when we left Brussels, but by the time we reached our destination, the drizzle had turned into a deluge. It was almost a two-hour drive to Nieuwpoort, a small town close to the Belgian port of the English Channel, but Julian managed to make it there in half the time.

The land was open and empty, with only a smattering of farms and cottages along the countryside. Fields of wheat were broken up by groupings of towering trees, and both of them swayed as a storm rolled in from the coast.

I worried about the crime scene with the weather the

way it was. Ash didn't last long against water or wind. But Julian assured me that it would be okay.

Half-walled fences of stone broke up the land and lined the narrow road we sped along. Julian turned the car sharply through a narrow break in the fence and directly into a field of grass toward a heavily treed area. Cars were already parked just outside the perimeter of trees, and our tires spit up mud so it splattered across our windows as we raced to meet them.

My boots squished down in the mud when I jumped out of the SUV. The air was considerably colder than it had been in the city. The wind cut through my clothes and whipped my hair around my face in disarray until I stepped into the shelter of the trees. The upper branches were so thick that water was unable to seep through. The ground was dry.

I followed Julian deeper into the wooded area, but I no longer needed him to guide my way. His memories were fresh in my mind, and I knew exactly where the remains were. Xana stood guard over them, her posture straight and her hands clasped tightly behind her back. Everything was utterly still around her. Not even the leaves dared to twitch.

Others of Julian's clan were spaced farther out, forming a wide circle around the scene in case there were intruders or The Destroyer decided to make another visit.

Four long piles of fine black ash were lined up next to each other. There was nothing else left to show that anything living had once been there, not even a shard of bone. I knelt down beside the first pile and put a teaspoon of ash in a clear plastic bag. I'd send each sample back home for Erik to analyze.

A protest formed on Xana's lips at disturbing the ashes, but I cut her off with a look. She knew her job. And I knew mine. I sifted through the pile with my hands, the ashes like silk between my fingers.

My knuckles grazed something cold and hard, and I knew what it was before I dusted the ashes away to see for myself.

A misshapen disc of melted silver gleamed against the blackness of the ash. I picked it up gently and rubbed it between my fingers. It had already hardened completely.

"What is that?" Julian asked, kneeling beside me.

"A piece of silver. If it's the same as the last Drakán victim there should be two inside all of the remains."

"I don't understand."

"The Destroyer feels as if these people have betrayed him somehow. These are the exact coins that Judas was given for betraying Jesus."

"Yes, shekels of Tyre. I have thousands in my hoard. They're not hard to come by for anyone who was alive during that time period."

"Great. That'll certainly narrow it down." The problem I had with finding suspects had everything to do with age. As the centuries wore on, fewer and fewer Drakán were born. So the older Drakán far outnumbered the young.

"Have you found many remains with the silver embedded in them?" Julian asked.

"I've only found the remains of one Drakán, period. Your

Jillian. All of the other crime scenes I saw were human, and if The Destroyer is truly forming an army, then it makes sense that these humans were simply meals. But it's impossible to know about the other clans and their missing Drakán. There could be hundreds of remains scattered all over the world, and I wouldn't know about it unless I had a vision like I did with Jillian. I'm still not completely sure why I dreamed of her."

"It's because she was connected to me. Even before you and I met for the first time, we were destined to be with each other. You recognized my power through her."

"Oh." His explanation made sense, and it was nice to have at least one of my questions answered. "As far as any other Drakán remains, you know as well as anyone that the other clans don't use my position as Enforcer. The Archos all choose to try and handle the problems themselves, or ignore them completely, just to keep me from coming into their territory. You've all made it very difficult to do my job over the centuries."

"Yes, we have," he said softly.

I put eight pieces of silver into a Ziploc bag, and then I went about the task of shoveling the remains of the four Drakán into separate wooden boxes, no bigger than a shoebox. There was nothing left to do for them except return them to their families and send them off in ceremony to the Realm of the Dead.

"Xana will take care of it," Julian said as I began to transport everything back to his car.

He lifted the small boxes from my arms and gave them to Xana. He tossed her the keys to his car with a flick of his wrist and grabbed for me. I dodged out of his way before he could take hold.

"Oh, no. I'm not doing that again," I said. "I'll ride back with Xana."

Julian's lips twitched, and I swore if he laughed at me that he was going to be sorry. He moved with a speed I could only envy and grabbed me around the waist. I didn't have time to fight back before we dematerialized into nothing.

We reappeared back inside the deep cavern built under the Chateau de Longévité. My head spun and I gasped for breath as I checked to make sure all my body parts had reassembled correctly. Julian sat on the edge of his desk, completely in control of himself, while I struggled to get things together.

"Stop doing that," I growled. Nausea roiled in my stomach, and my dragon was agitated and bumping against me, which wasn't helping matters any.

"It is a waste of time to drive in a car when I have a power such as this. Especially when it's a matter of urgency."

"What? Big bad Julian hasn't figured out how to stop time completely?"

The corners of his mouth quirked in my direction, no doubt amused. "I will ignore your unpleasantness for now. I find that becoming lifemated has made me quite agreeable."

I sputtered at his insult, and finally closed my eyes. I had to get my anger under control. New or uncomfortable situations always brought on my dragon rage. I opened my

shields, trying to draw on the calmness Julian was present-
ing, but I gasped as his magic practically crackled off his
skin. He wasn't calm at all. The fury inside him was wielding
a double-edged sword as it hacked viciously at his temper.

His rage swelled bigger and stronger, but had no outlet.
Guilt weighed him down so heavily I thought I might
drown in it. He hadn't been able to save his people. Hadn't
kept his promise of protection. And he blamed himself for
their deaths.

Julian rushed by me in a blur, and the walls trembled
with his fury. Stone crumbled, and his most precious
possessions flew from the shelves and shattered into
millions of pieces. The floor cracked into fissures beneath
my feet, and water seeped through the cracks. He whirled
like a cyclone, leaving nothing but destruction in his path.
He left no corner unturned. And I didn't try to stop him.

It was easy to understand in hindsight how I'd thought
him cold and cruel upon our first meeting. In truth, he was
anything but. His responsibility as Archos was great. And he
approached his duty with the respect it deserved. I knew for
a fact that Alasdair didn't feel for his people the way Julian
did for his own. Alasdair loved the power. And he loved the
yearly tax he was paid from each of his subjects to add to his
hoard.

It was then I remembered that Julian came from true
Drakán royalty. His father should have been king. And
Julian should be king now.

He stood with his back to me against the far wall. His
hands were splayed over the rough stone and his shoulders

heaved with every breath. I didn't know what to do for him. How to tell him that I finally understood.

I approached him slowly, avoiding the remains of his treasures as I went. I placed my hands on his back and felt the shudder that ran through him. I stroked him gently, calming his beast with my touch.

"I'm so sorry," I said. It was inadequate, but it was all I had to give him. I didn't like to see him hurt, and all I could think was that it was my duty to take his pain away. I ran kisses along his shoulder blades and put my arms around him in a hug.

The fight seemed to go out of him in a great whoosh, and I turned him so that he faced me. His expression was back to the impenetrable mask he wore when he didn't want anyone to know what he was thinking. I leaned up slowly, keeping my eyes steady on his as he watched me warily.

"Is this normal?" I asked. "This need I have for you?"

"I think so," he said, the anger inside him seeming to dissipate.

"I've never felt this before—this connection—as if I might die without you close to me. You pain is my pain. Your joy is my joy. Your desire is my desire."

"The archives of old say that every time we mate it is like a new discovery. It will never get old. Our joining will become a necessity. Like breathing."

He traced the outline of my tattoo with his fingers and the fire glowed under his touch. We fell together and I knew with every mating I was losing more of myself and loving more of him.

CHAPTER

TWENTY-TWO

Something woke me—not a vision or a dream, but a kind of knowing. I stretched carefully, and Julian's arms tightened around me. I looked up and saw he was staring at one of the destroyed bookshelves.

"Can they be replaced?" I asked. "Your hoard was like nothing I've ever seen before."

Magic tingled along my skin. Broken pieces of pottery and torn pages of books began to reassemble themselves. Shredded canvas knitted itself back together and shards of glass fit together like puzzle pieces. The remnants of his destruction swirled above us, and the room slowly put itself back together.

I laughed in sheer awe of his power. "You amaze me. I've never been very good at physical magic."

"You're better now that we've bonded. You'll have to start practicing. You never know when it will be useful." He traced circles over my back absentmindedly, his thoughts somewhere else.

"Tell me what's wrong." I leaned up on my arm so I could look down at him. His gaze was shuttered and he'd rebuilt his shields. He evaded my question.

"Did you know that this room was part of the original caverns my father hid his clan in after the Banishment? None of the other Archos were ever able to hunt him or his people. He protected them well until he stole away with my mother."

"What happened to them when he went away?"

"They became reckless. The need to hunt and survive without a leader drew them out of hiding. Many of them were slaughtered by the other clans. Others abandoned the clan completely and went out on their own. But this cavern stayed hidden. And when I'd aged and my time with the Faeries was through, Esmerelda brought me back here. My clan adopted her."

"That was a nice thing to do," I said. Drakán weren't known for their hospitable natures, especially with those who were different. With Esmerelda being the daughter of Thelos, one of their most hated enemies, it was very un-Drakán-like for them to even considering welcoming her to the fold.

"I've told you before that loyalty is very important to me. Esmerelda raised me, and it was her Fae grandfather who showed me how to rule. If Esmerelda had tried to raise me with her Drakán father, then I would have been killed long ago."

"What happened when you were old enough to return to

your clan?" I couldn't stop touching him. I had to have constant contact with his skin, and I could tell by the way he kept running his hands from the base of my neck all the way to my thighs and back up again that he felt the same.

"Xana had held things together as best as she could. We desperately needed numbers. And we needed more warriors. Times were much harder then than they are now, and human food was harder to find. The cities weren't as populated as they are now.

"I gathered everyone who was left and we expanded on this underground room, digging tunnels and building rooms. All of Belgium has caverns and secret passageways beneath it—an underground city where we once lived. I made everyone swear the blood oath, and I was immediately able to get a better grasp on their abilities, so I knew how to make them stronger. I culled out the strongest of the clan and trained them for battle. And when we weren't training, I gave orders for everyone to find strong-willed humans to mate with. It took more than two hundred years to build the clan back up to where we could defend ourselves if we were attacked."

"But you did it," I said. "You were meant to lead, Julian. I was wrong before to call you a tyrant. These people need you. All of the clans need you."

"Yes," he agreed. "The Drakán should be mine to rule, as they should have been my father's before me. And it is you who should be at my side as queen. If we don't take action soon, then our numbers will die out completely."

It took me a moment before I understood what he was really saying, and when I did I held his cheeks between my hands and looked directly into his eyes. I wasn't going to let him avoid this confrontation by closing himself off.

"Am I understanding this correctly? You want to ignore the Prophecy and declare yourself as King of the Drakán?"

"Not exactly. I would like to form a temporary coalition of all the clans to flush out The Destroyer. I would declare myself king and swear an oath to step down when The Promised Child was born."

This had the potential for disaster written all over it. Namely, it would be a cold day in hell before the other Archos deferred to Julian for anything. Alasdair had rather see our entire race destroyed than give power to anyone other than himself.

"I guess I'll be the voice of reason and ask how you think you can accomplish something like that. This very discussion is the reason we were banished in the first place."

He was quiet for a long time before he spoke again. "We are true lifemates, Rena."

"I know that."

A seed of fear planted itself within me. I shook my head in denial and pushed away from him. For the first time since we'd mated I couldn't bear to touch him. My blood ran cold as I realized what he planned—what he'd probably planned all along. I'd played very nicely into his hands. I was a fool.

I pulled the sheets around me so I was completely covered, but Julian lounged against the shredded mattress and sheets in naked splendor.

"Hear me out, Rena. You and I have already united two of the clans by our mating. You are the daughter of an

Archos. And I am more powerful than your father. It makes sense that I should lead both clans."

"Gods, what have I done?" I scrambled off the bed, trying to put as much distance between us as possible, but he grabbed the sheet and tugged me back. I let it go and went in search for my clothes. They were scattered across the floor, and I pulled them on hurriedly, my hands shaking so bad I could barely get the buttons through the holes on my blouse.

"You planned to take my father's clan all along," I accused. "As soon as you saw the mating fire and realized who I was and that I had no knowledge of the mating fire. Was the story of the mating fire in the archives Dimitris stole from my family? Because there's no mention of it in our new archives. I played right into your hands, didn't I?" I laughed bitterly at my stupidity.

"It's not like that, Rena."

"How do I even know this lifemate stuff is real? Did you strike a deal with the gods so they would bind us together?"

I'd heard stories that those who were powerful enough and had something in particular that the gods wanted could offer a trade for their help. I was willing to bet that Julian had several things the gods would be interested in.

"My clan will not follow you, Julian. They've spent millennia hating you."

He moved to the edge of the bed and sat along the side facing me. "Yes, but they'll follow you. Your father won't have a choice but to step down."

"He'll challenge me to a duel. Have you noticed the scars on my back? He fashioned a whip of liquid metal and sustained it with his dragon's fire. My skin didn't regenerate as it should have and I almost died. I wished I'd died. He did it because I'd displeased him in some way. I can't even remember why. Can you imagine what he'll do to me for trying to take his clan?"

Julian got out of bed and towered over me. Even with the fresh pain of his betrayal in my heart, I still wanted him. I knew in that second that if I had to go back to the moment where I had a choice of being Julian's lifemate or being executed, I would have gladly chosen death.

Pain flashed across Julian's eyes before his face became impassive and his voice grew colder. "You're stronger than Alasdair now. He can't win. You've been looking for the opportunity to pay him back for what he's done to you since you came into your Enforcer powers. You carry scars only because he fears your psychic power over him. He doesn't understand you, and he knows that there is something different about you—something not wholly Drakán—and it terrifies him. He holds no affection for you, but he keeps you close because he has no choice without breaking our laws. He knows you have not reached your full potential, and he's hoping that if your magic comes out of its dormancy that you'll share it with him. It's the reason he hasn't defied the Council and has kept you alive. I've seen inside his soul."

I shook my head in denial. There was nothing that special about me. That fact had never been more glaringly obvious than right now.

"You can feel the truth in my words, Rena. I cannot lie to my lifemate. Alasdair would have killed you if it wouldn't have meant his own death. Now is your chance for revenge."

The words whispered past his lips, and the temptation in them almost brought me to my knees. He knew how to entice me in more ways than just lust. My dragon was bloodthirsty, and I longed for revenge against my father for the torment he'd caused me over the years. My dragon was also covetous. She wanted to show her dominance over Alasdair and take the clan that belonged to him for her own.

"You're wrong if you think my people will follow me. I'm the Enforcer. I've been an outcast among my people for centuries. They fear me, and what I might do to them, even though I've defied Alasdair by helping many of them. I'll never have their complete trust or loyalty."

"Fear is oftentimes a great motivator. Especially for the Drakán. You undervalue your own worth, Rena. You fear your powers just as Alasdair does, and your people suffer for it. But when you learn to embrace them our race will follow you. For your wrath will be the things nightmares are made of."

My human nature warred badly with my dragon. My heart was broken. Where was the man who'd whispered words of affection to me? Where was the man who'd promised to protect me with his life? I was beginning to think that man had never really existed.

"You could have been honest with me from the beginning, Julian. How did you keep from laughing at my naïvety? You must think I'm an idiot to have felt sorry for you. To think that…" My voice choked on a sob.

"To think what, Rena?"

I was going to say that I thought he might actually care for me. It was pathetic to think that someone could actually love me after all these years. I didn't know why I'd ever considered the possibility.

"Nothing," I said. I hunted up my shoes and sat down to put them on. I had to escape to my own room for a while. Remove every trace of Julian from my body so I could get a grasp on my thoughts.

"Think wisely before you make any rash decisions," he cautioned. "This plan is a sound one, and it is what's best for our people. You'll see that once you think things through."

He came toward me, crowding me with his size and nakedness, but I held my ground. I'd never let him think he intimidated me.

"I don't want you to leave the chateau. It isn't safe outside these walls. My sources tell me that all of the clans have reported missing members, and they are not as well populated as this one. It would take very little to convince the other clans that we could lead them in a battle against The Destroyer and help find their missing people. Think of the power we would hold. Until The Promised Child is discovered the clans are ours for the taking."

Power was seductive to any dragon, and I was no exception. Julian's eyes gleamed with triumph and he knew he had me.

"Or forcing the issue now could cause a full-scale war among the clans. The gods could decide to destroy us all."

"We'll just have to take the chance."

My life had changed drastically in just a few short days. I remembered Calista's description of The Destroyer.

He is a great pretender. His power is one to be feared, but he is seduction reincarnate, and all will follow him into battle without knowing the truth.

I looked into the eyes of my lifemate and wondered again if he was The Destroyer. Only time would tell.

Something else he'd said bothered me, and I finally remembered what it was. "You said your spies reported that there are Drakán missing from all the clans. Who's missing from mine?" I asked.

"Your father has disappeared."

"That's not possible."

"He was taken from your home in the middle of the night. He vanished into thin air along with his hoard. Your brother witnessed the entire incident."

Fire simmered just under my skin, but it didn't escalate. I didn't know how I felt. I couldn't say I was sad to hear of Alasdair's disappearance because that would be a lie. But I knew his absence would leave the clan in turmoil. Because Erik had no power to call his own, the role of Archos would fall to me until someone challenged me for the position since I was Alasdair's only other child. Things were about to get bad.

"Fine," I said, as if there were only business between us. "I will order my clan to follow you in my father's stead." Getting them to obey me would be the tricky part. "How are you going to find The Destroyer?"

"With all of the clans gathered, we should be able to find the one responsible if he's among us. He would not be able to hide his power from Esmerelda. She is impervious to Drakán magic even though her own Drakán power is quite impressive. Between now and the gathering, I will teach you as much as possible about your abilities. You will need to know how to fight by using more than just your mental abilities."

I finally moved away from him and walked to the metal door that led out of the cavern and back up into the chateau —ready to escape from the bowels of the city.

"I need to make some phone calls," I said. "Where are we going to unite the clans?"

"I own most of Switzerland. It'll give us the privacy we need to train."

"That's handy. You've thought of everything, haven't you?"

"If I wasn't smart enough to plan ahead I'd be dead many times over by now."

I pushed my hand through the metal of the door and moved to follow with my body, but I thought of one more thing—an important thing.

"I want you to stay away from me once the clans are united. I need time to think. And I need time to observe how you deal with my clan. You're very good at clouding my judgment."

"Staying away from you will make what I have in mind quite…challenging."

"That's the point," I said as bitterness and anger clouded my voice. He'd used me and taken advantage of the human nature I'd wanted to embrace. I guess in hindsight he'd taught me an important lesson. I wasn't human. I was Drakán. I could learn to harden my heart as well as anyone.

"Rena," he said softly, taking a step toward me. Something that looked like pity lined his face, and I took a step back out of his grasp.

"Just stay away, Julian. I wouldn't want your grand plans to be ruined because you were distracted by the opposite sex. It's been more than one great leader's downfall."

"That's very true," he said. "But of course there's always our dreams."

TWENTY-THREE

I avoided Julian for three days—mind and body—before I finally had no choice but to listen to his instructions about the gathering clans. He'd been on conference calls and short trips for the last seventy-two hours to line things up for his takeover, so it hadn't been that hard to stay out of his way.

He cornered me late one night as I made use of the gym I'd found on the second floor of the chateau. Olaf had offered to spar with me, and I'd been more than happy to take my recent frustrations out on him. Olaf had had no idea what he'd gotten himself into.

My fury was great, and it was the first time I'd gotten to see what I was really capable of since Julian and I had mated. I was a lot stronger. I dodged Olaf's blows with time to spare, and my speed kept him off center and confused. The power behind my punches was debilitating, and Olaf was bloody and sweating by the end of it. When my foot hit him with a roundhouse kick to the ribs, mirroring the move I'd used on him the day I'd broken out of the chateau, it didn't feel like I was hitting cement. The sound of breaking ribs was like music to my ears, and Olaf toppled like a redwood in the forest.

"Impressive," Julian's voice called out from the other side of the room.

I'd been so focused on my fight that I hadn't even noticed when he'd entered the room. He was careful not to touch me as he came closer, and his shields were locked tight, just as mine were.

"That will be all, Olaf. Go and let your body heal."

Olaf bowed low to Julian and shot me a look that promised retribution. I was looking forward to it.

I moved across the room to put space between us and wiped my face with a towel.

"The increase in your power calls to me, Rena. We are not meant to be apart," Julian said once Olaf was gone.

I turned backed to him. "Get on with it, Julian. You've made your bed. I'm not in the mood to be messed with. Those days are over."

A growl rumbled low in his throat and his eyes rimmed red with fire. "You don't want to challenge me, lifemate. Your power is not great enough to defeat me. I could take you easily and make you want me. Don't underestimate my control."

"I know you're the alpha in this relationship. You don't have to prove it. But I won't submit to you. Yes, you can make me want you, but if you take me against my will there will be no end to the depths of my hatred for you. You've

239

gotten what you wanted from me. Be happy with that and move on."

He growled again and I could see the fine tremors that ran through his body where his beast wanted to break free. It was a testament to his power that he was able to hold back. I'd never known a Drakán who could control himself once his beast started to break free.

"The clans will begin gathering in three days' time," Julian rasped, every word measured and even. "Some of the Ancients are already forming hunting parties, hoping to track The Destroyer's scent. If they can bring it back to me I should be able to tell what Realm he and his army are hiding in."

My curiosity got the best of me. "How would you know which Realm he traveled to?" There were once eight Realms in our universe, but the number lessened by one after the Drakán Realm was destroyed. And then it lessened again after the gods obliterated Atlantis for destroying the Drakán Realm. I knew very little about the six remaining Realms other than what they were and what creatures resided there. It was another bit of lost history that disappeared when our archives were stolen.

"I'll know because I've travelled through the portals that take us from one world to the next. The scent of each Realm is unmistakable. Just as the Earth Realm smells of fresh meat, the Realm of the Gods smells of freshly fallen snow. The Realm of the Fae smells of trees. Oceana smells of sea salt, and the Shadow Realm smells of brimstone. Only the Realm of the Dead has no smell."

"I'd like to know about the other Realms," I said.

"Esmerelda told me the Drakán Realm hasn't been the only one to suffer at the gods' hands."

"Maybe if you decide to accept me back into your good graces I'll tell you about them someday. And despite what you thought when you came to my lands, I'm not the only creature in this world who has the ability to travel. It'll take all of our magic to defeat The Destroyer and save this world." He put his hands in his pockets and quirked his lips. "We're running out of places we can be banished to."

"Did you just make a joke?" I asked, incredulously.

"Apparently not a good one." He took a step forward and I took one back before I could stop myself. He kept coming toward me until we stood facing each other, barely any space between us.

"You might have a right to your anger, Rena. You know as well as I do that the want between us was there long before I thought of what our combined union would do for our power. But my desire will not go away. And neither will yours. The power that we've created with the mating fire is the best thing for our people. There's no need to make us suffer needlessly."

He leaned closer so his lips just barely touched my ear. I shivered and my dragon called to him. She'd been lonely.

"You've missed me, Rena. You may think you hate me, but your body knows the truth."

I pushed him back and retreated several steps. I didn't care if it made me look like a coward or not. Just the touch of him burned across my skin.

"Stop toying with me and just tell me what you want from me. I know you've spent the last three days deciding how you can use me to your advantage. Give me instructions and stop torturing my beast with your lust. It's cruel to keep doing so."

"You're the one punishing us both," he said. "But you're right. We don't have time for this now. I need you to go with Xana to Switzerland and begin greeting the clans as they arrive. You'll have a few days to settle in. It is your home as it is mine, and Xana will keep you safe."

"Will I be in danger?"

"You're going to have to act as queen. Just as I will act as king. The strongest of the clans will not be receptive at first. Our very lives will be tested. And you must not show them weakness. We are lifemates, and your anger at me will divide the clans even more than they already are, so have a care."

"So you're saying I have to fake it?"

"It'll be a new concept for you. I hope you're a good actress."

"Wow, two jokes in one day. I'm mated to a clown."

"If you ask nicely I'll let you juggle my balls."

He kissed me hard and left me standing there with my mouth open wide in shock.

TWENTY-FOUR

S witzerland was filled with pure misery and endless snow.

Once Xana and I left Belgium, an overwhelming emptiness settled in the pit of my stomach. It got worse with every mile that separated me and Julian—to the point that I spent a great deal of the flight either hanging over the toilet or wishing I was dead. Sometimes both. Gods, I hated flying. Julian owed me big time.

All in all, this little trip was a good test for me, because I knew in my heart that distance between the two of us was the only answer. I would eventually have to leave him and go back home. I had no other choice. The gods had made a terrible mistake in making us lifemates. There weren't two more mismatched creatures in the entire universe.

In addition to the nausea, I found I suffered from an amazing amount of guilt. Noah had left several messages on my phone since I'd mated with Julian. I hadn't had the courage to call him back. What was I supposed to say? Any attraction I'd felt to Noah was gone.

There were so many questions I had that were unanswered. I hadn't forgotten that I'd felt the same searing pain across my body with Noah that I'd experienced with Julian. Which made me wonder if I'd mated with Noah first if my desire for Julian would be obsolete. Would I have been Noah's lifemate? Did I choose the wrong man?

I figured it was best just to let whatever attraction had been between the two of us die a slow death. Despite what Noah thought about our destinies being entwined, I didn't really have room for any more alpha males on my relationship plate.

I arrived in Switzerland much like I'd arrived in Belgium. My clothes were a wreck, my hair hung down in my face, my skin was pale and clammy, and a Bellator was dogging my every step. I just thanked the gods that no one was there yet to witness my arrival.

By my third day there, surrounded by nothing more than snow and guards, I thought for sure I would either lose my mind or go on a destructive rampage through the nearest town just for a little excitement. The trepidation I'd felt at greeting the clans had turned to worry and uncertainty. No one had arrived, and I honestly wasn't sure if they were going to. Not even my own clan had shown, even after I'd called home and given the order as their new Archos to attend the Drakán Summit.

But one by one, as the sun settled over the mountains on the third night and a hard snow began to fall, the Drakán began arriving at the castle on top of Mount Drummondsey.

Mount Drummondsey was built like a resort town, except there were no humans who lived or worked there. It sat empty and unused most of the year. The main castle sat at the apex of the mountain, and as you traveled farther down the hill, small bungalows dotted the rough terrain. It was shielded by magic, and only dragons could see the haven through the clouds that rolled low over the mountains. The mountain was filled with wild game, so the hunting was plentiful and everyone's bellies stayed full.

The castle was six stories of gray stone, turrets, and towers. Private terraces and wood-burning fireplaces accompanied every room. It was lush and beautiful, and impossible to enjoy with all the hostility behind its walls.

Drakán came from all over the Earth Realm for two solid days, until every room in the castle and all of the bungalows were bursting at the seams. Julian had made it clear that it was too dangerous for human mates and children to attend the summit, and had forbidden them from even entering the country.

Most of the Drakán I welcomed didn't particularly want to be there, and they were more than happy to let me know the fact by causing as much mischief as possible. Arguments and fights broke out constantly between enemy clans, and I spent most of my time settling petty disputes.

"I saw it first!" A female Drakán roared as she held on for dear life to a tapestry that dated back to the days of William the Conqueror, clearly intent on adding the item to her hoard. She was dressed in a well-cut pantsuit of winter white, and her blond hair was pulled back in an elegant chignon. She spoke in her native Russian tongue.

"You lie," said another female in a lyrical hiss. Her auburn hair and Ancient green eyes were electric with anger. "I had it in me hands when you came and snatched it away."

I remembered what Julian said about acting like a queen and not backing down. I couldn't fight them like I would as if I were acting as Enforcer. My power to control the mind only went so far. I didn't have anything to back it up with other than finding another dragon to set them on fire. A queen would definitely have other tricks up her sleeve.

I drew on Julian's power for reassurance and cast it out at the two women. The magic weighed heavy on them until they had no choice but to drop to their knees in submission. I took the tapestry out of the blonde's hands and hung it back on the wall.

Both women looked at me with fire flaming from their eyes, and I could feel their beasts writhing in anger inside them. I sensed the Russian's powers and dismissed her. She was a weakling. She'd didn't even have the ability to call her dragon form. But I kept an eye on the red-haired Ancient. Her beast was close to the surface, and if she shifted before I got her under control I'd lose the upper hand.

Her magic swelled, tasting mine as I'd tasted hers, and she smirked as she was obviously unimpressed with what she'd found. I pulled hard on the thread that bound Julian and me, and our combined magic kept her beast contained. The smirk disappeared as she lost control of her magic. An invisible force pushed her head down low so she had no option but to bow before me. The Russian whimpered, but I ignored her fear.

I opened my senses further and absorbed the Ancient's anger and magic, until she was snuffed out like a candle. She lay prone on the floor, and her body tremored with aftershocks.

"This is my home, and the things in it belong to me," I told them, hoping Julian really meant it when he'd said what was his was now mine. "You will abide by my rules, or I will leave you as you are—weak and helpless—no better than human beggars. Have I made myself clear?"

Both women bowed as low as they could, their bellies touching the ground, and cried out their promises to obey. I released Julian's magic and my bindings on them dissolved. I walked away, and my hands didn't start shaking until I was behind the walls of my own room. Every step I took to secure Julian's position as king and my place beside him left us more open to challenges from other Drakán. I hoped to the gods we would be strong enough to defeat them all.

While I was playing hostess to the world's most horrible houseguests, Julian and the other Archos, minus my father, were closeted away in a private room discussing the terms of his plan to defeat The Destroyer.

I knew the exact moment when Julian told them he expected all the clans to unite and recognize him as king until The Destroyer could be defeated—the mountain trembled and the castle walls shook with their anger. Each

Archos roared out a resounding denial at his proposal, but Julian wasn't worried about their lack of cooperation. He told me things would work out, and he'd been right.

It wasn't long after dinner was over when the Russian Archos, Milos, disappeared from his room. There was no trace of him. One moment he was dining with his sister, and the next he vanished into thin air, leaving a hysterical Drakán behind who screamed her way through the castle. The feel of fear in the castle was oppressive as I ran quickly to find Julian and hear what had happened.

The remaining two Archos were already gathered in Julian's study by the time I got there. I didn't bother to knock as I walked through the shield Julian had erected around the room. I was technically Archos for my own clan, and had every right to be there. I didn't think about it as I walked into the room, but I instinctively made my way to Julian and stood at his side.

He put his arm possessively around my waist and pulled me close. "Rena, may I introduce to you Cale of the Éire and Andres of the Rumanus."

I nodded politely, but didn't speak. I wasn't sure of the dynamic Julian wanted to present. The two men looked at me dismissively.

Julian's voice hardened as he admonished the men for their rudeness. "Rena is my true lifemate. We are the first to share the blue mating fire since the time of the Banishment. You will treat her with the same respect that you would give me."

"It cannot be," Andres said. "We would have heard of such a phenomenon."

"You will be witness to it at the mating ceremony tonight," Julian said.

They looked at me this time with curiosity and something like wonder, but they both took a moment to bow low before me in proper respect before Julian let the other shoe drop.

"She is also the daughter of Alasdair. And she is the Archos for her clan until Alasdair is returned or his death confirmed."

Dragon fire whooshed beneath the skin of Cale and smoke curled from his nostrils. Andres wasn't as quick to catch on, so it took a moment before his rage matched Cale's.

"You bastard," Cale said. "You knew this would happen."

"I knew you would eventually see things my way," Julian agreed. "But do not accuse me of masterminding Milos' disappearance. The Destroyer has taken care of that all on his own. Circumstances have fallen into place and given me a powerful lifemate who holds her own clan. We are already united. There is no choice but for you to do the same. You cannot defeat the both of us."

Julian's words weren't negotiable, and the two Archos' fear and hatred of him was obvious. I opened my senses and read their thoughts. They both believed that Julian was The Destroyer, and they were only going to give in to his wishes to keep from facing the same fate as Milos.

Cale nodded stiffly. "I will go speak with my people."

"As will I," said Andres. "You give us no choice. Archos."

They both bowed and left the room.

I didn't have time to panic as events teetered on the edge of chaos just before sliding neatly into place. What I did have time to panic over was the formal ceremony Esmerelda had decided to hold in my and Julian's honor, declaring us to the entire Drakán nation as true lifemates.

The mating fire was briefly mentioned in the Ancient texts that the five warriors had created so their people would know the history of the Drakán Realm. Since Calista's mother had stolen all of our clans' texts and handed them over to the enemy, I was quite ignorant about our history, as were my clansmen who weren't Ancients. Calista and Alasdair had never found it necessary to record the time before the scrolls were stolen. The new archives began from the moment Alasdair took over as Archos.

As soon as Esmerelda had arrived at Mount Drummondsey, she'd started poring over the Ancient scrolls of Julian's clan. According to Esmerelda, once two Drakán had experienced the mating fire, a ceremony was supposed to occur so we could show our appreciation to the gods for giving us our soulmate and the opportunity to continue our race. I personally wanted to tell the gods to go to hell, but Esmerelda insisted that we follow through with the ritual. She reminded me it was never a good idea to make the gods angry.

"Relax, my dear," Esmerelda said. "This is just a formality. You and Julian have already been bound in every way that counts."

"Don't remind me." I hadn't touched Julian in almost a

week. Between the sexual frustration and the undercurrents of violence that pulsed through the castle, my nerves were stretched as tautly as they could go.

"This ceremony holds more than one purpose. It not only shows the clan what you and Julian have become, but it's also an event that will give them a united purpose. A true lifemate is something we all dream of."

"Right. A united clan. I'm just the sacrificial lamb."

Esmerelda took my hand and led me into the large ballroom where the ceremony was to take place. To say the atmosphere in the room was cold would be an understatement.

The ballroom was almost twice the size of the gathering room at Julian's chateau in Belgium, and all of the Drakán filled one room for the first time in our Earthly history. They stood next to each other and breathed the same air, but they weren't *together*. And they weren't happy.

Each clan stood off separately, their colors visible among the sea of Drakán. It was a field of black, red, green, white, and blue. They'd ignored the orders to attend in all black under Julian's colors.

Julian stood in the center of the room in front of an altar, his back to all the clans as he waited for me to join him at his side. He wore a beautifully cut tuxedo, and his posture was straight and proud. He'd pulled his hair back into a tail at the nape of his neck, and I fought the urge to reach up and unbind it so it fell around his shoulders. I loved it down. My mouth watered at the sight of him.

I wore a long, hooded red cape that tied at the neck and covered me from head to toe as I made my way toward

Julian. He helped me remove it, and there were audible murmurs through the crowd as they noticed I was dressed in black—signifying the union of the clans and my union to Julian.

My dress gathered at my right shoulder and flowed straight to the floor in layers of sheer fabric. My feet were bare. The tattoo down my left side was clearly visible. I'd pinned my hair up, and Esmerelda had stuck a red rose behind my ear to remind me where I'd come from. I ignored the accusatory stares from the clans, including my own, and I tried not to feel guilty at what I had done. This was Julian's show, and I had no more choices than our unhappy clans had.

I've missed you, Rena, Julian whispered through my mind.

He lifted my hand and kissed it softly. The touch of his lips against my starved skin sent electric shocks shooting to my very core. I barely stopped the moan before it escaped my lips.

When will you accept that you cannot run from me? We will never be as strong apart as we are together. Only when we're together does our true power show. Open yourself. You can feel their envy hitting our backs like waves against the sand. They know they cannot stop us now that we're joined.

I did as he said, and was almost knocked forward by the ferocity of emotions that came from the Drakán behind us. Waves of hate and despair. Anger and hope. And there it was—envy. Power rushed across my skin, and my dragon responded to it. She loved that others feared her. That they lusted after her mate. She was a selfish, greedy creature, as all dragons were, but the power that now ran in her blood did not lie. She was stronger. She was dominant.

My human self was more reserved. My conscience prickled at what I'd forced my clan to do. Something still didn't feel right about the whole situation. It was hard to keep my dragon wants and my human common sense separated, especially when faced with so many other Drakán.

I didn't look at him as I answered. *I'll accept that I can't run from you once you stop trying to manipulate me and my feelings. I will not cower before you and let you make my decisions, mate or no. If our clans continue to fight the change of being united, The Destroyer will win, and you'll have played right into his hands. If this plan of yours doesn't work, and your greed to become king destroys our people, I swear to the gods I will kill you or die trying.*

I didn't make threats idly. I meant every word of it.

I will protect you and our people, Rena. I promise you. I can feel you pulling away from me, fighting against the hold we have on one another. Leaving me will not help you on your quest to find out more about your powers.

Maybe not. But I need to do it anyway. You cloud my mind, and I can't trust you since you tricked me into handing you my clan on a silver platter. Getting as far away from you as possible is the best thing I can do for myself.

I've never been to America. I'll enjoy coming after you.

I fought the urge to growl and release my inner fire. Talking with Julian never got me anywhere except naked, and that wasn't an option right now. *I think we need to get this over with. My brother is seriously thinking of running you through with a sword. And I promise, he's very good at it.*

Yes, I know. I saw him fight in the Macedonian Wars. I am better.

Erik had barely spoken a word to me since his arrival. In his eyes, I'd betrayed him and our clan by becoming mated to Julian. It didn't matter that the choice had been taken out of my hands. Julian was our sworn enemy, just as the other clans were, and I was forcing them to rely on him for protection. Erik's eyes had blazed with an intense hatred I'd never witnessed before. And it was directed at me. Calista hadn't even bothered to show up. The rest of my clan avoided my gaze completely. All except Cal. He'd met my eyes with something resembling respect and understanding, and he'd given me a nod of encouragement before his father had pushed him out of my line of sight.

Panic began to set in as Esmerelda took her place behind the altar, and I gripped Julian's arm involuntarily. Things were starting to seem much too similar to a human wedding ceremony. And I was human enough to hold some stock in the ritual. Julian grabbed me around the waist and held me tightly against him.

Esmerelda had informed me that the scrolls had said it was the female Drakán's choice as to who performed the mating ceremony and read the sacred words. It was usually someone close to her—a father or brother. Emptiness and despair filled me when she'd told me this. I had no one who would be proud to stand in for me at a moment like this. Alasdair was gone, and from the looks Erik had given me he wouldn't have agreed if I'd asked. I'd been alone my entire life, and after this was over I'd be that way again.

I hadn't known what to tell Esmerelda when she asked

me who I'd chosen to read the scrolls. I thought of Julian and who he would have chosen if he'd been in my position. Esmerelda had been delighted when I'd asked her to take on the role.

Esmerelda pulled an ancient piece of parchment from a cylindrical tube made of ivory. It had been protected by magic over the centuries and was still in beautiful condition, the edges gilded with gold leaf and the penmanship in itself a work of art.

"My brothers, my Drakán," she began. Her voice echoed through the silence of the ballroom. "This is a night of great triumph for our people. It is a night that unites us all with the spirits of our ancestors, for the mating fire hasn't been witnessed since the time of the old lands. The gods have deemed Julian of the Belgae and Rena Drake, daughter of Alasdair of the Americas, worthy of each other—in spirit, mind, and body.

"And in keeping with the traditions of our homeland, a *stipis* will be offered to the Archos Julian, lifemate to Rena. What most valued gift shall be given to your mate this night?" Esmerelda asked me formally.

Esmerelda had told me that a *stipis* was a gift to your lifemate of the most precious possession you owned. The choice hadn't been difficult for me. It was something I carried with me always, and I found it odd that my dragon didn't seem to mind parting with such a valuable treasure.

My gift lay on the altar and was hidden under a piece of black velvet. I pulled the cloth aside and precious metal gleamed in the light. It was a torq, and two kinds of gold were melded together and shaped like the sun. A yellow diamond the size of a quail egg was perched in the center. The sun was attached to a chain woven of gold and linked with rubies.

"It is the only thing I have of my mother," I said clearly, so the entire room could hear. I turned the torq over. Latin was inscribed across the back. "*Amori, Ferocia, Venerato,*" I said aloud. "Love, Courage, and Respect. I give this to you freely, lifemate."

I picked it up, the gold cool between my fingers, and I placed it around Julian's neck. I made sure the chain lay over his collar so it didn't touch bare skin. He turned the sun over in his hands and studied it for a moment. His eyes met mine and the shock on his face was apparent.

Who was your mother, Rena? Julian asked. He sounded angry, and the rims around his eyes were beginning to turn red.

I looked at the torq again, trying to see what Julian did, but there was nothing there but precious metal and gems. *I don't know who she was. Alasdair has never spoken her name. I know she was royalty and killed shortly after my birth when the Ottoman Turks invaded Egypt. This torq was in my blankets when Calista came to take me away to live with the Drakán. Why? What's wrong?*

He studied me closely, weighing my words for truth.

Nothing, he finally said. And then aloud he said, "I accept this gift of my lifemate with deepest gratitude."

"Now it is your turn for the *stipis,*" Esmerelda said to Julian.

He nodded and pulled the cloth from his gift. Ancient parchment scrolls, much like the one Esmerelda read from, sat on the altar. I knew what they were without opening them. Tears came to my eyes.

I heard the gasps of some of the Ancients in my own clan. Julian had given me back our archives that had been stolen from my grandfather Niklos. These scrolls were the reason so many of my clan were dead. And Julian's message couldn't have been any clearer to those watching. The feud between all of the clans was over. For now.

"These belong to you," Julian said, and bowed low before me with great respect.

Thank you. I didn't have the voice to speak it aloud.

Julian took my hand and we stepped toward each other. I wanted to be alone with him, to show my appreciation for what he'd given me. To touch him the way my body had craved for the last few days. The conflict of emotions inside me was overwhelming. I was at war with myself. And though I could love Julian at this particular moment in time, I could also hate him for doing this to me.

He leaned down and kissed me softly on the lips. He absorbed all my anger—my hate—my sorrow. It was suddenly all gone, and there was only him. The blue mating fire started small and danced between our mouths. The crowd gasped and surged forward to see the fire they'd only heard of in legends. Until that moment many had thought this was a scheme Julian and I had come up with to take power over all the clans. This was the proof they needed to see that we truly were lifemates. And that we could lead them to victory.

I pulled back before things got out of control and my

clothes burned away. But Julian's eyes still held the passion of the flame, and I knew mine did as well.

"May your union be blessed and fruitful," Esmerelda said over the swell of voices. Everyone in the room repeated the sentiment. Esmerelda leaned down and picked up a squirming goat. She placed it on the altar, and held it by the scruff of the neck. "You shared flesh and blood with each other, and now you are bonded for life. One of you cannot live without the other. Bonding is a great sacrifice, and we will make another one here today in honor of it."

Her hand transformed into razor-sharp talons, and she sliced the goat's neck with a quick slash of her wrist. Blood poured across her hand and spilled onto the altar in a fiery wash of color. The coppery scent brought my hunger swiftly, and I could tell by the surge of bodies in the room they felt the same desire. Esmerelda dipped her finger in the blood and drew a line across my forehead. Then onto Julian's.

Two large chairs were brought out—both of them dark and heavy with ornate scrollwork across the back. A plush red cushion sat in each chair. Julian and I each took a seat.

Growls rose up from around us, and the tension in the room was high. The hunger was difficult to resist, especially among the youngest of our kind. I'd always relied on my abilities as Enforcer to control my beast. Others weren't so lucky. There would be a fight for the carcass as soon as the way was clear.

Five Drakán—their different colors signifying they'd been chosen from each clan—came and surrounded us. I grasped the arms of the chair as two of them bent down and lifted it high above them. The three others did the same with Julian. The crowd roared with a resounding cheer.

What the hell is going on? I asked mind to mind. There was no way he could have heard me over the noise otherwise. The crowd surged behind us up the stairs. The sound of gnashing teeth and snapping bones echoed over the celebration as the newlings attacked what was left of the goat.

The scrolls say it is tradition for there to be witnesses to the consummation to ensure the mating fire flames true.

Like hell, I growled. *I don't need witnesses. Besides, they already got to see the mating fire. They'll have to be happy with that.*

And I was so looking forward to putting on a show.

Very funny. I don't suppose I can get these guys to take me to my own room. It's not a good idea for us to stay together. The temptation is too great, and the pull between us is too strong.

So you keep saying, but I don't believe we have a choice in this matter. I'm sure we can find an extra blanket and pillow for you. The floor is probably quite comfortable.

He smirked at my predicament. I growled again and this time smoke curled from my nostrils.

The five Drakán lowered the chairs to the ground. I stood up slowly and faced the bedroom door, more scared than I cared to admit. Every time I mated with Julian I lost a little more of myself to him.

The door stood open, and all I could see was miles of bed dressed in black satin. The crowd of people behind us were eerily silent as they waited to see what I would do.

Julian's hand pushed gently against my lower back, and I went willingly into the room. It had been too long since he'd touched me, and my dragon rolled through me with joy and desire. He closed the door behind us and shut out the curious eyes of our people. We were completely alone, and I wouldn't be sleeping on the floor tonight.

"Why did you ask me about my mother?" I asked once we had privacy. I wasn't sure I really wanted to know, but I was trying to stall what was about to happen. I just wasn't ready yet, and I'd take all the damned time I needed.

Julian unbuttoned his jacket and slid it off his broad shoulders. He threw it over a black brocade chair and then untied the bow at his neck. He unbuttoned the top two buttons of his white dress shirt and untucked it from his pants. The ritual of undressing so casually in front of me seemed much too intimate.

"It's not important." He sat down in the chair and stretched his legs out in front of him, crossing his ankles.

"Oh, I think it is. For a moment, after you saw the torq, you looked at me as if you hated me. I don't call that nothing."

"I thought it seemed familiar. It was nothing, Rena."

He was lying to me. Maybe not lying exactly, but he was evading the truth. Which I'd always thought was the same thing.

"Did you know my mother?" I asked.

The possibility overwhelmed me. I'd always wanted to know more about her, and if Julian had known her all along, my wrath would not be containable. My anger smoldered just under my skin, and the grumble of my roar gathered low in my stomach. The betrayal was harsh and cutting, and I moved to attack just out of instinct.

"I did not know her," Julian said calmly. He spoke the truth and my anger died down so my fire became a gentle simmer. "It is just as I said. The torq seemed familiar to me. It reminded me of…less pleasant times."

I nodded and turned my back, breathing deeply to get myself under control. My emotions were all much too close to the surface. There was no reason for my anger to react so quickly. Something was happening to me. I'd felt the change inside me as soon as I'd given the torq to Julian. My hands longed to touch it again.

I pulled a pillow from the bed and went to rummage around in the wardrobe for an extra blanket. I was restless and unsettled. My dragon wasn't satisfied, and the fire just beneath my skin was jumpy.

I stood perfectly still as I felt the air shift behind me. I could feel the heat from Julian's skin as he stood just a hairsbreadth away from my back. Our bodies were separated by no more than an inch, but magic danced along our flesh, and it felt as if he was touching me everywhere. I tightened my grip on the pillow until my fingers penetrated the fabric and feathers tickled my fingers.

"No, Julian."

"Can you really say no, Rena? Your beast calls to me in anguish and need even as mine calls to you. Would you deny them pleasure?"

"Yes," I hissed. "You are making me someone I'm not comfortable being. I can feel myself slipping further and further away every time I lie with you. I don't know what powers are yours and what are mine. I don't know what I believe anymore. You've turned my entire world upside down and my family is in shambles. I'm a failure as an Enforcer because The Destroyer is still out there, killing our people and planning to take control of our world. And while all this is going on, all you have to do is touch me and I forget it all. I want to crawl inside you and spend the rest of my life there, and to hell with everyone else."

His magic moved over my skin and I put my hand against the wall to keep myself from falling over from the sensation.

"That's not the real me, Julian. You've made me something I'm not. An imposter. And I have this terrible feeling that our actions are going to bring the wrath of the gods against us like nothing our Drakán ancestors ever experienced."

"Fighting against your true nature and your powers is what's giving you this feeling." He pulled the pins from my hair and tossed them to the floor, and the thick mass tumbled around my shoulders and down my back. He pressed his nose against it and inhaled its scent.

"You cannot lie to me, Rena. For I've seen all of you. Everything you keep hidden in the furthest corners of your mind. You're afraid of letting your power take complete control of your mind. Fear is an emotion for prey, and it calls out to all predators. I am a predator."

I dropped the pillow and feathers plumed wildly into the air and floated down softly around us.

"You are so lovely." He inhaled my scent again and goose

bumps pebbled my flesh. "We are trapped inside these human bodies, Rena, but our hearts and instincts are those of an animal. Do you have any idea what I want to do to you right now?"

"Yes, but we are not full-blooded Drakán," I managed to say. "We are tainted by other blood, and these feelings I have are a result of that blood."

"Your dragon is stronger than you think. You are more than you think. Just as I am. We are intelligent and cunning. Selfish and loyal. Fighters and lovers. We are Drakán."

Fire erupted around us in a whoosh of blue flame.

"Do you deny what is between us?"

"Yes!" I shouted, even as my dragon battered against me in denial. I sobbed in silent gasps as my emotions warred within me.

Julian would always win these battles. I didn't have the strength to stop him. He kissed the nape of my neck and then bit down gently, the scrape of his teeth sending visible sparks along my skin.

"If you don't accept your own powers, how are you going to accept mine? Do you want me, Rena?"

I could only see the truth of my desire and his when our minds were connected like they were.

"You know I do," I said, resigned.

"Will you open yourself to your full power and give me everything you have?"

I nodded wordlessly.

"I need to hear the words, Rena. There will be no going back once you agree. I will take everything you have, and I will give you everything in return."

263

"Yes." The word was so soft it was almost silent.

Julian roared in triumph and we tumbled to the floor. A symphony of colors played behind my closed eyelids. The lights flickered in the room. Lightbulbs popped and tinkled to the floor, plunging us into darkness. The windows cracked and then shattered in a shower of glass. Snow swirled into the room like a blizzard, but didn't melt when touched by our fire. Water poured from the faucets and flooded onto the carpet, building until there was a lake beneath us and waves ebbed and flowed.

And then we collapsed in a heap together as the mating fire slowly died out.

The last thing I remember before submitting to sleep was that the powers that had unleashed in the room weren't familiar to me. They were like nothing I'd ever seen or experienced before.

The problem was, I didn't know if they'd belonged to me, or Julian. Either way we had a problem.

TWENTY-FIVE

" I 'm going to be formally presented to the clans as Archos," Julian said the next morning as he shook me awake.

I pushed his hands away and rolled over. It felt like we'd just gone to bed. I looked for the clock on the nightstand, but didn't see it there. The table was turned over on its side and the clock lay faceup on the floor. The red numbers glowed 7:15. I'd been asleep a little over an hour.

After we'd made love the night before—the first time— and let loose the powers that had brought the elements to crash down upon us, the magic that had seemed so destructive at the time calmly put things to rights again. The water drained and the carpet dried. The electricity came back on and the lights fixed themselves. The cracks in the walls sealed themselves, and the room was left almost whole.

I looked around and winced at the broken furniture and overturned plants that lay around the room. The elements hadn't caused the furniture to break. We'd done that all on our own, and Julian hadn't gotten around to putting things back together. No wonder I was so sore. And no wonder I'd spent the short time I'd been asleep trying to keep myself from rolling to the floor. The bed dipped down at an extremely weird angle.

"Gods, why does everything have to be so formal around here? And early," I added.

I was tired of the pomp and circumstance Drakán protocol seemed to demand. I missed my home and my solitude. I'd not had ten minutes of time to myself since I'd stepped foot inside Drummondsey Castle.

Julian was already up and dressed, and he brought a cup of coffee over to me and wrapped my fingers around the hot mug. My dragon immediately popped her eyes open and began to move around as the smell and heat reached her.

"Have you noticed that you're not very agreeable in the mornings?"

I growled and took a scalding sip before the coffee had had time to cool off. "Maybe if I ever got more than a couple of hours sleep at a time I'd be in a little better mood."

"Are you really complaining about last night?" he asked rubbing his finger across my bottom lip.

My lips twitched before I could help it. "Complaining might be too strong of a word." The cobwebs started to clear from my mind, and I finally took a long look at Julian. He'd dressed in another black suit and white dress shirt, but he'd forgone a tie and the collar sat open, exposing the strong length of his throat. His blue eyes were bright and alert, and he smelled like sin. He looked good. Really good.

He growled and moved across the room. "We need to be downstairs in twenty minutes, and your hair is..." He waved his hands above his head in a gesture that made me afraid to look in the mirror.

I pulled the covers off and put my feet on the floor, having every intention of going into the bathroom and making myself presentable, but Julian's eyes flared and I felt the lick of his magic against my skin before he could reel it back in.

"Twenty minutes is plenty of time," I said, getting a running start at him.

We were late, but it was to be expected.

I'd dressed quickly in a black strapless sheath that didn't leave anything to the imagination and a pair of needle-thin heels. Julian had been right about the state of my hair— indoor storms and broken furniture had made it interesting to say the least, and all I could do with it was brush out the tangles and pull it back in a tight bun at the nape of my neck. I slicked my lips with red and decided that was as good as it was going to get.

We walked into the ballroom arm in arm and swathed a path through thousands of Drakán to the center of the room. The Drakán closed around us in a wide circle. More Drakán had arrived overnight, and they stood shoulder to shoulder and hundreds deep. The clans were each still wearing their own colors, and each clan stood together so the circle around us resembled a rainbow wheel. But it was easily the color black that dominated the room. I hadn't realized how much the clans had diminished in numbers. Julian was right when he'd said his people were the only ones thriving.

I nodded to Cale of the Éire, who stood at the front of his clan. He was a tall man and thin as a reed, with a head of fiery curls and emerald-green eyes. The milk-white skin and red hair of his people were the result of centuries of confining their human mates and children to one small island. The Irish dragons were all varying shades of green, and they had the least in numbers. Cale was the grandson of the warrior Thelos, and he was Esmerelda's nephew.

My clan was also easy to recognize in the crowd. They wore our colors proudly, even though it made me angry that they'd defied my, and Julian's, direct orders. I was going to have to make my position clear and come down on them hard. I was their new Archos, and they would obey me. Or I'd make them sorry.

They showed more disrespect by not dressing formally —most wore jeans and sweaters. They lounged sullenly, with their arms crossed and their eyes defiant. Their arrogance and pride was obvious, and I realized how little I knew them. My job as Enforcer had kept me separated from them, and they only knew me for two things: the daughter Alasdair despised and the person who was called in when death was needed. Commanding them to join with Julian had been a bitter pill for them to swallow, but it was done and they needed to come to terms with it. Getting them under control was going to be a difficult job, and it was just another reason that I needed to leave Julian and go back home. He squeezed my hand as he felt the direction of my thoughts.

It will be all right. They are confused, and your brother is making things difficult, giving them ultimatums. They don't know who to follow.

I squeezed his in answer to his reassurance, and I tried to keep my mind off Erik. It just hurt too badly. I let my gaze wander around the rest of the room.

The Romanians all wore the traditional clothing of their country. The women wore white peasant skirts and blouses with a wraparound black apron. They wore no adornments or jewelry. The married women in the clan wore a white scarf to cover their hair. The men, who were far more scarce than the women, wore loose-fitting pants and shirts of white. They topped them with multicolored handwoven vests of wool. The Romanians were in sad shape—their numbers were small and they looked hungry. They weren't at all a healthy clan, in any aspect of the word.

Their Archos, Andres, stood proudly in front of them—a rigid man who was frozen for eternity as the picture of youth and vitality. It was common knowledge that his people were unable to breed. A Romanian child hadn't been born in more than two thousand years. He stood defiant in front of his remaining family, ignoring the needs of his withering people and condemning them to extinction.

The Russians were a different matter. Their numbers almost rivaled Julian's. Almost. The Russians had big problems. Lucian had been the warrior to form this clan. That part of the world had been vastly huge eleven thousand years ago, and he'd actually tried to start two different clans, hoping to stack the odds in his favor. He'd fathered hundreds of children in the lands that are now Russia and China, ruling over them both equally. But when he'd died, allegiances had been split. Both clans were considered equal in power, so there was no one who was strong enough to lead them both.

So while Milos was the true Archos in Russia, there were many loyal to Feng in China, though the Council had never agreed to make Feng an official Archos. Feng hadn't been invited to sit in on the meetings with Julian and the other Archos. But with Milos' recent disappearance, Feng had very handily stepped in and taken charge of both the clans. Russia's official color was white, and even those belonging to Milos should have been dressed in it. But instead they wore bright yellow. I could taste their fear, but there were none who were strong enough to challenge Feng.

Feng stood at the front of the group, a yellow silk suit covering his compact, muscled body. His ebony hair fell to his shoulders as straight as rain and his eyes were as black as coals and framed by thick lashes. He was an inch shorter than my own five foot four, but his attitude more than made up for his slight build.

If I'd thought Julian cold when I'd first met him, it was nothing compared to the expression on Feng's face. Feng was going to be trouble. It didn't take a psychic to figure that out.

I shivered as he held my gaze—there was a nothingness in the bleak depths of his eyes that terrified me. I could lose my soul in those eyes and never find my way back out. This man was cruelty itself.

Magic spilled across my skin and surrounded me, trying to seduce me with a flash of power that held no substance. It wasn't familiar magic. And I knew it belonged to Feng.

My eyes narrowed at his audacity. I reached deep down for my anger and it flowed to the surface and rippled off my skin. His thin lips smiled at my attempt to get him to release his hold over me and he pushed his magic at me harder—not gentle at all this time. I gasped and took a step back to steady myself.

"Release me," I whispered. The power of my words floated across the room and penetrated his shields. Feng was a child. Weak when faced with my psychic abilities. But Feng would not fight with honor.

His magic weakened and his brow furrowed in anger. He lashed out at me, but I was ready. I embraced the whip and slash of his power, much like I had with Julian, and I absorbed it. Feng's magic tasted different than Julian's had. It was bitter on the tongue—acidic.

Feng's magic vanished, and he stood powerless, humiliated in front of the Drakán by a woman. A myriad of emotions crossed his face—disbelief, rage, jealousy. But last was fear. And my dragon fed on it. He made the sign of devil horns in his left hand and pointed it at me.

"You are a magic succubus," he said. The words were spoken softly, but they covered the room like a blanket.

I'd never heard the term magic succubus, but I could tell by the stiffening in Julian's shoulders that he had. The power to absorb others' magic solely belonged to Julian

271

because he was of royal blood. I'd only recently acquired the skill once my dragon realized that Julian belonged to her.

"The archives tell stories of others like you," Feng spat. "You bring shame upon all the clans. Where do you really come from, Rena Drake? Have you sold your soul to the Shadow Realm? You are no Drakán with a power like that. You are evil incarnate and must be destroyed."

"You overstep yourself, Feng," I said. "I am the Enforcer. And I belong to Julian. You are no one. You belong to no one. And the people you've forced to follow you will cheer at your death. Remember your place."

His gaze locked on mine, and I stared him down. My dragon knew she was stronger, and she was going to force him to submit to her. The room was focused on our struggle of wills, but it was Julian who forced Feng's attention to be redirected.

"My lifemate can handle her own battles, Feng. But know that threats against her will bring the wrath of both our clans, for we are now united."

Julian took my arm and we both turned our backs on Feng. The ultimate insult, for to give your back to a dragon meant you didn't believe they were dangerous enough to worry about an attack.

Julian began the formal proceedings, even though he'd stripped the other Archos of their titles the day before.

"Welcome, Cale of the Éire and greetings to all of your people," Julian said, bowing formally and speaking the old language. He was following protocol that hadn't been used since the Banishment.

Esmerelda stood just behind me, and she translated for all of the newlings who had never heard the old tongue.

"Welcome Andres of the Rumanus and greetings to all of your people," he continued. We turned in the center of the circle to face the next group. "Welcome Feng of Ruskaya Zemlya and greetings to the people of Milos. And welcome, clan of my lifemate and the followers of Alasdair."

The tension in the room skyrocketed. Though Julian had greeted Feng, he had acknowledged him as a member of Milos' clan instead of acting leader of the Chinese and temporary leader of the Russians. But Feng did not attempt to release his magic again. He'd learned his lesson for now.

"Our people are in a great time of need," Julian said. "It is with hope and courage that you have all gathered together this day, for there is evil among us. The Destroyer must be stopped. Our people who still live must be returned, and those who are dead must be avenged. I have asked the impossible of you and here you are, standing before me. Now I ask another impossible task."

He turned slowly and made eye contact around the circle. The room swelled with anticipation. But underneath it were the dregs of resentment and fear. Julian stood strong and straight. My chest surged with pride that my lifemate was a true warrior—as fierce as the Drakán warriors who had breathed life into all of our clans—a leader to so many people.

My dragon whispered inside my head seductively, saying how wonderful it would be if he were our true king. I fought the urge to agree with her. The Promised Child would be our true king, and I needed to remember it, no matter how good the greed of power felt.

"I ask that we combine forces and hunt for our lost people. That we combine magic and seduce The Destroyer with its power, because the magnitude of such power will be irresistible to him. You will all follow me into battle when The Destroyer is found," he said with conviction. "You will follow me as one clan united, just as it was in the days of old—the days of the Realm of the Drakán."

"And then what?" someone yelled from the crowd.

I gasped in surprise, because I knew that voice. Erik came forward until he stood facing Julian like a gunslinger at dusk. His skin was pale, and dark circles rested beneath his eyes. He seemed thinner than when I'd left home, his face more gaunt. His pain was obvious, and the impotence of his power seemed pitiful in a room full of those who judged a person's worth by how much power they wielded.

"Erik. Don't do this," I said.

He'd been Alasdair's only son for two thousand years before I'd been born. Alasdair had never been a loving parent to either of his children, but he hadn't hated Erik. There'd been a bond between them that I'd never had. He was grieving for my father in his own way. But it was the wrong way.

My compassion for his situation was followed by frustration and anger. He shouldn't have questioned Julian's authority, especially since I'd already pledged our clan to join his. And he sure as hell shouldn't have been contradicting my orders to the rest of the clan.

"Stand back, Rena," he spat, not bothering to take his

eyes from Julian. "I don't answer to you. You've made your choice. I want our self-appointed leader to answer my question."

The crowd grew restless, and I could feel the stirrings of inner dragons throughout the room begin to waken and become interested in the violence that lay heavy across the room. Tension and anger poured from Erik. He stood before Julian powerless, his grief-stricken face desperate for his cause.

I cast my power out around him to soothe. And to search. Erik was close to losing his battle with being powerless. He'd been one of the greatest generals to ever fight for the Romans, but he'd been nothing as a Drakán. And he was tired of being nothing. He wanted to die.

"Well, my lord?" he said. "I asked you a question. What happens when we follow you into battle? Do you have grand plans for uniting us permanently? Of forcing us to bend to your will and controlling our minds as you did my sister's? Your powers of persuasion must be great for her to turn traitor to us all."

"Have a care, *castro*," Julian said. "You are speaking of my lifemate. And brother or no, I will not stand for it."

There were several gasps from the crowd, my own included. To be named *castro* was a terrible fate. To be named a *castro* meant that a Drakán had been castrated of his powers for displeasing the gods in some way.

"Call me what you will," he said. "I speak the truth. She betrayed us all for greed. To increase her own power."

"Would you not have done the same?" Julian asked. "It is our way. We are not a passive society. You have all forgotten what we used to be. Your human blood and human heart weakens you. I am strong, and the gods chose a mate for me who matched my strength."

There were several thoughtful nods from some of the Ancients in the crowd. I stepped forward to deny the accusation. To assure my people that I hadn't betrayed them because of power lust. Only because the gods had forced me to. But I stopped. I'd made a promise. I wouldn't interfere or undermine Julian's power in front of his people ever again. He wanted blind trust. And by gods he'd get it. We were in the middle of a volatile situation that could go from bad to worse if I chose now to open my mouth. Our immediate goal was to stay alive. I had the rest of eternity to hate Julian once that was accomplished.

Besides, Julian and I had already had this argument, and he knew exactly how I felt about having my choices taken away from me. I didn't know why or how we'd ended up as lifemates, but he'd had to have been behind it somehow, knowing this moment when he could declare himself would come.

I stepped back and felt Julian mentally sigh with relief. I took my place back beside him, but I couldn't bear to touch him just then. It wasn't his family he was destroying with words and magic. It was mine.

"Has it not occurred to you all that we cripple our entire race by continuing our feuds?" Julian asked the room at large. "Instead of mating with each other we are forced to mate with pure humans who dilute our blood even more. How will The Promised Child ever come to pass if we continue on this way?"

"You cloud the issues with your talk of The Promised Child," Erik shouted, turning the attention back on himself. "But I see through to what you really are. I have made peace that you and your lifemate would cause my death, but I will not cower and stand by while you destroy us all. You say that The Destroyer is among us, a creature more powerful than we can imagine. But I say that it is you, Julian of the Belgae, who has already destroyed us all. I name you The Destroyer."

The accusation lay like lead across the room, and then the room swelled with a whoosh of voices and frantic conversation. I felt the heat of fire as it burned angrily inside them and waited to break free. I glanced at Feng and saw he was smiling. We were making things very easy for him to step in and take over.

"Enough," Julian called out. The whip of power crashed across my body without warning. Julian had been shielding against me, keeping his emotions and thoughts from me, and I hadn't even realized it.

Erik went flying over the crowd and hit hard against the floor. The wood planks buckled under the force of his weight and the ground trembled as he hit, throwing everyone in the room off balance. I winced as I noticed one of the planks of wood had splintered and pierced through his chest.

"I will not be questioned by the likes of you, *castro*, unless you wish to challenge me. I have called everyone together because I have the power to do so, and your clan has been promised to me through your sister. You dishonor her with your disobedience. The Destroyer is clever at disguising himself. You were a champion fighting for the humans. But you are useless to us here. Go home and leave this battle for those who can win."

I was still tied to Erik, and I felt his flinch as Julian's words hit home.

Julian turned his back on Erik and took hold of my elbow, leading me toward the exit. I had to concentrate to put one foot in front of the other. I was numb.

"Is this what you wanted, Rena?" Erik yelled across the room. Pain laced his voice, and his breathing was erratic. "He could be the very one who took our father away from us. Yet you stay with him and condemn the rest of our people to be led to slaughter like cattle."

"You're wrong, Erik," I said, turning around to face him. I knew what I had to do, and hated myself in that moment almost as much as I hated Julian.

"I am your Archos, and he is my lifemate. He is not The Destroyer. He is the one who will save us all. Go home, Erik."

I held back the tears until I'd turned away from the room. The silence was deafening, and our footsteps echoed across the hard wood. It was the moment of truth for all the clans. They would have to decide if they were with us or against us. The line in the sand had been drawn.

"I will follow you into battle and fight at your side, Julian of the Belgae."

I recognized the thickly accented voice and dreaded what was coming next. Feng took a step forward and bowed mockingly, his hands placed in the position of prayer above his chest. "I will fight beside you, but when the battle is over we will have our own to contend with. I challenge you, Julian of the Belgae, for the kingdom of our people, until the day The Promised Child is delivered."

I stared at Feng and saw straight to his soul. To his future. And in it was Julian's death.

Julian returned Feng's bow and arrogantly raised his brow. There was a small smile upon his lips, and I realized he was elated at the prospect of a good fight.

"So shall it be," Julian said. The words rang like a death toll.

We exited the room. My legs shook and my heart thundered against my chest. Excitement shone in Julian's eyes, and I decided then and there that I would never understand the male psyche. My mind and my heart were both frozen. I either needed a good cry or a good fight.

I picked the fight.

CHAPTER

TWENTY-SIX

As soon as we crossed the threshold, I drew from Julian's magic and slammed the doors shut with a resounding thud. I sealed them with our combined powers and ignored the pounding that came from the Drakán on the other side. They could all stay in there forever as far as I was concerned.

"Are you out of your mind?" I said.

The calmness of my voice was the complete opposite of the turmoil that wreaked havoc inside of me. My inner dragon roared and fire spread beneath my skin. But something kept me from bringing her completely out and unleashing her rage against Julian. My dragon's anger was an aphrodisiac to Julian, and I knew he'd never get the point if I used her. So for the first time in my life, I sent her away.

But once I'd locked her away and could no longer feel my beast, magic still pulsed within me and filled me to bursting with the need to break free. It wasn't power I was drawing from Julian. It was my own. And it felt comfortable inside my skin like it had always been there. Maybe it had. The room dimmed to a soft glow around me, but the target of my rage stood out like a beacon. *Julian.* His eyes flared and he called on his dragon, but for once I didn't react as his animal came to the surface. It was as if I were no longer Drakán. And while there was a part of me that was terrified at the unknown, my body embraced it fully. And wielded it.

A great wind swept through the hallway from out of nowhere. Gale-force winds that tore priceless paintings from the walls. Antique vases crashed to the floor and shattered into tiny pieces. Julian's hair swirled violently around his face. But he kept his balance against the rage of my storm and leaned into it.

"How could you do that to Erik? Don't you have any compassion? You ridiculed him in front of everyone. Brought his greatest shame to light."

The hallway was long and narrow, and we faced each other like gunslingers. My dragon wanted to come out and play, but I held her back, reveling in the new power that coursed through my body. This power didn't need my dragon. Didn't want her. And it felt wonderful.

"I did what I had to do," he said. "Your brother is weak. And I would have lost ground with the other clans if I'd let him get away with questioning my authority. You know this. You'd been having the same thoughts about your own clan and their disobedience. Don't question my authority. You agreed to this, lifemate."

Thunder echoed in the narrow walkway and lightning crackled horizontally along the ceiling.

"What has come over you, Rena? You feel different." Julian didn't seem worried, only curious. "Your thoughts are projecting in shapes and colors. I can't read you."

"You're no longer welcome in my head. And besides, you did this to me. You asked me to give you all my power last night, to open myself to everything. This is my power. And it has nothing to do with the Drakán. This power is not something that is yours to control. I'm free of you."

"Not completely. You just aren't as fully mine as you once were. But we are still lifemates, and there's nothing you can do to change the fact other than sell your soul to the Shadow Realm."

"It's a tempting thought. You swore to protect my family, to treat them as your own."

"And I've kept my promise. Erik is still alive."

The violent wind rushed past me, the force of it aimed straight at Julian. But still he stood his ground. The chandeliers rattled and shook, and pieces of them slashed down around us like daggers. Another violent rumble echoed in the chamber and the windows cracked at the concussion of sound.

"Control yourself, Rena." Julian stepped aside as the chandelier fell from the ceiling and shattered at his feet. "You know I had no choice."

"And what about Feng? Could you not see your death in his soulless eyes, Julian? Could you not see mine? He is determined to see you dead. By any means possible."

"Sometimes we see the future because it is true. And sometimes we see the future because it is what we wish it to be. Which is it for you? Do you have so little faith in my ability?"

"Faith!" I screamed. "You have given me nothing to have faith in."

Heavy copper urns lined each side of the hallway. I put the force of my wind behind them and launched them at Julian's body one by one. He put both hands in front of him and the urns bounced off the shield he'd placed around himself. They fell to the ground impotently.

"You have used me, insulted my intelligence, planned my future, and risked us all, yourself included. My life force is connected to yours, and I do not wish to die because you are in the middle of a power struggle. What is there for me to have faith in? I am your lifemate, and you have treated me no better than a whore."

I brought my foot down hard on the wooden floor beneath me. It buckled with the force of an earthquake and rippled in waves toward Julian. I took advantage of him being slightly off balance and launched everything I could find that I hadn't already broken—vases, lamps, and an oil painting of a nude woman who looked far too satisfied with herself. Glass nicked the side of his temple, and blood ran freely down his face, but he swatted the items away with his magic.

"I'm beginning to grow tired of your tantrum. What is this really about, Rena?" he asked.

My anger vanished suddenly. The wind stopped and my

power died. The air was still and weighed heavily around us —the calm after the storm. I was exhausted and heartbroken, and I didn't know how to get through to Julian. How were we ever supposed to have a relationship when he didn't know the first thing about compassion, or love or trust? Tears fell silently down my cheeks, and I think I began to give up—on Julian, our people, and myself. I didn't have the strength left to guard my mind or my heart.

"You love me?" Julian asked, surprised.

Just the fact that he could be surprised over such a basic emotion told me all I needed to know. Julian was hopeless, and our relationship was less than that.

"Yes," I said. "But it doesn't matter. I believe the mating affected me differently than it did you. I can't seem to help it, though I want so badly to hate you. And I blame the gods for making me feel this way. Our lives are a diversion to them. Entertainment. And I'm tired of being played with."

"Don't do this, Rena."

"I've made my decision. I'll fight beside you when we face The Destroyer. But if we live, I will do everything in my power to release this bond we have. The gods are going to owe me one. I'm going to leave you and go back to my people. I don't know if my clan will have me after what I've done to them. I'm not sure it matters. But I will not stay to watch Feng kill you, and I will not live with a man who sees me as nothing more than a pawn in his game and feels even less for me."

I turned and fled the hallway, leaving chaos behind me. I didn't want to hear his response or his excuses. And I didn't want to give him the chance to talk me out of leaving. Julian had a way with words that made me lose sight of my own convictions.

The fight didn't help as much as I thought it would. I ended up having a good cry anyway.

CHAPTER
TWENTY-SEVEN

My luggage had been placed in the room next to Julian's—the one we'd thoroughly destroyed. As soon as I found the strength, I was going to collect my things and move to the other side of the castle. Or maybe one of the more private bungalows down on the mountain.

I stumbled into my room and locked the doors behind me, and I did the same to the door that connected my room to Julian's. My dragon stirred in sympathy and I felt her sadness at what had just happened. I tried to comfort her, and drew my Drakán magic around me so we could both be warm, and then I flung it outward to shield my room from intruders— mainly Julian.

The little black phone Noah had given me began to warble. I laughed bitterly and let it go to voicemail. I barely had the energy to breathe, much less speak. As soon as it stopped ringing I picked up the phone and dialed for my messages. I only had the one.

"Rena," Noah said. His out-of-breath voice was full of panic. I hoped everything was all right because I couldn't deal with anything else right now.

"Rena, you've got to call me back as soon as you get this. You've opened your powers, and I could feel them as if you were standing beside me. So could everyone else. To hell with secrets. I'll tell you whatever you want to know. You're walking around with the equivalent of a lit stick of dynamite. And the part of you you've kept hidden so long is now shining like a beacon for all to find you. There will be those who want to hunt you. And I promise, you won't want to meet them. You need to get away. Hide."

"Great." I rubbed my fingers in a circle at my temple to ease the headache that had formed there.

"I mean it, Rena. Call me back. I don't care what's going on with the Drakán. This is life or death. I can protect you. I'll talk to you soon."

The message ended and I realized it was the first time he'd openly acknowledged what I was. Not only did he know who I was, but he seemed to accept it. I looked at the buttons on the phone, trying to decide if I should call him back. I wasn't overly concerned about the life-or-death situation—it was pretty much par for the course with me.

I decided I'd call him later, stripped out of my clothes, and left them in a pile on the floor. I crawled between the cool sheets of my bed and snuggled into the soft mattress. My life was out of control and no one could fix it. Least of all me. Shuddering sobs wracked my body, and I hid my face in my pillow. I cried away centuries of pain—Alasdair, Erik, Julian. The men in my life who always found me just useful enough, but never truly loved me.

The tears finally took their toll and I fell asleep. It had been several days since I'd dreamed, and my stomach clenched in dread as the vision began. My dreams were only ever filled with others' horrors, and I couldn't handle it right now.

But when the vision came, the only person I saw was me.

It was as if a movie were playing out in my mind. The screen was split vertically down the middle by a line—half the screen was white—half was black. I stood in the center so I was covered by both light and dark. But I'd never seen myself as I looked. Half of my body—the half that stood on the dark side—was covered in silver scales. My mating tattoo was visible and scrolled intricately among them. The other half of me—the half on the light side—was human. And naked. But there was something different.

Another tattoo decorated the other side of my torso. The writing wasn't Drakán, but it was still beautiful. I didn't recognize the symbols. It started at the shoulder and formed a sleeve down to my wrist. It swirled around my stomach and curled up to my breast. It glowed cerulean blue.

A black dragon flew above me and circled around a sun that looked exactly like the torq I'd given Julian. But the sun had my eyes. A midnight-blue sky shining with stars covered the two of us like a blanket.

The stars shifted and spun until they formed the face of a woman. She was ethereally beautiful. Her hair shone silver in the moonlight and her black eyes twinkled with the stars.

With her she brought the scent of the lotus flower. Her eyes were kind and her touch gentle, and then her face transformed into that of a hideous beast just before she devoured us all.

I cried out at the emptiness she brought. She was desolation. True nothingness. And she'd swallowed me whole.

"Shh, my love," Julian's voice said as he tried to soothe me. Even in dreams I couldn't escape his voice. But I knew it couldn't possibly be him. I wasn't his love.

"Go away," I said, though I was glad my dream had shattered at the sound of his voice. I'd feared I'd be lost in the blackness forever. My body was wracked with chills and not even calling on my dragon fire could get me warm.

It wasn't until the bed shifted and I felt a hard body behind me that I realized I wasn't really alone. I woke slowly and stiffened at his touch.

"Why must you fight me, even in sleep?" he asked.

I didn't have an answer, so I stayed silent. We lay quietly a few more minutes until I began to relax. Then he spoke, and tension filled me once again.

"I have done you a great disservice, lifemate. I owe you an apology."

I turned over to face him, unsure if I'd heard his words correctly.

"Excuse me?" I asked.

"I apologize," he repeated.

"Why?" An apology seemed a little out of character for the man I'd come to know.

"You know only a portion of the man," he said, reading my mind. "We are still new to each other, and this union

289

will have many pitfalls because it is our nature to fight first and ask questions later. But I know that we were truly meant to be lifemates. I didn't bargain with the gods for you, I give you my oath, but I would do anything for them because they blessed me with you. It would be hell to spend eternity apart. And I do not wish for the time we have together to be in strife. The apology is mine to make, and I hope we can come to live in peace with each other if you decide you do wish to reside with me. I have never been close to a woman before. Or spent any time with them outside of the bedchamber."

"Why not?" I asked, curiously.

"Because women are the same. They are softer. It doesn't matter what culture or time period they come from. They want affection and love and to be showered with attention. I've never met a woman who I wanted to give those things to, and I wouldn't begin to know how to give them."

I knew this already because I'd seen his true feelings when we'd faced each other earlier. For all his age and wisdom, he truly had no knowledge of what those things were. He only knew of loyalty and obedience and matters of war.

"You may not realize it, but everyone wants love and attention and devotion," I said softly. "We all need it. Not just women. Without those things our souls would wither and die. Love can make us so much more than we already are."

His eyes became guarded, and the diamond-shaped pupil of his eyes shrunk to the size of pinpricks. "I'm not sure I can give you what you are asking, Rena. In my head I know that our people must come first, even above each other. But you are my lifemate and I can feel your pain. It overwhelms my senses until I can't think of anything but soothing you. I know that our life force is now shared, but I feel as if I am splitting my loyalties."

"I'm not asking you to neglect the needs of your people. I know you carry a great burden, and I will help you however I can. But I think if you will treat me as your equal and not one of your people to command, you'll find things like affection will come naturally. We should always try to please each other, and maybe the love will find its way. I've never experienced it either, but that doesn't mean I don't want it."

His skepticism was obvious, and I saw into his mind and heart before he could close it against me. He didn't see how it was possible I could ever become his equal. My power was less than his.

He chose his words carefully, trying to work his way around the temper I'd shown earlier and still get what he wanted. He was a master at manipulation. "I cannot promise you the love that you want. I do not understand it, and it appears as if it could be a weakness." I dropped my gaze and stared at the spot just above his collarbone because I couldn't bear to see the pity in his eyes.

He smoothed the hair back from my face, and his warmth sunk into the coldness of my bones. "I'll be forever grateful to the gods for choosing you for my lifemate, but love has no place in the midst of battle. I'm sorry that you have been burdened with such an emotion toward me."

"I'm not sorry," I said, finally coming to terms with my

emotions. Just because Julian didn't love me didn't mean I could stop loving him. Tears streaked down my face, and I hated that he was witness to my weakness. My dragon nudged at me gently, comforting me. She hurt too, and she didn't understand the other emotions that got in the way of the physical act of mating. Being tied intimately to Julian was all she needed to be happy. But I needed more.

"I don't like to see you cry. The archives say that it is my job to see to your happiness, as it is yours to see to mine. I have failed you."

He kissed each tear away gently, and licked the salty liquid from his lips. Dragon tears held many magical properties and were often used in healing. But nothing could have healed me at that moment.

I was going to have to suck it up. Julian and I were different. We didn't understand each other, but maybe the gods had something else in mind when they'd put us together.

"I must go," he finally said. "There are things that need to be tended to. Traps to be set."

"What do you need me to do?" I asked.

"My wish is that you stay here. I feel we are close to exposing our enemy, and I want you to be protected."

"How am I supposed to stand by you and fight when I'm locked in a room? Your orders were that every man and woman would fight. I cannot be an exception to the rule."

"And you won't be. But we have not found The Destroyer yet. The gods are fickle beings and could see fit to make things difficult for us. Remember that the Prophecy was not their original creation, but given to us by the goddesses. There's no guarantee they'll honor the words that have fueled our existence for the last eleven thousand years."

"That's a cheerful thought," I said.

"The reason I came to you here was to tell you that The Destroyer has delivered more Drakán. Their ashes are lined neatly at the base of the mountain."

I threw the covers off, ready to jump out of bed and go examine the scene, but Julian put a hand on my arm to stop me.

"The ashes have already been gathered and dispersed to their clans. Two pieces of silver were found beneath each pile of ash, just as before." Julian's shields all of a sudden grew taller and more impenetrable, and I knew something else had happened.

"What is it?" I asked.

"The Destroyer's scent was on his victims. He left a trail. His army is ready, and he wants us to follow him so they'll have the advantage in the fight."

"Who is it?" I asked excitedly. "Did you recognize him? Where is his army?"

Julian hesitated, and I tasted the lie before the words came out of his mouth.

"I don't know, but I'm going to follow his scent out of this Realm and see where he's waiting for us. I'll come back and gather our warriors once I've found his hiding place. I'll be gone awhile. Stay here until then. No one is to be trusted."

He was already dressed and walking out the door before I could call him out on his obvious lie.

"I'll stay on one condition," I said before he could escape. I'd learned a thing or two from Julian in the time I'd spent with him, and if I wanted answers I was going to have to play dirty. Julian turned and lifted his eyebrow in wait.

I felt the blue mating fire erupt from beneath my skin and I crawled off the bed so I was naked—fully exposed to him body, mind, and soul.

"I'll stay here if you'll come back to me tonight."

A devilish smile played on his lips. He bowed arrogantly before walking out my door.

Two could play this game. I knew he'd be back.

The snow fell in big fat flakes and the gentle hush cocooned the mountain as it piled higher and higher. I'd showered and slathered on lotion the scent of honeysuckle. I was past the point of exhaustion, but I was revved at the same time. We were close to finding The Destroyer. I could feel it. And so could my dragon. She was restless and wanted to hunt. But I'd promised Julian I'd stay in the castle.

My body had finally gotten its warmth back after the vision I'd had. I was clueless as to what it meant, but something told me that Noah might have some of the answers. One problem at a time though. As soon as I dealt with The Destroyer, I'd have time to deal with Noah.

I bundled up in my blue satin pajamas and terrycloth robe. I pulled on a pair of warm socks and slippers and made sure the magic that I'd put on the doors into my room was sealed tight. I had no idea how Julian had broken through them and ended up in bed beside me. I hadn't felt him breach them at all.

I poured a large glass of wine and went out the glass French doors that led onto my balcony. It was cold, and puffs of white left my mouth with every exhale, so I let the dragon fire beneath my skin spread outward. I touched the logs in the outdoor fireplace with my hand and they burst into flame. I went to each corner of the balcony and did the same thing to the braziers. Someday I was going to get Julian to teach me how to breathe fire from my mouth. It could come in handy.

This was the first time I'd been out on my balcony, and I hadn't realized it was connected to Julian's suite next door. I looked over the edge of the balcony. Hazy clouds rolled below me, and when they passed by and cleared the view I stared straight down into nothingness. It was an endless drop. Drummondsey Castle had literally been built out of the mountain.

I heard the quiet shuffle of footsteps behind me and smiled to myself. Maybe there was hope for Julian yet if he couldn't stay away from me this long.

"Someday you're going to have to tell me how you keep breaking past my shields," I said with my back still turned. "I know they're strong."

"Are you so enamored by your mate that you're no longer able to think of anyone else?" Erik asked.

I whirled around and wondered how long he'd been standing there. "Erik! What are you doing here? I thought you'd left."

"Not yet. The rest of the clan isn't as eager for me to

leave as you are. I'm a scientist—a healer for our people. I don't suppose it ever occurred to you to keep me around in case there was a need."

Actually, it hadn't occurred to me. Not since I'd seen what Esmerelda's Faerie salve could do.

"So you truly have put your clan from your mind," he said, reading the guilt from my face.

"No, of course not. But a lot has happened in just a short period of time. You have to give me time to adjust. My entire life has been turned upside down and rearranged without my permission."

"It didn't look like you were protesting Julian's wishes too vehemently to me. His marks are all over you. The mating has changed you. I wonder if you even have a mind of your own anymore. Or are his thoughts automatically yours?"

"You're being cruel, Erik. I understand you're upset, but none of this is my fault."

"Then come with me," he said.

"What? Why? Where would we even go?"

"Come with me and I'll show you," he said. Power and magic slithered along the edges of the balcony until we were completely surrounded. It was a power like none I'd ever felt before. It burned to the touch, but at the same time made me yearn for more. But that couldn't be because Erik didn't have power.

"I can show you things Julian could only hope for, powers that he's never dreamed of."

Erik walked toward me slowly, and I moved back until I

stood against the railing. His eyes were bleak and empty of emotion, but he moved with purpose.

And then I picked up on something I'd managed to miss for the last five hundred years—something everyone had managed to miss. Erik wasn't powerless. Erik had a lot of power, more than me and more than Julian. He'd been shielding everything, and up until now he'd been powerful enough to hide exactly what he was. The Drakán powers I wielded had blinded me to what he was, but my other powers, the ones Julian had awoken in me with our lovemaking, sensed Erik for what he was.

"Oh, gods," I whispered.

"What's the matter, Rena? Dragon got your tongue?"

"I don't understand. How did this happen? How did you hide it?" I asked.

He looked confused for a moment before he realized what I was talking about. "You can see through my illusion?" he asked. He wasn't upset. Just curious.

"I can see through it so clearly that I don't understand how you've hidden it your entire life." I took a step forward, my anger making me careless. "Destroyer." My dragon roared, and I pulled my power tight around me like a cloak. His magic sizzled against mine, and sparks began falling amid the snow.

"My, my, someone has some new powers. Even your mate hasn't been able to detect the strength I keep buried deep within. Though he did follow the trail across the Realms I set up for him just as I'd planned. I couldn't approach you if he was hanging around here, now could I?"

"Erik, we're family. Don't do this."

His laugh was cruel and slithered across my skin. This was not the brother I'd known, and even though the truth was staring me in the face, reality was sometimes hard to accept.

Then I had a moment of panic. I was standing in front of The Destroyer. Alone. I'd never actually expected to have to fight him by myself.

"I can smell your fear, Rena. It makes me hungry. Tell me you aren't afraid of your own brother."

"You are not my brother."

"Sure I am. As much as we both hate it, Alasdair is our father." Erik spat on the floor at the mention of his name.

"You're insane."

"Tsk, tsk. Insults will not get you into my good graces. I was hoping you'd come with me of your own free will. No one could ever match the power of the two of us together. I've known since your birth that you would be special. Your Drakán powers are average, but you're carrying a little something extra aren't you? And I want those powers badly. I hope you don't struggle when I rip them from your body. Who was your mother, Rena? I still haven't been able to get Alasdair to tell me, and I've thought of several rather inventive means of torture."

"I don't know who she was!" I yelled. I was getting a little tired of being asked the question. Erik had brought up a good point though. I was going to have to find out who she was if I lived long enough. These new powers obviously had everything to do with her.

"Pity."

"It was you who killed Jillian and the other Drakán,

wasn't it? You who sent those bastards to attack me, while you watched from the safety of the house."

"Guilty." He shrugged sheepishly and smiled. "If Calista hadn't shown up and had one of her visions, I'd already have you under my control, and you'd have never bonded with your lifemate."

My dragon writhed with anger, and I was past the point of trying to coddle Erik's unstable emotions. "The pieces of silver were a little overly dramatic, don't you think?"

"I thought it made things more interesting. You certainly got the point I was trying to make before you betrayed your own clan."

"I'd hardly call any Drakán who refused to follow you guilty of betrayal. I'd call them courageous. If anything, I'd call you the betrayer. Our race is sacred, and you are making us extinct."

"I'm making us stronger. We deserve to have a Realm of our own. This one is as good as any, and the humans are unnecessary. The Drakán can make this land thrive and we can gain back what we once had. I'm the only one who knows the way it can be done. All you have to do is follow me."

"I'll never follow you. The Promised Child is our future."

"I knew Judas. Did I ever tell you that?" he asked, changing the subject while at the same time reminding me what I was to him.

"I'm sure you were good friends. You have so much in common."

"Sarcasm seems inappropriate, considering your life rests in my hands."

"Go ahead and kill me," I said, calling his bluff. He'd already told me he wanted my power. There was no way he'd kill me without taking it first. And that would take time.

His expression had been full of mocking humor, but his composure began to crack at my taunts. He snarled and his face became that of a monster—but not Drakán at all. His eyes became soulless orbs and the green of his irises glowed with insanity.

"Where's Alasdair?" I asked. "Where are the others you've taken? We've only found the ashes of a few. Have the others joined your army?"

"Yes, most of them were more than happy to join my army once I promised them I could give them a new Realm of the Drakán. The ones who chose not to follow me have become part of a little experiment. I'm more powerful now than I've ever been since I've found a way to steal others' Drakán powers. Most of my experiments are still alive. Alasdair too. You've already found the ashes of the ones I've finished with."

"How did you do it?"

"I told you I was a scientist, Rena. You always looked at me with pity whenever I said it. But I'm a genius. And modern technology is a marvel. I've built a machine that steals others' powers and makes them my own. I just drain their powers away until all that is left is an empty husk of what they used to be. No better than a human. It's very painful I'm told.

"You see, I've started my own kingdom, Rena. And there I get to be king. Do you know how easy it is to procreate when Drakán mate with each other instead of humans?"

"No," I answered. My mouth had gone dry at the thought of what Erik had been creating all these centuries.

"The Drakán will soon outnumber all the other Realms put together, and when they do I'll be lord and master over all. My machine should work on all the creatures of the Realms. No one will be able to come close to the powers I'll have. Can you imagine a Drakán who has the combined strength of all the Realms in the palm of his hand?

"My patience has paid off, and my kingdom is vast. I'm sick of hearing the prophecy of The Promised Child, and I'm tired of waiting for the gods to take us out of these forsaken lands and return us to where we belong. I have made my own deal with the gods, and I can feel their fear of me, just as I can feel yours. So I'll ask you one last time, Rena. Will you come with me?"

"Never." I relaxed and let the power rush through my body—my other power. The snow that swirled around us changed direction and fell harder, faster, until it was almost impossible to see through the white wall it created.

"Then I'm left with no choice but to take you by force," he said. "You don't think I'd allow such untapped potential to walk away freely when it could be mine, do you?"

A flash of light cut through the snow and gathered in Erik's hands, sparking yellow and orange and red and traveling back and forth between his palms like an electrical current. The fireball grew in his hands.

I kept my power ready, waiting to see what he was going to do. Thunder roared through the sky and an explosion of light blinded me for just a moment. But even a moment was too long.

Something hit me with the force of a Mack truck. My body slammed against the railing hard enough to bend the iron bars, and I collapsed to the ground in a heap. Erik's insane laughter skittered across my skin. I had to think of something, or I was as good as dead.

I looked down at my body and tried to evaluate the damage as best I could. I was half numb and silvery scales lay across my stomach. That wasn't a good sign. I knew from reading the archives that when our human bodies sustained a mortal blow, we reverted to dragon form to heal the damage. I needed to shift completely, but I couldn't hold my concentration long enough to do so. My dragon nudged me frantically, trying to get me to make the change. She was covered in blood.

Erik gathered another bolt in his hands. I put the thought of my dragon away. She wasn't the one who could win this fight. I steadied my breathing and drew in on my power, building it from the depths of my belly and pushing outward. I saw what I wanted in my mind, and then it happened. I disappeared. I was completely invisible. My body no longer whole, but instead tiny particles. I was the air, and I controlled it all.

"That's quite impressive, Rena. I think I'll enjoy taking that power from you very much."

I gathered my energy and hovered just above the ground, so as not to leave tracks in the snow. I moved behind him and knew I'd have to act quickly, whatever I chose to do. The effort to hold myself invisible was taking its toll on my wounded body. The pain was overwhelming.

"Reeeena. Come out, come out wherever you are."

I stayed perfectly still and tried to give my body a little longer to heal.

"You know this moment was destined to happen, Rena. As soon as the goddess gave the Prophecy to our ancestors, our lives were all laid out before us. I was predestined." He tossed the fire bolt up in one hand and caught it with the other, waiting for me to show myself. "I can wait you out, Rena. My patience is infinite. Let me tell you a little story about how cunning the gods are."

My body shook with the effort it took to maintain my invisibility, and the other elements were going crazy. Snow, wind, and sleet flew in different directions and lightning crackled across the sky in horizontal streaks.

"Did you know my mother knew she was supposed to give birth to The Destroyer?" Erik asked. "The goddess who delivered the Prophecy to the warriors came to her one night in a dream and told her this was her destiny. She was told by the goddess that the outcome of the Prophecy was not foretold, and that she must raise me not to be defeated, but to triumph."

I wanted to ask why the goddess would plot against us, but the gods and goddesses had never had reasons for the things they did unless it somehow benefitted themselves. It didn't sound like they wanted The Promised Child to be delivered, whatever their reasons were.

"So my mother plotted secretly to get herself with child. Alasdair had shown great cunning and power when he'd manifested the ability to travel and saved his people. She knew he was strong and that his children would be as well. But she was the daughter of another clan, and she knew he'd rather kill her than bed her.

"Alasdair had already ruled for several millennia by that time and he still hadn't fathered a child. He fell in lust with Caesar's wife, Claudia, and my mother's spies told her Alasdair planned to take Claudia back to his lair and mate with her his until she grew with his child. So my mother struck a bargain with the gods to be taken in Claudia's place.

"She disguised herself as Claudia and waited for Alasdair to come for her. Alasdair found her in the garden, and he kidnapped her, just as she'd planned. It only took a month before she conceived. She kept up the illusion of her true identity until I was born. Alasdair took me from her birthing bed, and literally dropped her back in Rome. He never knew she was really Drakán—the gods had disguised her scent. My mother eventually found me and nurtured my powers. It was she who had the ability to hide my powers from Alasdair until I was old enough and strong enough to do it myself. The rest is pretty much history," he said, his maniacal laughter growing more and more out of control.

Erik circled the balcony, watching for any sign of movement. He inhaled deeply and the flames I'd cast in the fireplace and braziers burned out into plumes of smoke. My new powers were going out of control. I was too drained to keep a handle on the elements that raged around me, and a blizzard was whipping snow around the mountain and it was accumulating at an alarming rate on the balcony floor.

I'd held out as long as I could. My body began to rematerialize, and he waited patiently as snow flurries fell and collected around me.

"Gotcha," Erik said and lifted his arms to send another blast my way.

My human body reappeared naked, so I quickly shifted into my dragon form. I moved with unimaginable speed and ripped my claws across Erik's torso, dodging the ball of fire aimed in my direction. His blood sprayed across the cold ground in an arc of crimson drops. It glittered in the moonlight like wet rubies, and his flesh lay in tatters over muscle and bone. He roared with anguish. Fire spewed from his mouth, and his fist came straight at me. I didn't have time to dodge.

I knew I was hurt badly when there was no pain. I flickered back and forth between my human form and my dragon—finally ending up as human—naked and torn. Blood trickled down the corner of my mouth and dripped in a rhythmic pattern on the snowy white ground. I knew my jaw was broken because I couldn't open my mouth to scream. I was choking on my own blood.

I fought to stand up straight and confront my brother, my enemy. I wouldn't die like a weakling on the ground.

"I'm taking you with me, Rena," he hissed. "You can't defeat me. I am The Destroyer of Prophecy, and I will not be beaten."

I will not let you take my powers for your own. I'll die first. I wasn't able to speak because my face was too swollen. Blood pooled rapidly in my mouth. I couldn't spit it out fast enough to keep from drowning. If this was my fate, so be it, but he would not use my powers against others as long as I had a breath in my body.

He gathered the light between his hands once again, and I prepared myself for another blow. But instead of aiming his deadly hands in my direction, he pointed them toward the sky. An arc of light shot from his fingertips and cracked the night in two pieces.

Time stopped. Snow flurries stood still in the air, and the drops of blood that dripped from my body and face were suspended between time and space. My body became sluggish—as if I were under water—trapped inside some invisible hourglass looking out at the real world.

The light from his hands spread across the night sky. And out of the darkness appeared a portal—a circle of undulating liquid silver that shone brighter than the sun. I would die, by his hand or my own, before I went through it with him.

"Enough games, Rena," he said and started toward me.

I didn't know what kind of games he was used to playing, but being beaten to death wasn't on my list of fun things to do. I scooted away from him as far as I could go until I reached the balcony edge. I only had one option. I had to fly.

I took a deep breath and fell over the ledge of the balcony into a free fall down the side of the mountain. I watched in slow motion as Erik made a grab for me and yelled my name. But he was too late.

I realized something on my way. I was able to scream after all.

CHAPTER
TWENTY-EIGHT

E rik didn't follow me down the side of the mountain.
Instead he cursed my name and vanished inside
the portal, closing it behind him with a thun-
derous reverberation that echoed through the sky.

I shifted quickly, sighing in relief as my body had more
room for my injuries in dragon form. I stretched out to my
full length and roared as bones popped in and out of place.
Panic consumed me. I still couldn't fly, even drawing on
Julian's power. My mind raced, and I opened myself to my
other power. My dragon didn't like this magic because it
didn't come from her, and she tried to push it away. But I
wouldn't let her.

The wind began to blow from the bottom of the mountain. I blanked my mind and put all my strength into
focusing on the wind, so the air moved faster. I controlled
the pressure as it swirled around me, and the air held me

steady. I was flying. Sort of. The only problem was I didn't know how to land.

I hovered just outside the bottom floor of Drummondsey Castle, and I floated in front of a large plate-glass window and looked into a room with an eerie blue light. It took me a minute to figure out what I was looking at, but when I did I heaved a sigh of relief.

I flew straight at the window, and the plate glass shattered into a million pieces. I didn't even register the new cuts. I already had too many to count. I landed at the bottom of Julian's Olympic-sized swimming pool like a ton of bricks. I was unconscious before I reached the bottom.

I woke up throbbing from head to toe. The lights were out and total darkness filled the room. The kind of darkness that made you search deep within yourself to see what you were really made of. I didn't like what I found, and I panicked at the black that came at me from every direction. It reminded me too much of the vision I'd had about me and Julian and the beautiful monster who'd devoured us. I'd never been afraid of the dark before, but now I was terrified.

I moaned, and several candles flickered on around the room. Esmerelda stood over me and held a cup up to my lips. I swallowed and sputtered as the foul-tasting brew went down.

"What is that?" I croaked, pushing it away. I didn't need any more torture.

"Don't worry, dear, the taste won't last for long," Esmerelda said.

"I need to see Julian," I rasped out. My throat was on fire and my jaw was still sore.

"I know. He's been pacing outside the door since he felt you beginning to stir. He's been worried about you."

"Hmmph," I said. "Worried I'll take him down with me more than likely."

"I don't think so," she said. "I think a man who stays by your side and barely sleeps for two days has to at least care a little."

"Two days!" I said. "Do you know what can happen in two days' time? Why didn't you wake me sooner?"

I threw the covers back and swung my legs to the floor, but they were too weak to support me. Bile rose in my throat and I broke out in a clammy sweat. Black dots danced in front of my eyes as I fell to my knees.

"I tried to wake you up. We all tried to wake you up, but no one could get through to you. I used all the Faerie medicine I had with me, and it still took you this long for you to wake up. I've never seen anyone have injuries bad enough that they couldn't be healed by magic and our own physical healing capabilities. Your body caught fire twice and tried to burn itself to ash, but Julian linked with you and shared some of your pain. It's a good thing I had the sudden urge to take a dip in the pool."

"I really need to see Julian," I said again.

I put my head between my knees since I was already on the floor, and I got the nausea under control. Esmerelda helped me up, and I crawled back under the cool sheets and

I closed my eyes. The door clicked open quietly and I felt the pull between us as Julian's footsteps got closer. I pushed my pillows up against the headboard and sat up. Slowly.

"You have a way of keeping a dragon on his toes, Rena," Julian said in a disapproving tone. The hollows of his cheeks were more pronounced than normal and dark circles ringed beneath his eyes. He wore black slacks and a black T-shirt, and I realized it was probably the most casual I'd ever seen him. He looked tired, and far underneath the gruffness of his voice was worry and relief.

"I know you're not making this out to be my fault," I said. "He's been here with us the whole time, and it's not like I could have kept him out of my room. He's The Destroyer for the gods' sake."

He sat next to me on the bed and my magic flared. I could feel the acceleration of my body's healing just by being close to him. He took my hand and rubbed his thumb across the pulse in my wrist in soothing circles.

"I failed to protect you," he said.

I looked away at the intensity of his guilt and closed my eyes. Julian was a good man, and it was me that had failed him. It was my family who was responsible for so much pain, and I should have somehow recognized what had been going on in my own house.

I squeezed his hand before letting it go. Once I told him what I knew, he'd probably never want to touch me again.

"I have to tell you something."

"That your brother is The Destroyer and has managed to hide the fact from all of us?"

My eyes filled with tears and I blinked rapidly to get rid

of the evidence. Julian sighed and took my hand again. He stretched out beside me, careful not to jostle me too much, and pulled me against him so he held me in an embrace.

"How did you know?" I asked.

"You were unconscious, naked, and bleeding when I first carried you up here. You gained consciousness just long enough to tell me Erik was The Destroyer."

"You don't seem surprised."

"I knew something wasn't right from the moment you showed up in my lands. The things my spies sent me about Erik made my instincts go on alert. He was always a suspect. But when I met him face-to-face I was sure I was wrong because I couldn't detect his powers."

"You checked up on us?" I asked incredulously.

Julian gave another sigh. "Rena, you were an open book to me from the moment you stepped off the plane. You have never had any secrets from me. But I had to check out your clan."

My head began to pound and my anger wanted to take control, but I didn't have the strength.

"Maybe you should just start at the beginning and tell me what happened," he said.

"Could I have something to drink?" I asked after I'd reined my temper in. None of this was Julian's fault. I had to remember that.

I could sense Julian's impatience at the delay, but he went to the small fridge in the corner of the room and got me a bottle of water. My mouth was as dry as dust and my stomach hurt from hunger.

"I was waiting for you out on the balcony," I began,

finding the label on my water extremely fascinating so I wouldn't have to look in Julian's eyes. "I was thinking of you and not paying attention to anything around me. I didn't even know he was behind me until he started speaking."

"He's a *Viator*," Julian said. "You wouldn't have heard him unless he wanted you to."

"I don't know, when he opened the portal it made the mountain shake. It sounded like the sky had been torn in two."

"One doesn't need a portal to travel through human time. But to travel between the Realms is the gift of a double-edged sword. To travel between the Realms means to give up part of your soul with each crossing. When you say it sounded as if the sky had been torn in two, that's because it was."

I looked up at him with worry. "What about you? You traveled between the Realms earlier when Erik left the trail for you to follow. What will happen to your soul?"

"Are you worried about my soul, Rena?" He touched my cheek and smiled slightly. "It's only a small piece. I haven't made it a habit of traveling through the Realms over the last several millennia. And the piece of my soul that was taken was for a worthy cause."

I took a long drink of water and sat up against him a little straighter. I was already feeling stronger. My jaw had full mobility now, and it was getting easier to speak.

"Erik was so strong. I couldn't defeat him, and I refused to go with him. My only choice was to jump over the edge of the balcony and pray for a miracle."

Julian ran his fingers through his hair in a gesture of

frustration. "As soon as I left you to travel between the Realms I got a bad feeling. I'm not connected to you once I leave this Realm, but the loss of you was overwhelming. I knew I had to get back as quickly as I could.

"You took a thousand years off my life when I saw Esmerelda dragging you out of the water. I couldn't figure out what was going on. The pool was colored red with your blood. You weren't moving. Your fire began to burn without your knowledge. It would have swallowed you whole and turned you to ash if I hadn't been there to absorb it."

"I'm sorry." The words seemed inadequate.

"I was gone between the Realms long enough to get a good sense of his trail. I know where he's hiding his army. We need to go into battle as soon as you're healed. Two days have passed and more of our people have disappeared. We cannot waste any more time."

"He has more than an army. He has a kingdom. He's been mating Drakán to each other for centuries, building his numbers. He's created a machine to drain the powers of those who don't agree to fight for him. It makes them human. He's determined to steal the powers from all creatures and make himself king over all the Realms."

Julian's face showed the first sign of legitimate surprise I'd ever seen before he quickly masked it. "Then we must stop him."

"But will we win?" I asked.

"If we don't, we will die trying. The Drakán deserve to have peace and power restored to them. Now that you're awake, Esmerelda's medicine should restore most of your strength by this evening. Rest for a while. Those of us who can change form will meet and go after The Destroyer at midnight."

"I assume you know how to find him?" I asked.

"He's taken possession of the Realm of the Gods."

Which meant the gods had chosen sides, or they'd finally met their match and were too afraid of Erik to do anything but hand over their Realm without a fight. Whatever the case, they weren't going to be any help to us. So praying was probably out of the question.

CHAPTER
TWENTY-NINE

I'd healed as much as I was going to by the time midnight rolled around. We gathered, thousands strong, cramming into the ballroom and spilling out into the halls. A hushed murmur whispered its way through the crowd, building to an overwhelming roar of sound. The scent of anticipation and fear was strong, and the hunger for flesh and blood lay heavy in the air.

Despite the impressiveness of our numbers, less than a thousand of us could actually shift to dragon form and take flight. Human blood had weakened us all more than we'd thought. But we needed numbers, and it was decided those who couldn't shift would remain in their human forms and ride through the Realm on the backs of their dragon brethren. I had no idea what to expect from Erik's army. We could only hope that if we couldn't outnumber them, we could at least overpower them.

Julian raised his hand high up in the air, and the room

went silent. I looked at the Drakán standing around me. I didn't know most of them—a scary thought considering a few days ago they would have tried to kill me, and now they'd be fighting beside me.

Feng stood against the wall, watching Julian with a malice and calculation in his eyes that made his position clear. He wore black sweatpants and a sweatshirt with the sleeves cut out. A tattoo of a dragon snaked all the way up his arm and rested its head on his shoulder. He looked deadly and dangerous, two traits we needed on our side when fighting The Destroyer and his army. I only hoped Feng didn't decide to change his allegiance once we went through the portal.

Xana, Olaf, and the other guards all stood behind Julian —Esmerelda and I flanked his sides. I worried about him destroying another piece of his soul by taking us through the portal, but it was he alone who could make the sacrifice to save the very people who despised him.

"I have asked you all to do the unthinkable," Julian said. "The Destroyer was one of us. And he betrayed us to strengthen his own power and treat us no better than slaves. We will not let the Drakán race falter. And we will not forsake The Promised Child by letting this impostor deceive you. You are strong. And you are ready to fight. *Porro Ago Drakán.*"

Long Live the Drakán. The crowd repeated the sentiment with a resounding cheer.

A familiar crack echoed through the room. The ground shifted and the plaster on the walls split and crumbled. The portal swirled and opened to reveal a liquid silver hole in the middle of the room. Gasps sounded from all the Drakán. Besides myself and Julian, it was the first time any of them had seen a portal to another Realm.

The Drakán around me began to shift into their dragon forms. There were dragons of all colors—all shapes—all sizes. Julian's black dragon was massive and towered over all those around him. Xana and the other guards were also in varying shades of black—some lighter, some darker, some duller, some brighter—but none had the onyx sheen and breathtaking beauty of their leader.

Esmerelda was the color of a shiny copper penny. Even though the Drakán clan she was born to was green in color, the Fae blood that ran through her veins made her unique. Her form was dainty and feminine despite her increased size, but Esmerelda had seen many battles before. She was a seasoned warrior, and she was as deadly as anyone in the room.

Feng stood just to Julian's right. His scales a dark golden yellow. Tiny spikes ran the length of his spine and tail. Not for the first time I wondered about the ancestors we all shared that helped shape our destiny. Feng's guards showed the mixed heritage of Prince Lucian's two races. The Chinese dragons were shades of yellow. The Russians were shades of white.

Cale of the Éire stood to the outermost side of the group, surrounded by a handful of his own guards. He looked to be reconsidering his decision to risk his life and his former clan. His dragon was emerald green. His guards were shades of the same green, from sea foam to the color of Irish fields at night, and their hesitation was obvious.

I couldn't stop the despair that overwhelmed me as I looked over my clan and saw my father and Calista both absent. Not to mention Erik, though we'd see him very soon. The clan varied in color—from the palest pink to brick red. But not me. The silver of my scales didn't belong to any clan. Which was why Julian and I both thought it would be best if I transported through the Realm in my human form. As far as my clan was concerned, I'd never been able to shift, and we wanted them to keep thinking that for now. Seeing the silver of my scales would not help me get control over the disobedient group.

Andres of the Rumanus and his blue clan only had a few dozen Drakán who could shift, but they all pushed through the crowd, eager to be one of the first through the portal. I climbed on Esmerelda's back and all the other Drakán who were still in human form did the same. Some carried swords in scabbards and others were relying on nothing but their physical strength.

Julian gave the signal and the dragons took flight. I held on for dear life as the wind rushed across my cheeks and Esmerelda launched herself just behind Julian into the liquid silver portal. As soon as we left our Realm I was completely cut off from all that existed in that world. I couldn't help but look back as the last of the Drakán came through and the portal closed behind us.

THIRTY

he Realm of the Gods

T I hadn't known what to expect once we crossed through the portal and into the Realm of the Gods. Julian had explained to me earlier that it was an ever-changing place—a place that reflected the gods' and goddesses' wants and needs. It was a place where they could honor themselves. They could alter it at their foolish whims, much like they liked to do with the lives of their people.

The Realm of the Gods had always seemed like a foolish waste of space to me—a place where only the gods and goddesses could reside while there were so many others of us who were floundering without a Realm to call our own. But I guess they felt they were entitled since they'd been the ones to create the Realms in the first place.

I thought for sure the Realm of the Gods would be a place much more sinister, considering The Destroyer had made the changing Realm his home. A place that epitomized everything he stood for—violence, anger, hate, and cruelty. I expected darkness and monsters lurking around every corner. Thrones of fire and fury. Eerie sounds and helpless cries from those who were being held against their will. But my expectations came nowhere near the reality.

The Realm of the Gods was a place of sheer beauty. A beauty so pure that it almost brought tears to my eyes. It was light and brightness all rolled into one—a city of ice with crystal palaces that gleamed like diamonds and streets made of freshly fallen snow. White covered every surface. It would have been glaringly bright had there been an illuminating source to reflect off of them.

Julian had explained that the Realm of the Gods had neither sunlight nor moonlight, so all who passed through its gates would not fear death.

"This was not what I was expecting," I said to the copper dragon beneath me.

No, but many times it is the unexpected that can be the biggest threat. Keep your eyes open.

There was a field with hills and valleys covered in snow below us—pristine in its beauty. There were no trees, no blue skies, just endless clouds and fields of white. As we soared through the sky the hills rose and fell below us.

I hunkered low over Esmerelda's back so we could fly faster, and I struggled to keep my eyes open and on everything around me. Riding on the back of a dragon was not a way to cure a fear of flying. Her powerful muscles bunched and flexed beneath me, and Julian moved closer, touching my leg briefly with his black scales to ease my discomfort.

We passed over the last hill and my adrenaline surged.

A castle made of glass and white stone sat nestled between two hills. It was circled by a crystal-clear lake and guarded by a drawbridge made of diamonds. White dragons launched themselves from the rooftop and came at us in a fury. Thousands of them. These dragons weren't the same white as the Russian clan. These were of the purest white, never varying in shade. And they were our mortal enemies.

They charged us in straight lines—hundreds upon hundreds of them for as far as the eye could see. Erik had always been a great general. He knew how to win battles.

All of our dragons dropped the human Drakán they carried to fight their own battles on the ground. Erik hadn't been a hundred percent successful in his breeding experiments because it looked like there were still many in his kingdom who couldn't shift form, just as many of ours couldn't.

Julian led his dragons back up into the sky. He was dead center of the pack. Feng and his best warriors flanked Julian's right, and Xana and our best warriors flanked his left. The others under Julian's command quickly got into formation so they mirrored the white dragons.

I growled in anger as Cale and his people held back. It was too late for them to change their mind. They were trapped in this Realm. And they would either fight or die. Esmerelda and I came up behind them, and she roared her displeasure, forcing them to take their place in the battle lines.

I knew what my job was. I'd had to fight for it, but in the end I had won. Esmerelda and I were to find the prisoners and release them—though most of them would be no better than humans now. Their fragile human shells were going to make their escape all the more difficult.

Have a care, lifemate, Julian whispered through my mind. *I would be most displeased with you if you injured yourself again.*

It was the last thing I felt from him. He closed himself off completely, and the loss of him was almost debilitating.

Snap out of it Rena, Esmerelda said. *He'll be fine. You must see to your tasks now.*

Esmerelda and I veered off from the group and flew down to the castle. I held on tight as she made a smooth landing in freshly packed snow. The sounds of battle came from above—the clang of razor-sharp claws as they hit against each other like swords—the gnashing of teeth—the ripping of flesh.

I watched as the first drops of blood fell from the sky and marred the pristine snow with red. The Realm of the Gods was white and beautiful no more.

CHAPTER

THIRTY-ONE

rakán fought Drakán across a battlefield of snow as Esmerelda and I made our way closer to the drawbridge that led into the castle. Red-scaled dragons fought furiously against the Drakán who guarded the inner gate, and Esmerelda and I slipped by while they were preoccupied and entered the castle.

White marble, veined with the palest gray, lay beneath our feet. The walls were white stone. The ceilings were made of glass, so every floor above us was visible. We could see straight into the sky. Straight into the carnage of the battle raging overhead.

The large foyer split in three directions, forming three hallways—one to the left, one to the right, and one down the middle.

"We should split up," I said.

Esmerelda was still in her dragon form so she spoke to

my mind. *Julian told me I wasn't supposed to let you out of my sight.*

"Every second will count if we're going to free our people. We might already be too late to save them."

She finally agreed. *I'll take the right.* The shiny copper of her dragon got a running start before taking flight again and spiraling down the long hallway.

I pushed out my dragon powers, searching for something that would lead me to my people.

I took the left.

The white stone seemed to be some kind of natural power source, illuminated from within. But the farther I went down the hall, the less light there was. It was almost as if the marble was dying. But that couldn't be possible. How could an inanimate object die?

Torches were placed along the wall, well used and recently lit. My inner fire lit and spread through my body. I touched a hand to the first torch and it burst into flame. I exhaled gently and the flame whooshed down the entire hallway, lighting every torch that came into its path.

The smell of pitch was strong as it burned. Rats scurried across the floor and scattered from the light. I looked down and saw the carcasses of their dead. At least our people had had some source of food.

I ran at full speed down the long hallway until it finally opened into a spacious room. This room wasn't white like the rest of this Realm. It was drab and gray. Dingy. Smoke and scorch rings stained the walls. The stench of blood, infected flesh, excrement, and death dropped me to my knees. I breathed in through my mouth, but the cloying smell coated the back of my throat, thick like syrup.

I lifted my head slowly and looked around the room. A choked sob escaped before I could control it. Large cages hung and swayed from the ceiling. Dozens of men and women—Drakán—were inside them; their naked bodies huddled together for warmth. There were tables with restraints in the middle of the room stationed next to beeping machines. Arm and leg shackles were attached to bloodstained walls. Erik had taken our sacred people and made them no more than lab rats for his twisted mind.

I stumbled to my feet and ran toward the first cage. I wondered why they hadn't tried to break the flimsy iron bars that held them prisoner, and then I remembered that they were no longer the powerful creatures they'd used to be. Iron was nearly unbreakable by human standards.

I stood in front of the locked cage and called my power with a vengeance, ripping the iron door from its hinges. Cries for help and weeping filled the room as I went from cage to cage. The stronger prisoners helped the weak to their feet and walked them toward freedom. But there were some who remained motionless on the ground. They would never see freedom again.

There was a man who'd carried many of the weaker out and returned for more. He was too thin, his ribs prominent and his skin slack, but he held an inner strength that gave him a purpose and a reason for living.

"Who do you follow?" I asked him as I opened the door of the last cage.

"Julian is my Archos," he replied. "But I am less than nothing to him now that my powers are gone."

"Julian will not think so," I assured the man. "He is here fighting for all of you now. Tell me, have you seen Archos Alasdair?"

He curled his lip in revulsion.

"Tell me what has been done with him. Julian is my lifemate. And Alasdair is my father. I must know if he still lives."

He looked like he wanted to ignore my pleas. "If it is as you say and Julian is truly your lifemate, then I can do nothing but fulfill your request. Your father has been held in solitary," he said, pointing to the far corner of the room. "He was quite the troublemaker."

The man turned to walk away with the other prisoners, but he turned back before he reached the long white hallway. "Your father never turned his back on his clan. He tried to take the brunt of the punishment for his people before the madman broke him. There is honor in what he did. You can be proud of that." The man limped away and didn't look back again.

I hadn't noticed the thick metal door in my hurry to release the other prisoners. This was not a cage but a closet. Part of me was afraid to open it and see what waited on the other side.

I placed both hands against the cold steel, but I couldn't feel him—couldn't feel anyone. I held the padlock in my hand and drew my fire until all that was left was molten metal. The hot metal burned against my skin and it would leave a scar if I didn't remove every trace of it. The door swung open, and the man who hung from the shackles didn't resemble my father at all. This man was old. His hair was solid silver and his face was deeply lined with age.

"Alasdair?"

He struggled to lift his head, but when he finally did it was my father's silver-streaked eyes that stared back at me. My eyes. They no longer had a diamond-shaped pupil. They were human eyes. Erik had succeeded in stealing all of my father's powers for his own.

"Rena." Alasdair's chapped lips cracked and bled with the movement. "You are too late. I am less than nothing now. And it is a good thing I no longer have my strength, for I would kill you if I could. Erik told me you have given my father's clan away to the son of his most hated enemy. I despise the ground you walk on."

"You have the nerve to despise me when your own son is The Destroyer and killing all of our people?" I stood back and wondered what I should do. "Should I leave you to rot? Is that what you want from me? It would serve you right if I did after what you've done to me."

"I...don't...want anything from you." His every breath was harder than the next. "I should have killed you when I had the chance."

"It's a shame you didn't. Because now I'm here to make sure you live and suffer for the rest of your pitiful life." I unfastened his manacles and he fell to his knees.

"Even now your pity makes you weak," he said as I helped him to stand. "Just like your mother."

"What?"

I didn't get the opportunity to ask any more questions.

Something powerful rammed against us and knocked us across the room into the hard stone wall. I heard the crack as the wall gave from the force of my body. My head took the brunt of the fall, and I was dazed for a moment. I looked over at my father and saw his eyes open and empty, staring straight ahead.

His death had been quick after all. The skin around his heart was singed. His body hadn't turned to ash because he was human.

I rubbed at the back of my head, and my hand came away smeared with blood. My rage poured from my skin, and my power sent the metal cages hanging from the ceiling into an eerie dance. I looked around for the person responsible. Erik leaned casually against the far wall, hidden in shadow. I got to my feet, ready to face him once and for all.

Erik walked toward me. He was covered in blood. It was matted in his hair, and it dripped down his chin and the tips of his fingers with every step he took. I couldn't see any open wounds so I knew the blood must be someone else's.

"Are you wondering whose blood decorates my body, Rena?" he asked. "I think the color of Julian's blood looks good against my skin. Don't you agree?"

I shook my head in denial. I couldn't believe it. Wouldn't believe it. I'd know if Julian had been killed, though panic filled my soul at how completely he'd cut himself off from me. Would I have even felt it if he'd fallen? Would I die the same instant he took his last breath?

"I don't believe you," I said.

"I haven't killed him yet. I thought I'd save him for last. He was a very worthy opponent, but as you can see..." He shrugged and more blood spattered from his hands into the air.

My power stirred within me. My dragon coiled tightly. She wanted justice. She wanted to fight. Erik smiled, the blood on his teeth and lips a harsh reminder of what I was fighting for. He was as still as a snake ready to strike. His own power stretched just under the surface. He was waiting for me to make the first move.

There was a blur of movement in front of Erik. It happened so quickly I wasn't sure if I'd actually seen anything at all. But then I saw a tiny hand holding a heart. A beating heart. Erik's heart.

Erik was still on his feet. He hadn't registered what had just happened to him. He looked around in confusion, his eyes already going cloudy with unconsciousness. Esmerelda stepped around from the back of his body where his large frame had been hiding her. She held his heart out and he finally looked at it.

He raised his head sluggishly and opened his mouth to speak. The words wouldn't come. Esmerelda looked him in the eyes and blew him a kiss of fire. She laughed as he turned to ash.

My mouth hung open in shock. Esmerelda had just killed The Destroyer. And it had been way too easy.

"Get real, Rena. Did you honestly think this idiot was The Destroyer?" she asked. She kicked at his smoldering ashes. "Someone so careless and foolhardy that he had to take the powers of others just to make himself stronger? The true Destroyer needs no one's powers but her own."

"How can Erik not be The Destroyer? He told me the

story of my father and the woman who pretended to be Claudia so she could give birth to him. Erik fulfilled the Prophecy."

"I was that woman, Rena. Erik was my son. And I knew from his conception that he'd be necessary for my plan to work. My deception was not easy. I've been patient for thousands of years, planned everything to the last detail. I knew from the beginning that Alasdair would get me with child. And I knew I would deliver him a son. Just as I know it is your and Julian's son who will become The Promised Child. It is why you must both die. But I had to wait for the two of you to join before I could put my plan into action. If the possibility of The Promised Child did not exist between the two of you, then I'd have to wait for another pair of life-mates to come along and put the Prophecy in motion."

I had a vision of a boy with dark hair and aquamarine eyes, the same little boy I'd seen in the vision I had after Julian and I had first met. I knew she spoke the truth. *Our son.* I screamed out in protest as the vision faded away and the image of Julian's torn and bloody body replaced it.

"How can you be The Destroyer?" I asked. "You are not the Descendent of two Drakán. You are Fae."

"I told you that Prophecies were vague. It never says specifically that The Destroyer needs to be a Descendent of two Drakán—the race of the Descendents isn't mentioned at all."

"Gods," I breathed out. She'd set herself up in the perfect position and waited patiently for thousands of years. *A great pretender.* It was the last coherent thought I had.

An invisible vise gripped around my body and brought

me to my knees. My organs were being crushed. No oxygen could get to my lungs, and my mouth opened and closed, gasping for air.

The power Esmerelda possessed overwhelmed me. I couldn't beat her. I was nothing compared to what she was. Erik's power paled in comparison to hers. She released her hold slightly so I could take a breath. But while the vise around my body loosened, I began to feel other things. She began to slowly peel the skin away from my body. Tears mingled with my blood. I couldn't pray for death to come fast enough. She held me immobile with her powers, but I was still able to scream. I screamed until my voice went hoarse.

The look on her face became one of excitement and I braced myself for worse pain. My muscles separated from my bones with wet pops. Injuries involving muscles were always the hardest to heal, even for dragons. I didn't want to end my life this way. I wanted the possibility of that child to still exist.

I gathered what was left of my power and tried to heal myself.

"Tsk, tsk," Esmerelda scolded. "Don't waste your energy. You won't last nearly so long if you do. And what fun would that be?"

I ignored her and embraced my power. I kept it wrapped snugly around me. Esmerelda's hold lessened slightly. She was playing with me, but the relief the slight respite gave me was welcome. I drew from everything I had, but when Esmerelda laughed at my attempts I realized that she knew my powers better than I did. My dragon stirred restlessly, wanting to fight, but I didn't call to her. I called to the other power. The power that was nameless, but grew stronger inside me every day.

"Oh, so you've found it," she said. "I was wondering how long it would take for you to notice. The bond with Julian made it easier, no doubt."

"What are you talking about? What do you know?"

"It's a shame Alasdair couldn't have told you who your mother was before he died."

"Who was she?"

"Your blood is unique. Much like mine. Do you know the stories of how the Realm of the Drakán came to fall?" she asked.

My throat was raw, and I was to the point of pain where only numbness existed. "Yes," I rasped out.

"Tell me," she demanded.

I swallowed the bile that rose in my throat and tried to regulate my breathing before I answered.

"The Drakán stopped growing intellectually because of their selfish natures. They became greedier for things. Not for knowledge. They only relied on their brute strength in battle. And when the Atlanteans accused us of killing their queen's infant son and declared war on us, the Drakán ultimately couldn't defeat the Atlantean inventions or the strength of their magic. Their rage and determination was too great, and the Realm of the Drakán fell into nothingness."

"That's right. And who is every Drakán's sworn enemy?"

"The Atlanteans," I answered automatically.

The Realm of the Drakán had been a barren land, filled

with volcanoes and black porous rock—a land that suited its inhabitants in every way. It was the volcanoes that had surrounded our Realm and the lava that flowed within them that we drew our magic from. It was an impenetrable Realm that no enemy could ever breach because the dragons' psychic powers could sense when the Realm was going to be invaded, and the Drakán would have their armies ready and waiting to fight.

But it was one woman who'd had the power to destroy us.

I knew the tales of how the Atlantean queen had sacrificed herself and destroyed our race to avenge the death of her child. She hadn't listened to reason when my ancestors claimed their innocence. All that mattered was her vengeance. The queen had figured out a way to block herself from the dragons' psychic powers, and she'd flown through the portal to the Drakán Realm undetected. She'd fought the fire of our volcanoes with ice.

My mind finally got a grasp on what Esmerelda had been hinting at. I shook my head in denial, then immediately wished I hadn't because the pain was so great.

"It's impossible," I said. "The gods completely destroyed Atlantis as punishment for the queen's actions. I've never heard about there being any survivors."

"The Drakán Realm was completely destroyed too, but here we are. Why is it so hard for you to believe the Drakán are not the only creatures hiding in the Earthly Realm?"

I'd heard something similar to that before. Noah. He'd known all along what I was. And now I knew what he was.

"Your mother was Atlantean royalty, Rena. It was her

mother who sacrificed herself and destroyed our Realm. Our forefathers' brute strength was no match for her invention of ice combined with her control over the elements. She destroyed the entire Realm with ice and fire. The five warriors were very lucky to escape with their lives. No one else did. Julian recognized the symbol on the torq you gave him. He also knows who you are."

At the mention of my lost heritage, the unknown power I'd been wielding surged around me. It pulsed in time with my heart and fed my blood. I gasped as I felt the hatred inside me. It recognized the Drakán as its enemy and wanted to kill it. It recognized the dragon inside me and wanted to kill her too. No wonder I'd always felt so many conflicting emotions over who I was.

I soothed my power and let her know that the dragon inside me was a friend, and she calmed, though she didn't like it. My dragon nudged against me, not wanting to be forgotten, and I felt the thread of Julian's power. It pulsed with his life force. He was alive. I pulled his magic to me, absorbing his powers.

I'd had enough. My body had had enough. It was time to fight or die. The red glow of my fire erupted around my body and spewed from my mouth. Black smoke curled from my nostrils. The air around me whipped with gale-force winds, and lightning flashed in arcs just over our heads. But Esmerelda laughed at me and held me tighter in her grasp.

I could feel the urgency in Julian's magic, and I knew he wanted me to take more from him. I drew his magic in until it filled me to bursting. Esmerelda's eyes widened in surprise, as she felt the link that existed between me and

Julian. My Drakán magic was powerful, but it was my Atlantean magic that would destroy her.

The pressure in my chest built to the point of bursting, and the castle walls began to crumble around us. Esmerelda's hold on me lessened as she moved to dodge chunks of flying granite.

Rocks filled the doorway, blocking our only exit, and I flinched as the stones blew into the room like bullets and turned to dust as they made impact. It wasn't my magic that had caused the explosion. Julian staggered into the room with a gray cloud of dust and debris. His dragon form was gone, and his naked body was badly damaged. Blood dripped steadily down his side and was smeared across his face and neck. His arm hung limply down at his side— useless. But he was alive.

Esmerelda raised her hand and gathered her fire in the palm of her hand. She pointed it toward Julian and sheer terror for his life forced me to fight harder against her bonds. Julian stumbled to his knees, and I screamed his name. A ball of orange flame grew larger and larger, and as the intensity of its heat grew, the color changed from orange to white. It looked as if she held a bolt of lightning in her hand.

I pulled the thread between us harder, finding the strength to stand on my own two feet, while praying for a miracle. And then Julian did something so unexpected I almost staggered beneath the shock of it. He shoved every ounce of power he had through the thin thread that bound us. It was painful and at the same time invigorating. The rush was euphoric. But the rush didn't last long.

Julian had given me his power and left himself with none. He was no better than a human now, and his wounds were mortal. I embraced his power with my own and shoved everything I was—Drakán and Atlantean—into Esmerelda. The fire consumed us both. Her laughter grew and raised chills upon my skin. But her laughter died as my flame grew hotter. The red flame turned to orange—then yellow—then blue. No one could survive the power of the mating fire.

Her body blurred through the flames, the intensity of it uncomfortable even for me. My body hurt, and I wasn't sure Julian would live, even if I succeeded in killing Esmerelda. But he had to live. We both had to live. I thought of the lost Promised Child and fought harder through the pain.

When the blue flames around us turned almost white, Esmerelda released the vise around me and my lungs and organs took a great sigh of relief at the loss of pressure. She reached toward me with her hand, and I knew if I let her touch me that it would be the end. She would take my heart with her into the Realm of the Dead and then I would have no choice but to follow her.

I stomped my foot, displacing the ground beneath me, and moved my arms back and forth in a gentle sway, controlling the elements in a dance that was unfamiliar and second nature both at the same time. The ground shook with the force of my power. The once-beautiful white castle crumbled to ruins, and large stones fell dangerously close to our bodies.

As Esmerelda's hand moved closer, I slashed out with the vicious claws of my silver dragon, ripping out her heart and crushing it to dust. I pushed my power harder and the stone walls crumbled faster, crushing her under their weight. Her shrill screams of terror pierced my soul and vibrated over my skin. I blew one last breath of fire and watched as her body went up in flames.

I fell forward on my hands and knees. My body was slicked with blood and sweat, but the walls were still falling and I had to protect Julian. I shoved his power back down the thread. His body jerked as he accepted it, and the renewal of energy gave him strength so his wounds began to heal. I wished I could have said the same for my own. I was completely spent.

He crawled toward me and covered my body with his own. He used his magic to erect a shield around us and protected us from the falling rocks. I huddled beneath him on the cold marble floor and waited to die.

Then as suddenly as it started, the wind stopped blowing and the rocks stopped raining down on us. The lightning ceased and the thunder faded out with one lingering rumble. Everything around us was completely still —there wasn't even the sound of a pebble falling in the rubble.

The calm before the storm.

An ominous crack reverberated across the entire Realm, and the floor began to shift beneath us.

We must leave this place before we are destroyed with it, Julian said.

He shifted back into his dragon form, and I whimpered as he pulled me gently into his arms. He launched us straight up, where the ceiling of the castle had once been, and into the eerie whiteness of the sky. Another crack sounded. Then another.

I felt a rush of magic against me as Julian opened the liquid silver door of the portal, and I sighed in relief as it shimmered before us. The dragons who'd survived the battle grabbed the walking warriors and the human prisoners on their backs and fell in line behind us.

Just before we went through the portal, I looked back at what had once been the Realm of the Gods. It was completely destroyed, and it would soon be nonexistent. A dark cloud of black was gaining on us, slowly rolling over the pristine whiteness until the dark completely consumed the white. Big chunks of the Realm broke off and were being sucked into the blackness like a vacuum.

Hurry, Julian called out to his people.

I felt his muscles bunch beneath me and we soared toward the portal just as another crack sounded. The Realm of the Gods trembled with fear. It thrummed like a tuning fork as it shattered, deafening us with its resonance. It began to spiral in on itself, losing light and color in the black hole of nothingness as we raced to escape it.

For a moment, I wasn't sure we had escaped.

I groaned in pain as we landed in a heap in the middle of the ballroom we'd started in, and Julian quickly shifted back to his human form. He buried his face in my neck, and I could feel his body tremble with each shuddering breath he took. Other dragons and warriors began filling the space around us until everyone who was still alive had made it through. Julian closed the portal with a wave of his hand and a resounding cheer went up around us.

I found the strength to lift up my head and looked around the room. We were significantly less in numbers than what we'd been, and I knew we all had a long road ahead of us trying to rebuild.

I looked down at my body. It wasn't pretty. I'd have new scars to add to the ones on my back. I lifted my head and finally found the courage to look at Julian. His gaze was somber and his eyes colder. I could already tell Esmerelda's treachery would make a new stumbling block for us. It would be harder than ever to get him to open himself to love after what she'd done.

I held the sides of his face between each hand and kissed him gently. "We're alive."

And that was good enough for me.

CHAPTER
THIRTY-TWO

I waited at the boarding gate inside the airport for my flight back home with a mixture of trepidation and sadness. My wounds were healed for the most part. At least the ones on the outside.

I had to go home. There were things to see to. I was still the Enforcer, and although Julian was still acting as Archos for all five clans, my people needed me. They'd faced too much upheaval lately and their behavior was getting out of control. Yes, Julian and I were stronger together, but since there were no immediate conflicts to deal with between the clans, I figured it was the perfect time to go home. I needed the comfort of my own hoard. And I needed to figure out a way to deal with my new powers and who they made me. Without Julian.

Recognizing the other half of my blood has brought me a peace I'd not thought possible. I now understood why the push and pull between my human and dragon was so strong. They were natural enemies. I'd need help learning how to embrace them both. I was hoping Noah might know someone I could talk to—a mentor I could spend some time with to teach me how to grow in my powers.

The results of what happened in the Realm of the Gods were bittersweet. I discovered, after we returned back to the Earth Realm, that I'd absorbed some of Esmerelda's powers while we were locked together in combat. I had no idea if I'd keep them forever or if they'd slowly fade away. Whatever the case, I now had enough Drakán power to keep my clan in line and get them on the path of becoming a healthy clan.

Julian had been busy the last few days as well. He'd decided to set up a community for all those who'd lost their powers due to Erik's experiments. We had no clue what their lifespans would be, but they all seemed to be aging—some of them frighteningly fast. Julian was determined to give them peace and comfort until their lives ended.

I'd destroyed the Realm of the Gods with the strength of my and Julian's combined powers. The curtain had been completely torn down between our two worlds. Needless to say, the gods were angry. Now that The Destroyer was gone and they no longer feared that power, I had a feeling they'd be showing themselves a little more boldly. I had no idea where they'd be making their new home until they could build a new Realm. I just hoped it wasn't here. But that was a battle I'd have to face another day. I just hoped they gave me a little warning first.

I checked my watch and tapped my foot nervously as I waited impatiently for the boarding call. I stood alone, staring out the large windows, watching the planes come in. My scent reeked of danger and violence as it never had before, and even the humans sensed it, so they kept their distance.

My carry-on was gripped so tightly in my hand that my knuckles turned white. I was doing the right thing. And if the idea of being separated from Julian made me feel nauseated, it only proved to show that I'd become too dependent on him. I felt the tingle of magic along my spine before I heard his voice in my mind.

Do you really think running away is the answer?

I shivered as if his words had actually whispered across my skin. I had less than five minutes before I'd be safely inside the plane.

It seems like someone who could defeat The Destroyer shouldn't be such a coward.

"I need a little space, Julian," I whispered. "I haven't forgotten what happened between us before we entered the Realm of the Gods. I need more from you than you're willing to give, and I'd rather separate myself now before it becomes too hard."

You need to give me a chance to show you what I'm willing to give. I'll not stop wanting you. That should be enough for now.

"Believe me, it's not. I also haven't forgotten that you lied to me about who I really am. I'm Atlantean, Julian. That will never change. Can your dragon accept that?"

You are Drakán, Rena. My dragon doesn't see you as anything but that. You can't blame me for keeping those details from you. I knew it would only conflict you more. You already feel my absence. How long can you live without me?

I didn't answer. I had no idea how my body would react to being so far apart. But I had to let the two halves of my powers figure out how to coexist peacefully. Without throwing Julian in the mix. My Atlantean magic had already made it clear that it didn't care for Julian.

It sounds to me like you're playing with fire. Make sure you don't get burned. I'll give you the time you need to get things straightened out with your clan. But if you take too long I will come after you. You are my lifemate. We belong together. And I will not live without you.

"I love you," I said, unable to keep that from him.

He didn't answer and shut the door to his mind. I'd felt it before he'd put up his shields. But it couldn't be helped.

"Goodbye, Julian," I said before getting on the plane. I didn't look back. I knew I'd see him soon.

343

ABOUT THE AUTHOR

Liliana Hart is a *New York Times, USA Today,* and Publisher's Weekly bestselling author of more than eighty titles. After starting her first novel her freshman year of college, she immediately became addicted to writing and knew she'd found what she was meant to do with her life. She has no idea why she majored in music.

Since publishing in June 2011, Liliana has sold more than ten-million books. All three of her series have made multiple appearances on the New York Times list.

Liliana can almost always be found at her computer writing, hauling five kids to various activities, or spending time with her husband. She calls Texas home.

If you enjoyed reading this book, I would appreciate it if you would help others enjoy this book too.

Recommend it. Please help other readers find this book by recommending it to friends, readers' groups and discussion boards.

Review it. Please tell other readers why you liked this book by reviewing.

Connect with me online:
www.lilianahart.com

ALSO BY LILIANA HART

JJ Graves Mystery Series

Dirty Little Secrets

A Dirty Shame

Dirty Rotten Scoundrel

Down and Dirty

Dirty Deeds

Dirty Laundry

Dirty Money

A Dirty Job

Dirty Devil

Playing Dirty

Dirty Martini

Dirty Dozen

Dirty Minds

Addison Holmes Mystery Series

Whiskey Rebellion

Whiskey Sour

Whiskey For Breakfast

Whiskey, You're The Devil

Whiskey on the Rocks

Whiskey Tango Foxtrot

Whiskey and Gunpowder

Whiskey Lullaby

The Scarlet Chronicles

Bouncing Betty

Hand Grenade Helen

Front Line Francis

The Harley and Davidson Mystery Series

The Farmer's Slaughter

A Tisket a Casket

I Saw Mommy Killing Santa Claus

Get Your Murder Running

Deceased and Desist

Malice in Wonderland

Tequila Mockingbird

Gone With the Sin

Grime and Punishment

Blazing Rattles

A Salt and Battery

Curl Up and Dye

First Comes Death Then Comes Marriage

Box Set 1

Box Set 2

Box Set 3

The Gravediggers

The Darkest Corner

Gone to Dust

Say No More

Made in the USA
Middletown, DE
28 August 2023

37501521R00199